ASHES
OF THE CITY

Quinton Taylor-Garcia

ARPress
45 Dan Road Suite 5
Canton MA 02021
Hotline: 1(888) 821-0229
Fax: 1(508) 545-7580

Ordering Information:
Quantity sales. Special discounts are available on quantity purchases by corporations, associations, and others. For details, contact the publisher at the address above.

Printed in the United States of America.

ISBN-13:   Softcover   979-8-89676-019-1
                     eBook   979-8-89676-020-7

Library of Congress Control Number: 2024925443

Table of Contents

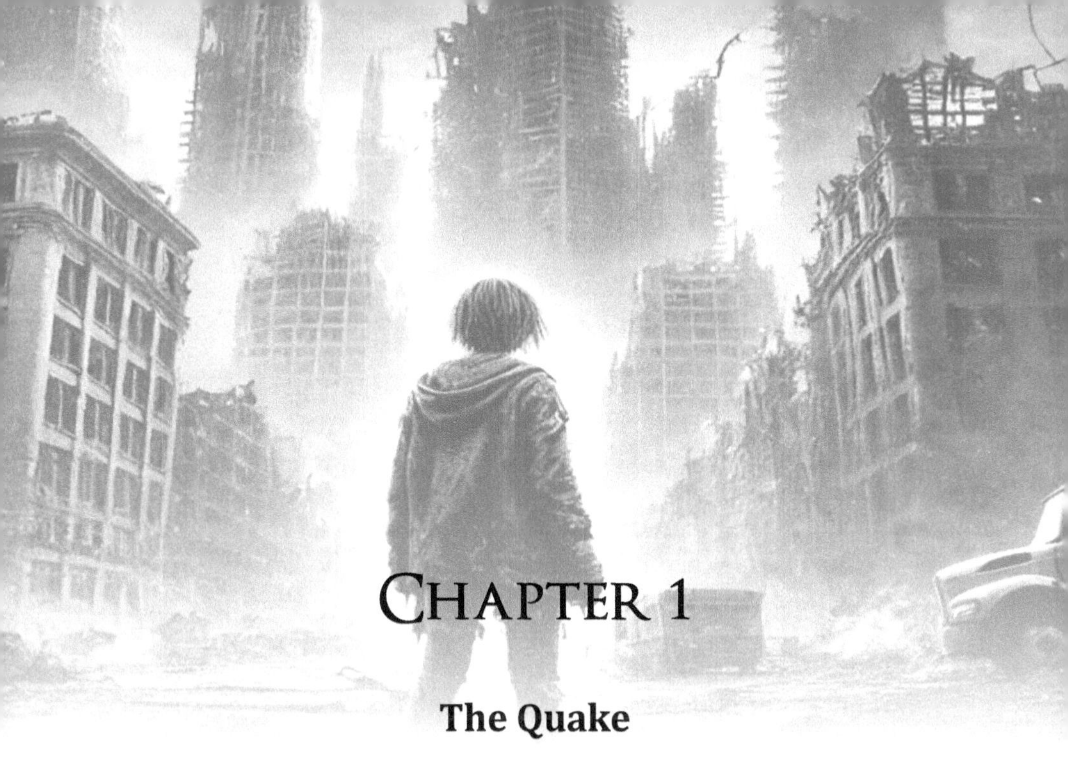

CHAPTER 1

The Quake

The city skyline loomed before them, a jumble of glass and steel piercing the overcast autumn sky. Maya squinted against the cool breeze, her ponytail whipping as she turned to face her classmates.

"Alright, everyone," she called out, her voice calm but authoritative. "Let's stick together and stay behind Mr. Callahan. We don't want anyone getting lost in the crowd."

As the group of high school students shuffled forward, Maya felt a familiar presence at her side. Riley, her best friend, nodded in agreement.

"Good call," Riley said, her green eyes scanning the busy sidewalk. "I've got the map pulled up on my phone, just in case."

Maya smiled, grateful for Riley's practical nature. She was about to respond when a sardonic voice cut through the chatter.

"Oh please," Jace scoffed, rolling his eyes. "We're not kindergarteners. Some of us can actually take care of ourselves."

Maya's jaw tightened. Jace always had to challenge everything, his rebellious streak as predictable as it was irritating. She took a deep breath, reminding herself to stay patient.

"It's not about babysitting, Jace," she explained. "It's about being responsible and looking out for each other."

As they waited at a crosswalk, Maya noticed Tariq hanging back from the group, his dark eyes taking in every detail of their surroundings. She wondered what was going through his mind, wishing he'd open up more.

"Hey, guys!" Benji's cheerful voice cut through her thoughts. "Why did the scarecrow win an award? He was outstanding in his field!"

A chorus of groans and chuckles rippled through the group. Maya couldn't help but smile, grateful for Benji's ability to lighten the mood.

As they crossed the street, Maya's mind drifted to the day ahead. She felt a mix of excitement and nervousness about leading their group project. Would everyone cooperate? Would Jace try to derail things?

"Earth to Maya," Riley's voice brought her back to the present. "You okay? You looked lost in thought there."

Maya nodded, forcing a smile. "Just thinking about the presentation. I hope it goes well."

"It will," Riley assured her. "You've got this. And I've got your back, remember?"

Maya felt a surge of gratitude for her friend's unwavering support. As they approached the museum entrance, she squared her shoulders, ready to face whatever challenges the day might bring.

Little did she know, those challenges would be far greater than any high school project could prepare them for.

Maya's gaze swept across the bustling city street, her eyes narrowing as she noticed something peculiar. A flock of pigeons suddenly took flight, their wings beating frantically against the air. She frowned, a strange uneasiness settling in her stomach.

"Did you guys see that?" she asked, her voice low and tense.

Riley glanced up from her phone. "See what?"

"The birds. They just... took off." Maya shook her head, trying to shake off the odd feeling. "It's probably nothing."

Jace snorted, his blue eyes glinting with amusement. "What, you some kind of bird whisperer now, Maya?"

Before she could retort, a faint rumble echoed in the distance. Maya froze, her heart rate quickening. "Did you hear that?"

"Hear what?" Benji chimed in, his usual jovial tone tinged with confusion. "The only thing I hear is my stomach growling. When's lunch?"

Maya's brow furrowed as she scanned their surroundings. The busy sidewalks, the honking cars, the chatter of pedestrians – everything seemed normal. And yet...

"I don't know," she muttered, more to herself than the others. "Something feels off."

Riley placed a reassuring hand on her shoulder. "Maya, you're probably just nervous about the presentation. Take a deep breath, okay?"

Maya nodded, trying to force a smile. But as they continued walking, she couldn't shake the nagging feeling that something was terribly wrong. The distant rumbling seemed to grow stronger, a subtle vibration beneath her feet that no one else appeared to notice.

"Guys," she started, her voice trembling slightly. "I really think we should-"

"Oh, come on," Jace interrupted, rolling his eyes. "Stop being so dramatic. You're always trying to control everything, aren't you?"

Maya felt a flash of anger, but before she could respond, Tariq spoke up for the first time. His voice was quiet, but there was an undercurrent of concern that made everyone pause.

"I feel it too," he said, his dark eyes meeting Maya's. "Something's not right."

The group fell silent, the tension palpable. Maya's mind raced, torn between her instincts screaming danger and the fear of looking foolish in front of her classmates. As the rumbling grew louder, she made a decision.

"We need to find shelter," she said firmly, her leadership instincts kicking in. "Now."

The earth roared to life beneath their feet, a primal scream that shattered the world around them. Maya's legs buckled as the ground heaved, sending her sprawling onto the cracking pavement.

"Get down!" she yelled, her voice barely audible over the deafening rumble.

Buildings swayed like trees in a gale, windows exploding outward in a shower of glass. The air filled with dust and debris, choking Maya as she struggled to breathe.

"What's happening?" Benji cried out, his usual humor replaced by raw panic.

Maya's heart pounded as she tried to process the chaos. This can't be real, she thought. We were just on a field trip. How did everything go so wrong so fast?

"It's an earthquake!" Riley shouted, her practical mind cutting through the confusion. "We need to get away from the buildings!"

Jace's sardonic laughter cut through the din. "No shit, Sherlock! Any other brilliant observations?"

"Shut up, Jace!" Maya snapped, her frustration with him momentarily overriding her fear. "This isn't the time!"

The ground lurched again, and Maya heard the sickening crunch of concrete giving way. A nearby storefront collapsed, sending a fresh wave of dust billowing towards them.

"Move!" Maya screamed, her instincts taking over. "Everyone, move now!"

As they scrambled to their feet, Maya's mind raced. Where do we go? How do we stay safe? The city she knew was transforming into an alien landscape before her eyes.

Tariq's quiet voice somehow reached her through the cacophony. "The park," he said, pointing. "Open space. Less danger from falling debris."

Maya nodded, grateful for his clear thinking. "Good idea. Let's go, stick together!"

As they stumbled towards the relative safety of the park, Maya couldn't shake the terrifying realization that their lives had changed forever in the span of mere moments. The world was quite literally crumbling around them, and she had no idea how they were going to survive.

Maya's heart raced as she guided the group towards the park, her eyes darting frantically between her classmates and the crumbling buildings around them. The acrid taste of dust coated her tongue, but she forced herself to speak clearly and calmly.

"Stay low! Cover your mouth and noses!" she called out, demonstrating by pulling her shirt collar over her face. "And watch for falling debris!"

As they moved, Maya scanned the group, counting heads. Twenty-three, twenty-four... where's twenty-five? A jolt of panic shot through her when she realized someone was missing.

"Wait!" she shouted, halting the group. "Where's Benji?"

A muffled cry answered her question. Maya whirled around to see Benji pinned beneath a fallen street sign, his face contorted in pain.

"I'm okay," he gasped, attempting a weak smile. "Just... stuck. Don't suppose anyone wants to play a quick game of limbo?"

Maya rushed to his side, assessing the situation. The sign's heavy, but not impossible to move. We need to act fast.

"Riley, Tariq, help me lift this," Maya commanded, surprised by the authority in her own voice. As they positioned themselves around the sign, she locked eyes with Benji. "On three, we lift, and you crawl out. Ready?"

Benji nodded, his attempt at humor fading as the gravity of the situation set in.

"One... two... three!" Maya strained, muscles burning as they lifted the sign just enough for Benji to scramble free.

As they helped Benji to his feet, Maya felt a wave of relief wash over her. But the moment was short-lived as another aftershock rocked the ground.

"Keep moving!" she urged, supporting Benji as they resumed their trek to the park.

I can't believe this is happening, Maya thought, her mind reeling. How am I supposed to keep everyone safe? What if I make the wrong decision?

Despite her doubts, Maya pressed on, her sense of responsibility overriding her fear. As they finally reached the relative safety of the open park, she turned to face the group, trying to project a confidence she didn't feel.

"Okay, everyone sit tight and catch your breath," she said, her voice only slightly trembling. "I need to check if anyone's hurt. Riley, can you help me?"

As Riley nodded and moved to assist, Maya took a deep breath, steeling herself for whatever challenges lay ahead. The world had changed in an instant, and she knew that this was only the beginning of their struggle to survive.

Maya had barely begun assessing injuries when Jace's voice cut through the tense atmosphere, sharp and defiant.

"Who put you in charge anyway?" he called out, his piercing blue eyes locked on Maya. "Last I checked, we don't need a self-appointed leader telling us what to do."

Maya's heart raced, but she fought to keep her voice steady. "Jace, we need to work together right now. It's not about being in charge—"

"Isn't it?" Jace interrupted, taking a step closer. His broad shoulders were tense, his jaw set. "You're barking orders like you know what's best for all of us."

Maya's mind whirled. How can he be so combative at a time like this? She took a deep breath, willing herself to remain calm.

"I'm just trying to help," she said, meeting his gaze. "We're all scared, but—"

"Speak for yourself," Jace scoffed, his voice dripping with disdain. He turned to address the group, his charismatic presence drawing their attention. "Listen up! We can't rely on anyone but ourselves now. The world's gone to hell, and playing nice isn't going to keep us alive."

Maya watched in disbelief as several students nodded, clearly swayed by Jace's words. This can't be happening, she thought, panic rising in her chest. We need to stick together, not turn on each other.

"Jace, please," she pleaded, reaching out to touch his arm. He jerked away as if her touch burned.

"Don't," he growled. "Your way is going to get us all killed. We need to be smart, be tough. Anyone who can't keep up is dead weight."

The harshness of his words sent a chill down Maya's spine. She could see the fear in the eyes of those around her, could feel the group fracturing before her very eyes.

What do I do? she thought desperately. How do I keep us together when he's tearing us apart?

As another aftershock rumbled beneath their feet, Maya realized that the earthquake was just the beginning. The real challenge would be surviving each other.

As Maya's mind raced, searching for a way to counter Jace's influence, Riley suddenly stepped forward. Her green eyes flashed with determination as she addressed the group.

"Everyone, listen up!" Riley's voice cut through the murmurs of uncertainty. "We can argue about leadership later. Right now, we need shelter and supplies. The school's partially collapsed, but the east wing looked stable. We should head there first."

Maya felt a surge of relief at Riley's intervention. Thank God for her level-headedness, she thought.

"Riley's right," Maya said, her voice steadier now. "Let's move. Watch for falling debris and help anyone who's injured."

As they made their way towards the east wing, Riley fell into step beside Maya. "We should check the nurse's office for first aid supplies," she said in a faint voice. "And the cafeteria might have some non-perishables."

Maya nodded, grateful for Riley's practical suggestions. "Good thinking. Can you take a small group to the nurse's office? I'll lead the rest to the cafeteria."

As they walked, Maya's mind whirled. How long will we be stuck here? What if help never comes? She pushed the thoughts aside, focusing on the immediate needs of the group.

"Maya," Riley said softly, touching her arm. "You've got this. We'll figure it out together."

Maya managed a small smile, drawing strength from her friend's confidence. "Thanks, Riley. I don't know what I'd do without you."

As they reached the east wing, Maya turned to address the group. "Okay, everyone. Let's split up and gather what we can. Stay in pairs, be careful, and meet back here in 15 minutes. We'll make a plan once we know what resources we have."

As Maya finished giving instructions, Benji's voice piped up from the back of the group. "Hey, guys, I know this is bad, but look on the bright side," he said, his crooked smile visible even in the dim light. "At least we don't have to take that algebra test tomorrow, right?"

A few nervous chuckles rippled through the crowd. Maya felt a small wave of relief; Benji's humor, however ill-timed, seemed to ease some of the tension.

"Yeah, and think about all the cool earthquake-themed TikToks we can make now," Benji continued, miming holding up a phone. "Hashtag apocalypse vibes, am I right?"

This time, the laughter was a bit more genuine. Maya caught Benji's eye and gave him a grateful nod. As the groups began to disperse, she overheard him quipping to a nearby classmate, "I always wanted to star in a disaster movie. Didn't think I'd have to live through one, though."

But as they made their way through the debris-strewn hallways, Benji's jokes became less frequent. Maya glanced back to see him staring at a collapsed section of the ceiling, his usually cheerful face etched with worry.

"You okay, Benji?" she asked softly.

He startled, then forced another smile. "Yeah, just... thinking about my mom. She works downtown. I hope she's alright."

Maya's heart clenched. She hadn't even had time to worry about her own family yet. "I'm sure she is," she said, trying to sound confident. "Once we get some supplies, we'll figure out how to contact everyone."

Benji nodded, but his eyes remained distant. As they reached the cafeteria, he mumbled, "If there's anyone left to contact."

Maya pretended not to hear, but Benji's words echoed in her mind as they pushed open the heavy doors. The cafeteria was a mess of overturned tables and scattered food. As they began to search for anything salvageable, Benji's usual stream of jokes had dried up entirely.

This is bad, Maya thought, watching him methodically stuff cans into a backpack, his face grim. If even Benji can't find something to laugh about...

She shook her head, forcing herself to focus on the task at hand. They had to stay positive. They had to survive. But as she caught sight of Benji's hunched shoulders and furrowed brow, she couldn't shake the feeling that their ordeal was only beginning.

Tariq's eyes narrowed as he scanned the chaos unfolding before him. Dust swirled through the air, obscuring his vision and coating his throat. He swallowed hard, observing the others through the haze.

Maya's voice cut through the din, sharp and authoritative. "Everyone stay calm! We need to find shelter and assess injuries."

Jace scoffed, his rebellious nature on full display. "Who made you the boss? We should be looking for a way out of here."

Tariq's gaze darted between the two, noting the power struggle beginning to form. He pressed his lips into a thin line, weighing the merits of each approach silently.

Riley's practical tone chimed in. "Maya's right. We need to regroup before we do anything else."

As the others bickered, Tariq's mind raced. The earthquake had changed everything in an instant. The rules that once governed their lives were shattered like the buildings around them. He knew that in this new reality, survival would depend on more than just following orders or acting rashly.

Benji's attempt at humor fell flat, his usual smirk replaced by a grimace. "Well, I guess we can kiss that history test goodbye, huh?"

Tariq's eyes lingered on Benji's faltering bravado. Even the class clown couldn't find levity in this situation. The gravity of their circumstances was sinking in for everyone.

As Maya began organizing small groups to search for supplies, Tariq hung back. He watched intently as some gravitated towards her leadership, while others, inspired by Jace's defiance, began to form their own cliques.

This is how it starts, Tariq thought. The formation of alliances, the seeds of conflict. He knew he'd have to choose his allegiances carefully if he wanted to survive.

A distant rumble signaled an aftershock, sending a fresh wave of panic through the group. Tariq remained still, his expression unreadable as he continued to observe. He'd always been an outsider, and now, that detachment might just be his greatest asset.

The aftershock subsided, leaving an eerie silence in its wake. Maya stood frozen, her ponytail askew, dust settling on her shoulders. She gazed at the devastation surrounding them, her voice barely above a whisper.

"Is... is everyone okay?"

No one answered. The group of students huddled together, their eyes wide with shock and disbelief. Riley, ever practical, was the first to break the silence.

"We need to check our phones," she said, fumbling in her pocket. "Call for help."

Maya nodded, snapping out of her daze. "Good idea, Riley. Everyone, check your phones. Try to reach emergency services."

The air filled with the frantic tapping of fingers on screens and muttered curses. Jace's voice cut through the tension, sharp and angry.

"It's useless. No signal. We're cut off."

Maya's heart sank as she stared at her own phone's blank screen. She thought of her parents, her little sister. Were they okay? Did they know what had happened? The weight of their isolation crashed down on her.

"Maybe... maybe it's just temporary," she said, trying to keep her voice steady. "The cell towers might be down, but-"

"Face it, Maya," Jace interrupted, his blue eyes flashing. "We're on our own now."

The reality of their situation began to sink in. Buildings lay in ruins around them, dust still swirling in the air. The once-bustling street was now a wasteland of broken concrete and twisted metal. And they were alone in the middle of it all.

Benji let out a nervous laugh. "Hey, at least we don't have to worry about that pop quiz in English now, right?"

His attempt at humor fell flat, met with blank stares and uncomfortable silence. Maya could see the fear creeping into their eyes, the panic threatening to take hold.

She took a deep breath, pushing down her own terror. They needed a leader now more than ever.

"Okay, listen up," she said, her voice growing stronger. "We may be cut off, but we're not helpless. We need to stick together and figure out our next move."

As Maya spoke, she couldn't help but notice the way Jace rolled his eyes, arms crossed over his chest. She knew he'd be a problem, but right now, unity was their only hope for survival.

"First things first," she continued, "we need to find shelter and take stock of our supplies. Riley, can you help me organize search groups?"

Riley nodded, already moving to Maya's side. "On it."

As they began to divide up tasks, Maya felt a flicker of hope. They might be isolated and scared, but they weren't broken. Not yet. And as long as she had anything to say about it, they never would be.

Maya watched as the group dispersed, following her instructions with a mix of nervous energy and trepidation. As the last student moved out of earshot, she felt her confident facade begin to crumble.

She leaned against a crumbling wall, her breath coming in short, panicked gasps. The weight of what had just happened—what was still happening—crashed over her like a tidal wave.

"What am I doing?" she whispered to herself, her voice barely audible over the distant rumble of aftershocks. "I'm just a high school student. How am I supposed to keep everyone alive?"

Her hands trembled as she ran them through her disheveled hair. The faces of her classmates flashed before her eyes—scared, confused, looking to her for answers she wasn't sure she had.

"Maya?" Riley's voice cut through her spiraling thoughts. "We've got the first group ready to search for supplies."

Maya quickly straightened, forcing a calm expression onto her face. "Great, thanks Riley. I'll be right there."

As Riley nodded and turned away, Maya caught a glimpse of her own reflection in a shattered window. The girl staring back at her looked older, more haggard than she remembered. Was this what leadership looked like?

"You can do this," she murmured to herself, clenching her fists at her sides. "You have to do this. Their lives depend on it."

With a deep breath, Maya stepped away from the wall, ready to face whatever challenges lay ahead. But as she walked towards the waiting group, a nagging voice in the back of her mind whispered doubts she couldn't quite silence.

Jace leaned against a crumbling wall, his piercing blue eyes scanning the group of shell-shocked students huddled nearby. A slight smirk played on his lips as he pushed off the wall and sauntered towards them.

"Hey," he called out, his voice carrying a casual confidence that seemed out of place in the chaos. "Anyone else think sitting around waiting for help is a waste of time?"

A few heads turned, eyes wide with uncertainty. Jace ran a hand through his unruly dark hair, his rugged appearance somehow more fitting in this new, broken world.

"Look," he continued, gesturing to the devastation around them, "the rules we lived by yesterday? They don't mean shit now. We need to take action, find food, weapons—anything that'll keep us alive."

Sarah, a quiet girl from his math class, spoke up timidly. "But Maya said we should stay together, wait for rescue—"

Jace cut her off with a sharp laugh. "Rescue? You really think anyone's coming for us?" His voice lowered, taking on a persuasive tone. "We're on our own now. The strong survive, the weak..." He let the implication hang in the air.

A murmur of agreement rippled through the small crowd. Jace's eyes glinted with satisfaction.

"I'm heading out to scavenge what we need," he announced. "Who's with me?"

As hands began to raise tentatively, Jace felt a surge of power course through him. This was his moment, his chance to rise above the rubble and take control.

"Trust me," he said, his voice a mix of charm and underlying threat, "stick with me, and I'll make sure we not only survive but thrive in this new world."

The seeds of division were sown, and Jace could almost taste the sweet flavor of growing influence. In the back of his mind, he knew Maya would oppose him, but that only fueled his determination. Let her cling to her outdated morals—he would do whatever it took to come out on top.

Maya's heart raced as she watched Jace's group splinter off, their determined faces a stark contrast to the fear and uncertainty etched on the others. She took a deep breath, squaring her shoulders.

"Listen up, everyone," she called out, her voice steady despite the tremor in her hands. "We need to stick together. It's not safe out there, and we're stronger as a unit."

Jace's mocking laughter cut through the air. "Stronger? Or just easier targets?"

Maya felt a flash of anger but pushed it down. "We need to find shelter, assess our resources. Riley, can you help me organize a headcount?"

As Riley nodded and moved to her side, Maya caught sight of Benji's worried expression. "What about food? Water?" he asked, his usual humor absent.

"We'll form search parties," Maya assured him, "but safely, in groups. No one goes alone."

She could see the doubt in some faces, the pull of Jace's words tugging at their resolve. Maya's stomach churned with anxiety, but she pressed on.

"I know you're scared. I am too," she admitted, her voice softening. "But abandoning each other isn't the answer. We can survive this if we work together."

As she spoke, Maya's mind raced. How long could she hold them together? What if Jace was right, and her approach was too cautious? The weight of leadership pressed down on her, suffocating in its intensity.

"Maya," Tariq's quiet voice broke through her spiraling thoughts. "There's a community center two blocks over. It might have supplies, and it's built sturdy."

She nodded gratefully. "Good thinking. Let's move out, stay close, and watch for aftershocks."

As the group began to move, Maya caught Jace's eye. His smirk sent a chill down her spine, a silent challenge that whispered of battles yet to come.

Maya led the group through the shattered remains of their once-familiar city, her heart sinking with each step. The devastation was beyond anything she could have imagined. Crumbled buildings lined the streets, their jagged silhouettes stark against the overcast sky. The acrid smell of smoke and dust filled the air, making her eyes water.

"Oh god," Riley whispered beside her, her voice trembling. "It's all... gone."

Maya swallowed hard, fighting back her own despair. "We need to focus on what's still here," she said, more to herself than to Riley. "Look for anything useful – food, water, medical supplies."

As they rounded a corner, the full extent of the destruction hit them. Cars lay overturned, some crushed beneath fallen debris. The road had split open, creating a chasm that stretched as far as they could see.

Jace's voice cut through the eerie silence. "Well, isn't this just peachy? Good thing we have our fearless leader to guide us through this wasteland."

Maya bit back a retort, instead turning to the group. "Spread out, but stay within sight of each other. Call out if you find anything."

As the others fanned out, Maya's mind raced. How were they going to survive this? Where would they find enough food and water for everyone? The enormity of the task before her was overwhelming.

Benji's voice snapped her back to reality. "Hey, guys? I think I found something."

They gathered around a partially collapsed convenience store. Through the broken window, Maya could see shelves of food and water.

"Nice work, Benji," she said, offering him a small smile. "Let's see what we can salvage."

As they carefully made their way inside, Maya couldn't shake the feeling of hopelessness that threatened to engulf her. The city they knew was gone, replaced by this nightmarish landscape. How long could they hold out? And at what cost?

Maya stepped carefully over the shattered glass, her eyes scanning the dimly lit store interior. "Okay, everyone, let's gather what we can. Focus on water and non-perishables."

As the group spread out, Jace's voice cut through the quiet rustling. "Why are we wasting time with this small-scale scavenging? We should be hitting bigger targets."

Maya turned to face him, her jaw tightening. "Because every little bit helps, Jace. We don't know how long we'll be on our own."

"Exactly," Jace retorted, his blue eyes glinting dangerously. "Which is why we need to think bigger. There's a warehouse district not far from here. That's where the real supplies are."

Riley stepped between them, her voice low and practical. "Guys, we need to focus. Fighting isn't helping anyone."

Maya nodded, grateful for Riley's support, but she could feel the tension building. As she reached for a can of beans, her hand trembled slightly. She's right, we can't afford to fight now, she thought. But how long can I keep everyone together?

Tariq's quiet voice broke through her thoughts. "I found some first aid supplies."

"Great work, Tariq," Maya said, forcing a smile. "Let's gather everything we can carry."

As they worked, Maya noticed Benji's usual jokes were absent, replaced by a grim determination. The weight of their situation was settling on all of them.

Suddenly, Jace's voice rang out again. "This is ridiculous. We're wasting time on scraps when we should be securing real resources. Who's with me on hitting the warehouse district?"

To Maya's dismay, several heads turned towards Jace, nodding in agreement. She felt a pit forming in her stomach. This is it, she realized. The moment where everything could fall apart.

"Jace, we need to stick together," she argued, trying to keep her voice steady. "Going off on our own is dangerous. We don't know what's out there."

"And staying here, playing it safe, is going to get us all killed," Jace shot back. "Sometimes you have to take risks to survive."

Maya looked around at the conflicted faces of her classmates. The unity they'd shared in the immediate aftermath of the quake was crumbling before her eyes. How do I hold this together? she wondered desperately. How do I keep us from tearing each other apart?

Maya closed her eyes for a moment, taking a deep breath. When she opened them, she found herself staring at the cracked pavement beneath her feet, a stark reminder of how quickly their world had shattered.

"Listen," she said, her voice low but firm. "I understand the fear. I feel it too. But rushing headlong into danger isn't the answer."

She looked up, meeting the eyes of each person in the group. Some nodded, while others averted their gaze.

"We're stronger together," Maya continued, her words gaining strength. "If we split up now, we're just making ourselves more vulnerable."

Jace scoffed, crossing his arms. "And what's your brilliant plan then, oh fearless leader? Sit here and hope for rescue?"

Maya felt a flicker of anger, but pushed it down. Now wasn't the time for petty conflicts. "No," she replied evenly. "We scout our immediate area first. Look for stable shelter, clean water, and any supplies we can safely reach. Then we plan our next move."

As she spoke, Maya noticed Riley nodding in agreement. It gave her a small boost of confidence.

"I know it's not exciting," Maya admitted. "But it's smart. And right now, being smart is what's going to keep us alive."

She paused, looking at the devastation around them. The weight of responsibility pressed down on her shoulders, threatening to crush her. But she couldn't let it. Not now.

"I can't promise it'll be easy," Maya said softly. "But I promise I'll do everything I can to keep us safe. All of us."

The silence that followed was deafening. Maya's heart pounded in her chest as she waited, praying she'd said enough to hold them together.

Finally, Emma spoke up. "I'm with Maya," she said quietly. A few others murmured agreement.

Jace rolled his eyes. "Fine. We'll play it safe. For now." The threat in his voice was clear.

As the group began to move, following Maya's instructions, she allowed herself a moment of relief. But the pit in her stomach remained. This was just the beginning, she realized. The real test was still to come.

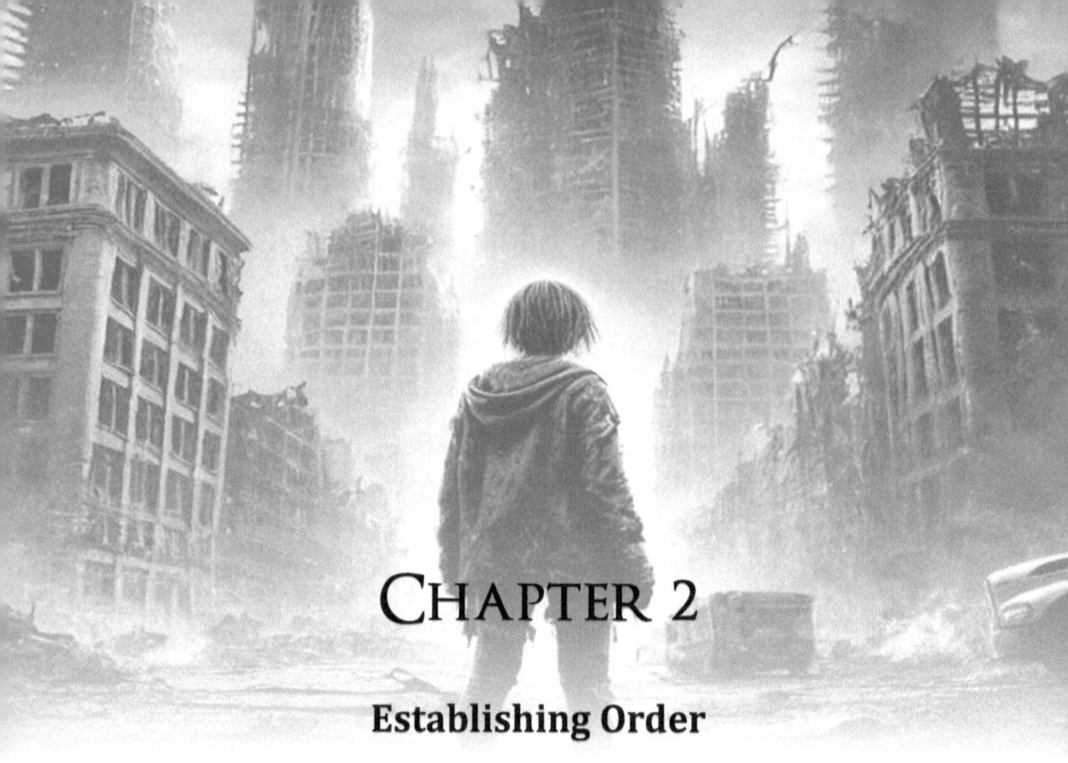

CHAPTER 2

Establishing Order

The dust settled, revealing a world transformed. Maya stood atop a mound of rubble, her eyes scanning the devastation that stretched in every direction. The once-familiar cityscape had been reduced to a jagged wasteland of twisted metal and crumbling concrete. Her classmates huddled nearby, their faces etched with shock and disbelief.

Maya's heart raced as she struggled to process the enormity of what had happened. She had always been the one others turned to for guidance, but this... this was beyond anything she had ever faced.

"What do we do now?" Emma's trembling voice broke the eerie silence.

Maya opened her mouth to respond, but the words caught in her throat. What could she possibly say? How could she reassure them when she herself felt so lost?

"We need to find help," she managed, her voice sounding small and uncertain even to her own ears. "Maybe there are emergency services nearby."

As she spoke, Maya's gaze fell on a group of her classmates who were gathering around Jace. His confident stance and animated gestures contrasted sharply with her own hesitation.

"Help isn't coming," Jace's voice carried across the rubble. "We need to look out for ourselves now."

Maya felt a flicker of irritation. "We don't know that," she countered, trying to inject some authority into her tone. "We should stay together and wait for rescue."

But even as she said it, doubt gnawed at her. The city around them was silent, save for the occasional groan of settling debris. No sirens wailed in the distance, no helicopters circled overhead. What if Jace was right?

"Maya?" Emma's voice pulled her from her thoughts. "What should we do?"

All eyes turned to her, expectant, desperate for direction. Maya felt the weight of their gazes, the crushing responsibility of their lives in her hands. She had always prided herself on being dependable, on having the answers. But now, faced with the stark reality of their situation, she felt woefully unprepared.

"I... I think we should..." Maya began, her mind racing. She needed to say something, to take charge, but the enormity of the task before her was paralyzing. How could she possibly make decisions that might mean life or death for her friends?

As she wrestled with her doubts, Maya caught sight of a small group breaking away, following Jace as he headed towards a partially collapsed building. The sight sparked a surge of determination within her. She couldn't let the group fracture, not now when they needed unity more than ever.

"We need to stick together," Maya said, her voice stronger now. "That's the most important thing. We'll figure out our next move, but we do it as a team."

The words sounded right, but as Maya looked out over the ruined city, she couldn't shake the feeling that she was in way over her head. The responsibility of leadership had never felt so heavy, so terrifyingly real.

Maya took a deep breath, steeling herself against the wave of self-doubt threatening to overwhelm her. She looked at the faces around her, a mix of fear, confusion, and hope etched into their expressions. Her own fear threatened to choke her, but she swallowed it down.

"Okay, listen up," she said, her voice steadier than she felt. "We need to get organized. First things first, we need to take stock of what we have and who needs medical attention."

As she spoke, Maya's mind raced. What if she made the wrong call? What if her decisions got someone hurt... or worse? The weight of their lives pressed down on her shoulders, threatening to crush her resolve.

"Riley," Maya called out, spotting her friend in the crowd. "Can you start checking for injuries? Anyone who's hurt, send them to Riley."

Riley nodded, her usually cheerful face now set with determination. Maya felt a flicker of gratitude for her friend's steady presence.

"What about food and water?" someone called out. "We don't know how long we'll be stuck here."

Maya's stomach clenched. They were right, of course. But admitting that felt like admitting defeat, like acknowledging that rescue might not come anytime soon.

"Good point," Maya said, forcing confidence into her voice. "We'll need a team to search for supplies. But be careful - no one goes anywhere alone, and don't take unnecessary risks. The buildings aren't stable."

As she gave out instructions, Maya's inner voice nagged at her. Was she doing enough? Was she making the right choices? The responsibility felt crushing, but she pushed through, knowing that showing weakness now could unravel everything.

"We're going to get through this," Maya said, meeting the eyes of those around her. "Together. We just need to stay calm and work as a team."

The words sounded hollow to her own ears, but she saw a glimmer of hope in some faces. It was enough, for now. Maya squared her shoulders, ready to face whatever came next, even as doubt gnawed at the edges of her resolve.

Maya turned to survey the group, her eyes scanning for any immediate tasks they could tackle. That's when she noticed Jace, standing slightly apart from the others, his arms crossed and a skeptical look on his face. As their eyes met, he shook his head almost imperceptibly.

"Alright, let's start by—" Maya began, but Jace's muffled voice cut through her words.

"Waiting around isn't going to save us," he muttered, just loud enough for those nearby to hear. A few heads turned towards him, curiosity and uncertainty flickering across their faces.

Maya felt a flare of irritation. "Jace, do you have something to add?" she asked, trying to keep her tone neutral.

He shrugged, a casual gesture that somehow managed to convey defiance. "Just saying what we're all thinking. Rescue? In this mess?" He gestured at the chaos surrounding them. "We need to focus on surviving right now, not sitting on our hands."

A murmur of agreement rippled through a small cluster of students near Jace. Maya's heart sank. She knew he had a point, but his words threatened to undermine the fragile sense of order she was trying to establish.

"We're not just waiting," Maya countered, her voice firmer now. "We're organizing, assessing our situation. That's crucial for our survival too."

Jace's blue eyes locked onto hers, challenging. "And how long do we do that before we actually start doing something?"

Maya felt trapped. Push back too hard, and she'd look defensive. Agree, and she'd lose control of the situation. She took a deep breath, buying herself a moment to think.

"We're doing something right now," she said finally. "But you're right, we need to be proactive. That's why I want volunteers to start searching for supplies. Carefully," she added, emphasizing the word.

Jace's expression didn't change, but he gave a short nod. "I'll lead a team," he said, already turning to gather a few of the students who had seemed receptive to his earlier comments.

Maya watched him, a knot forming in her stomach. She'd maintained control, for now, but Jace's quiet resistance felt like the first tremor before another quake. How long before the ground shifted beneath her feet again?

Maya watched as Jace moved through the group, his tall frame and confident stride drawing eyes to him. He leaned in close to a few students, speaking in hushed tones, his piercing blue eyes intense. She couldn't hear his words, but she saw the effect they had—nods of agreement, worried glances in her direction.

"We need to be smart about this," Jace's voice suddenly carried, loud enough for her to hear. "Sitting around isn't going to keep us alive. We need food, water, medicine—now."

A murmur of agreement rippled through those gathered around him. Maya felt her chest tighten.

"Jace," she called out, trying to keep her voice steady. "We agreed on a careful approach. Let's work together on this."

He turned to her, a slight smirk playing on his lips. "Of course, Maya. We're all in this together, right? But some of us are ready to take real action."

Maya's mind raced. She needed to regain control of the situation, but how? "Okay," she said, forcing herself to sound calm. "Let's divide into small groups. We'll cover more ground that way."

As she spoke, she noticed Jace already organizing his followers. They huddled around him, hanging on his every word as he pointed to different areas of the ruined city.

"Remember," Maya called out, her voice wavering slightly. "Stay close, stay safe. We don't know how stable these buildings are."

Jace's group was already moving out, their determined strides a stark contrast to the hesitant movements of the others. Maya felt a cold dread settling in her stomach. She'd lost this round, and she knew it.

"What now?" Riley asked quietly at her side.

Maya swallowed hard. "We stick to the plan. We stay organized, we stay careful." But even as she said the words, she wondered if Jace's way might be what they needed to survive in this new, brutal world.

Maya took a deep breath, steadying herself as she surveyed the devastated landscape before them. The once-familiar streets were now an alien maze of twisted metal and crumbling concrete.

"Let's move," she said, her voice carrying a forced confidence. "Stay close and watch your step."

As they ventured deeper into the city, Maya's heart raced. Every creaking building and shifting pile of debris sent a jolt of fear through her. She tried to mask her anxiety, but her hands trembled slightly as she helped a classmate over a fallen streetlight.

"This is insane," muttered someone behind her. "How are we supposed to find anything useful in this mess?"

Maya turned, meeting the skeptical gaze of a girl she recognized from her chemistry class. "We'll find what we need," she assured her, hoping her voice didn't betray her own doubts. "We just have to be patient and thorough."

As they rounded a corner, Maya gasped. A school bus lay on its side, windows shattered and metal frame twisted beyond recognition. The sight hit her like a physical blow, driving home the reality of their situation.

"Oh god," she whispered, her composure cracking. For a moment, she saw herself not as a leader, but as a scared teenager way out of her depth.

Riley's hand on her shoulder snapped her back to the present. "You okay?" he asked softly.

Maya nodded, swallowing hard. "Yeah, I'm fine," she lied, forcing herself to focus. "Let's check that convenience store across the street. There might be some supplies left."

As they picked their way through the rubble-strewn street, Maya's mind raced. How long could she keep this up? How long before everyone realized she was just as lost and terrified as they were?

"Stay alert," she called out, as much to herself as to the others. "We're all we've got right now."

The acrid smell of smoke assaulted Maya's senses as they approached the convenience store. Broken glass crunched beneath their feet, and the eerie silence was punctuated only by distant rumbles of collapsing structures and the occasional whimper from one of her classmates.

"Watch your step," Maya warned, her voice barely above a whisper. She pushed aside a fallen shelf, revealing rows of crushed snacks and spilled beverages. "Grab anything that's still sealed."

As the group spread out, Maya's gaze drifted to the world outside. The once-familiar skyline was now a jagged silhouette of half-standing buildings and twisted metal. Cars lay abandoned at odd angles, some crushed beneath fallen debris. In the distance, plumes of dark smoke rose ominously against the gray sky.

"I can't believe this is real," Emma murmured beside her, eyes wide with shock.

Maya squeezed her friend's shoulder. "I know. But we have to stay focused."

Internally, Maya's thoughts raced. How could they possibly survive in this apocalyptic landscape? The weight of responsibility pressed down on her, threatening to crush her resolve.

As they exited the store, their meager supplies clutched in shaking hands, Maya led them down another debris-choked street. The path ahead was treacherous, blocked by a tangle of fallen power lines and chunks of concrete.

"We can't go this way," Maya announced, her heart sinking. "We'll have to double back and—"

A low rumble cut her off, growing in intensity. The ground beneath their feet began to tremble.

"Aftershock!" someone yelled.

Maya's instincts kicked in. "Everyone, away from the buildings! Now!"

As they scrambled to relative safety, Maya's facade of calm finally cracked. She closed her eyes, terror washing over her in waves. When would this nightmare end?

Maya's eyes snapped open as the tremors subsided, her heart still racing. She scanned the group, relieved to see everyone unharmed. But the momentary panic had shaken her resolve, and she knew the others could sense it.

"Well, that was fun," Jace's sardonic voice cut through the tense silence. He stepped forward, his piercing blue eyes challenging Maya. "So, what's the brilliant plan now, fearless leader? More aimless wandering?"

Maya bristled, fighting to keep her voice steady. "We need to find a safe place to regroup and—"

"Regroup?" Jace scoffed, gesturing at the devastation around them. "Look around, Maya. There is no safe place. We need supplies, and we need them now."

She felt the others' eyes on her, waiting for her response. Maya's throat tightened as she struggled to find the right words. "I understand we're in a desperate situation, but—"

"But nothing," Jace interrupted, his voice growing louder. "See that apartment building over there? It's still standing. We should be raiding it for food, water, anything useful. Not wandering around hoping for rescue that might never come."

Maya's mind raced. Part of her knew Jace had a point, but the thought of breaking into people's homes felt wrong. "We can't just start looting," she argued. "What if there are still people inside? What if—"

"What if we starve waiting for your moral compass to point us in the right direction?" Jace shot back, his words laced with venom.

The air crackled with tension as the two locked eyes. Maya could feel the group's uncertainty, their loyalties beginning to waver. She had to decide, and fast.

"Okay," she said finally, hating the taste of compromise on her tongue. "We'll check the building, but carefully. We don't take anything unless we're absolutely sure it's abandoned. Agreed?"

Jace's smirk was triumphant. "Now you're talking sense. Let's move."

As they approached the looming apartment complex, Maya's stomach churned with unease. She prayed she wasn't leading them down a dangerous path, even as a small voice whispered that this might be their only chance at survival.

Maya's heart sank as she watched a small cluster of students huddle around Jace, their heads bent low in conspiratorial whispers. His words, though inaudible, carried an unmistakable undercurrent of discontent that rippled through the group.

"We should have gone in already," one of Jace's followers muttered, just loud enough for Maya to hear. "Every second we waste out here is—"

"Is time spent ensuring we don't make a fatal mistake," Maya interjected, her voice steady despite the tremor in her hands. She scanned the crumbling facade of the apartment building, searching for any signs of life or danger. "We need to be smart about this."

Jace's laugh was sharp and mirthless. "Smart? You call this smart?" He gestured broadly at the group, huddled and uncertain in the shadow of the looming structure. "While we're out here playing it safe, someone else could be clearing out everything useful inside."

Maya felt a flicker of doubt, but pushed it aside. "We stick to the plan," she said firmly, meeting Jace's challenging gaze. "Safety in numbers, remember?"

"Safety?" Jace scoffed, his voice carrying to the entire group now. "There's no safety anymore, Maya. Only survival. And your way? It's going to get us all killed."

A murmur of agreement rippled through some of the students. Maya's chest tightened as she saw the fear and uncertainty in their eyes. She knew she had to act, to reassert her leadership without becoming the dictator Jace was painting her as.

Taking a deep breath, Maya stepped forward. "I hear your concerns," she said, addressing the entire group. "And you're right, we need to act. But we do it together, watching each other's backs. That's how we've made it this far."

She turned to face the apartment building, her mind racing. "We'll split into teams. Two to search, one to keep watch. Rotate every fifteen minutes. No one goes anywhere alone, understood?"

There was a moment of tense silence before a chorus of quiet agreements answered her. Maya exhaled slowly, relief mingling with the weight of responsibility.

As the group began to organize, Jace brushed past her, his voice low and menacing. "Nice save, princess. But don't think this is over. When things get really tough—and they will—they'll see you for what you really are: a scared little girl playing at being a leader."

Maya clenched her fists, fighting back the urge to lash out. Instead, she met his gaze steadily. "We'll see about that, Jace. For now, let's focus on what matters – keeping everyone alive."

As Jace moved away, Maya closed her eyes briefly, steeling herself for whatever challenges lay ahead. The game had changed, and she knew that from now on, every decision would be a tightrope walk between unity and control.

Maya's eyes scanned the desolate cityscape as they ventured deeper into the heart of downtown. The eerie silence enveloped them, broken only by the occasional crunch of debris under their feet. Towering skyscrapers, once alive with bustling activity, now loomed like silent sentinels over the devastation.

"It's so... quiet," Riley whispered, her voice barely audible. "I never thought I'd miss the sound of traffic."

Maya nodded, her throat tight. "Yeah, it's unsettling. Keep your eyes open, though. We don't know what—or who—might be out here."

As they rounded a corner, the full extent of their isolation hit them. A sea of abandoned cars stretched before them, their owners long gone. Shattered storefronts gaped like open wounds, their contents spilled across the sidewalks.

Benji kicked at a broken piece of concrete. "This is hopeless. How are we supposed to survive in this... wasteland?"

Maya felt a flicker of irritation, quickly suppressed. "We survive by sticking together, Benji. One step at a time."

She closed her eyes briefly, fighting back a wave of despair. How long could she keep up this facade of confidence? The weight of their isolation pressed down on her, threatening to crush her resolve.

Opening her eyes, Maya spotted a partially intact convenience store. "Let's check it out. There might be supplies we can use."

As they approached the store, the silence seemed to deepen. No hum of electricity, no distant sirens, no chatter of people going about their day. Just the sound of their own breathing and footsteps echoing off the empty buildings.

Maya's mind raced. How long would it be before help arrived? Would it ever come? She pushed the thoughts aside, focusing on the immediate task at hand.

"Riley, you and I will go in. Benji, keep watch out here. If you see or hear anything unusual, give a sharp whistle. Got it?"

Benji nodded glumly, while Riley gave a determined "Roger that."

As they entered the store, the darkness closed in around them. Maya fumbled for her flashlight, its beam cutting through the gloom. Shelves lay overturned, their contents scattered across the floor.

"This is insane," Riley muttered, her voice tight with tension. "It's like we're the last people on Earth."

Maya swallowed hard, fighting back her own fears. "We're not. There have to be others out there. We just... we just need to hold on until we find them."

As they gathered what meager supplies they could find, Maya couldn't shake the feeling of being watched. The silence pressed in on her, amplifying every small sound. She knew it was just her imagination, but the weight of their isolation felt almost tangible in that moment.

Stepping back outside, Maya took a deep breath of the cool autumn air. The overcast sky seemed to mirror the group's mood, gray and oppressive.

"We'll get through this," she said, as much to herself as to the others. "We have each other. That's more than a lot of people might have right now."

But as they moved on, the empty streets stretching endlessly before them, Maya couldn't help but wonder how long their unity would last in the face of this overwhelming desolation.

Maya's eyes darted from one storefront to another, searching desperately for any sign of life or functioning technology. "There," she pointed, her voice a mixture of hope and uncertainty. "That electronics store might have something we can use."

The group hurried inside, their footsteps echoing in the eerie silence. Shattered glass crunched beneath their feet as they navigated through toppled displays.

"Spread out," Maya directed, her voice wavering slightly. "Look for anything that might work—phones, radios, anything."

As they searched, Maya's mind raced. We need to contact someone. Anyone. She picked up a smartphone, its screen cracked but intact. Her fingers trembled as she pressed the power button. Nothing.

"Any luck?" Riley called from across the store.

Maya shook her head, frustration building. "Keep looking."

Minutes stretched into what felt like hours as they combed through the debris. Each failed attempt chipped away at Maya's resolve.

"It's useless," Jace's voice cut through the silence, dripping with disdain. "We're wasting time here."

Maya's jaw clenched. "We have to try, Jace. We can't just give up."

"Why not?" he challenged, stepping closer. "Face it, Maya. No one's coming to save us. We need to save ourselves."

As their eyes locked in a silent battle of wills, Tariq observed from the shadows. His gaze flicked between Maya and Jace, noting the subtle shift in the group's dynamics. Some students nodded in agreement with Jace, while others huddled closer to Maya.

Maya felt a knot forming in her stomach. She's losing them, she thought, panic rising in her chest. But what if Jace is right? What if no one's coming?

"One more try," she said aloud, her voice firmer than she felt. "Then we'll reassess our plan."

As Maya turned away, Tariq's eyes narrowed. The seeds of conflict had been planted, and he wondered how long it would be before they took root and tore the group apart.

Maya trudged through the rubble-strewn streets, leading her weary group back to their temporary shelter—a partially collapsed school gymnasium. The fading light cast long shadows across the devastated cityscape, mirroring the growing darkness in Maya's heart.

As they entered the gym, the weight of responsibility crashed down on her shoulders. Maya's eyes scanned the tired, scared faces of her classmates. Some huddled in small groups, whispering among themselves, while others sat alone, staring blankly at nothing.

"Alright, everyone," Maya called out, her voice steadier than she felt. "Let's regroup and figure out our next move."

As the students gathered around her, Maya's mind raced. Do we wait for rescue that might never come, or do we start planning for long-term survival? The question burned in her mind, demanding an answer she wasn't sure she had.

"What's the plan, Maya?" a voice called out from the crowd.

Maya took a deep breath, buying herself a moment to think. "We... we need to consider our options," she began, her words careful and measured. "We've been waiting for help, but..."

"But it's not coming," Jace interrupted, his voice sharp. "We need to face facts and start taking care of ourselves."

Maya felt a flash of irritation. "We don't know that for certain, Jace. There could be rescue efforts underway that we just can't see or hear yet."

As she spoke, Maya's mind whirled with possibilities. If we wait, we might miss our chance to secure resources. But if we focus on long-term survival, are we giving up hope too soon?

"I think," Maya continued, her voice growing stronger, "we need to find a balance. We can't just sit here and do nothing, but we also can't abandon the possibility of rescue."

She looked around at the faces watching her, some nodding in agreement, others skeptical. The pressure of their expectations weighed heavily on her.

"What do you suggest?" someone asked.

Maya squared her shoulders, planning. "We'll split our focus. Some of us will work on improving our shelter and searching for supplies. Others will keep trying to make contact with the outside world."

As she laid out her plan, Maya felt a mix of relief and trepidation. Was this the right choice? Or was she just delaying the inevitable?

"It's not enough," Jace muttered, loud enough for everyone to hear.

Maya met his gaze, steeling herself. "It's a start, Jace. We need to work together if we're going to survive this."

As the group began to disperse, Maya felt the weight of her decision settling on her. She'd made her choice, for better or worse. Now she just had to hope it was the right one.

Maya's shoulders sagged as the weight of her decision settled over her. The cool autumn air whispered through the cracks of their temporary shelter, carrying the acrid scent of smoke from distant fires. She closed her eyes, trying to calm her racing thoughts.

"Hey," a soft voice cut through her internal turmoil. Maya looked up to see Riley's freckled face, her green eyes filled with concern. "You're doing the right thing, you know."

Maya let out a shaky breath. "Am I? It feels like I'm just... guessing."

Riley placed a reassuring hand on Maya's arm. "Listen, we need to focus on the basics first. Safe shelter, food, water. That's not just survival, it's smart leadership."

"You really think so?" Maya asked, her voice barely above a whisper.

Riley nodded firmly. "Absolutely. Look, why don't we start by organizing search parties? We can scout for secure locations and gather supplies at the same time."

Maya felt a small spark of confidence ignite within her. "That's... actually a great idea. We could cover more ground that way."

As they began to discuss the details, a commotion near the shelter's entrance caught their attention. Jace's tall figure loomed in the doorway, his blue eyes glinting with a dangerous excitement.

"While you're all sitting here playing house," he announced, his voice dripping with disdain, "my team and I are going to hit up that convenience store we passed earlier. Who knows what kind of supplies we might find?"

Maya felt her jaw clench. "Jace, we need to be careful. We don't know if those buildings are structurally sound after the quake."

Jace's smirk was razor-sharp. "Sometimes you have to take risks to survive, Maya. But don't worry, we'll bring back enough for everyone... if there's anything left."

As Jace and his followers filed out, Maya's mind raced. Should she stop them? Force them to stay? The idea of fracturing the group further made her stomach churn.

"Let them go," Riley said quietly. "We need to focus on what we can control."

Maya nodded, her resolve strengthening. "You're right. We'll stick to our plan. Unity is what will keep us alive in the long run."

As she turned to address the remaining group members, Maya silently vowed to prove that compassion and cooperation could triumph over chaos. The path ahead was uncertain, but she was determined to lead them through it, one careful step at a time.

Maya paced the length of their makeshift shelter, her footsteps echoing in the eerie silence. The weight of responsibility pressed down on her shoulders, making each step feel like wading through mud. She glanced at the worried faces around her, trying to muster a reassuring smile that didn't quite reach her eyes.

A commotion outside broke the tense atmosphere. Jace's booming voice carried through the air, followed by excited chatter and the sound of rustling bags. Maya's heart sank as she stepped out to face the returning group.

Jace strode in, arms laden with supplies, his followers trailing behind him like eager puppies. His blue eyes gleamed with triumph as he dumped his haul on the ground.

"Look what we found!" he crowed, gesturing to the pile of canned food, bottled water, and first aid supplies. "While you were all sitting pretty, we actually did something useful."

Maya fought to keep her voice steady. "That was incredibly risky, Jace. You could have been hurt, or worse."

Jace scoffed. "But we weren't. And now we have what we need to survive."

Some of Maya's group members eyed the supplies hungrily, whispering among themselves. She could feel their doubt growing, questioning her cautious approach.

"We need to think long-term," Maya argued, her hands clenching at her sides. "Raiding every building in sight isn't sustainable."

"And what's your brilliant plan?" Jace challenged, stepping closer. "Wait for rescue that might never come?"

Maya's mind raced, searching for the right words to regain control of the situation. But as she looked around at the conflicted faces surrounding them, she realized the damage was already done. The seeds of discord had been planted, and she could only hope they wouldn't take root.

Maya took a deep breath, steeling herself. "We're stronger together, Jace. Cooperation is our best chance at survival."

Jace's eyes narrowed. "Cooperation? That's your grand plan?" He turned to address the group, his voice rising. "While Maya here wants us to hold hands and sing kumbaya, the world out there is falling apart. We need action, not wishful thinking!"

A murmur of agreement rippled through some of the students. Maya felt a knot form in her stomach as she watched doubt flicker across faces she'd come to rely on.

"We can't just turn on each other," Maya countered, her voice wavering slightly. "That's exactly how we'll—"

"How we'll what?" Jace interrupted, his tone mocking. "Survive? Because from where I'm standing, your leadership is going to get us all killed."

The words hit Maya like a physical blow. She struggled to maintain her composure, acutely aware of all eyes on her. This was the moment she'd dreaded – her authority openly challenged; her decisions questioned.

"I'm trying to keep us safe," she said, hating how defensive she sounded.

"Safe?" Jace laughed bitterly. "Look around, Maya. There is no 'safe' anymore. It's survive or die, and your way? It's a death sentence."

Maya watched helplessly as several students nodded, moving to stand closer to Jace. The fracture in the group was becoming a chasm, and she felt powerless to stop it.

'They're slipping away,' she thought, panic rising in her chest. 'Everything's falling apart, and I don't know how to fix it.'

Maya retreated to a quiet corner of the warehouse, her body sagging against a stack of crates. The dim light filtering through dust-covered windows cast long shadows across her face, accentuating the exhaustion etched into her features. She closed her eyes, allowing the weight of the day to settle over her like a heavy blanket.

"What am I doing wrong?" she whispered to herself, her voice barely audible over the muffled conversations of the group.

Opening her eyes, Maya gazed out at the scattered remnants of her once-united team. Small clusters had formed, some huddled around Jace, others casting uncertain glances her way. The sight sent a pang through her chest.

"I can't let this fall apart," Maya murmured, her resolve hardening. "We need each other now more than ever."

She straightened, squaring her shoulders. As she did, her gaze fell upon a discarded first aid kit. An idea began to form.

"Hey, everyone," Maya called out, her voice steadier than she felt. "I think we should take inventory of our supplies. It'll help us plan better."

A few curious faces turned towards her. Even Jace paused his conversation, eyebrow raised.

Maya continued, "If we work together, we can get it done quickly. Plus, it'll give us a clearer picture of where we stand."

She held her breath, waiting. After a moment, Riley stepped forward. "I think that's a good idea," he said, offering Maya a small smile.

Slowly, others began to nod. Even some of Jace's followers looked interested.

As the group began to organize, Maya felt a flicker of hope. 'It's not much,' she thought, 'but it's a start. We can rebuild from here.'

She knew the road ahead would be challenging, fraught with conflicts and challenging decisions. But as she watched her classmates working side by side, Maya felt her determination grow.

'I won't let Jace's way win,' she promised herself. 'There has to be a better path forward, and I'm going to find it.'

Maya's eyes scanned the dimly lit warehouse, taking in the sight of her classmates sorting through meager supplies. Her heart clenched as she realized how little they had. Despite the momentary unity, she could feel the underlying tension, like a fault line ready to rupture.

"We're running low on water," Riley reported, his voice tight with concern.

Maya nodded, her mind racing. "We'll need to organize a scavenging team," she said, trying to keep her voice steady. "But we have to be careful. The aftershocks—"

"Careful?" Jace interrupted, his blue eyes glinting dangerously. "While we're being 'careful,' we're going to die of thirst."

Maya felt a surge of anger, but she pushed it down. "We need to work together, Jace. Recklessness could get people killed."

"And your caution already has," he shot back.

The words hit Maya like a physical blow. She thought of the classmates they'd already lost, faces flashing before her eyes. For a moment, doubt threatened to overwhelm her.

'No,' she thought fiercely. 'I can't let him win. I can't let fear rule us.'

"Listen," Maya said, her voice low but firm. "I know you're scared. We all are. But turning on each other isn't the answer. We're stronger together."

She could see the conflict in some faces, the wavering loyalty. It was now or never.

"I promise you," Maya continued, her resolve strengthening with each word, "I will do everything in my power to keep us alive and united. But I need your trust. I need your help."

The warehouse fell silent. Maya held her breath, feeling the weight of leadership pressing down on her shoulders. In that moment, surrounded by the rubble of their former lives, she silently vowed to find a way through this chaos, no matter the cost.

As the quiet stretched on, the looming specter of conflict hung heavy in the air. Maya knew that this was just the beginning. In this fractured, devastated world, every decision, every moment could tip the balance. But she was ready to face it head-on, for the sake of them all.

CHAPTER 3

The First Night

The ground heaves beneath Maya's feet, a low groan emanating from the earth's depths. Dust rains down from the cracked ceiling as the aftershock rattles the group's tenuous shelter.

"Get down!" Maya shouts above the rising cries of panic. "Move away from the walls!"

She lunges forward, grabbing a younger student by the arm and pulling her under a sturdy table. Around her, the others scramble for cover, their faces pale in the flickering light of the dying flashlight.

Jace stands amidst the chaos, his jaw clenched tight. He meets Maya's gaze across the room, a challenge in his eyes. As the tremors subside, he steps forward, his voice cutting through the whimpers and ragged breaths.

"This is what happens when we just sit here waiting for someone to save us," he says, his tone laced with scorn. "We're sitting ducks, and Maya's 'plan' is going to get us all killed."

Maya bristles at his words, but a flicker of doubt sparks in her gut. She pushes it down, rising to her feet. "We need to stay calm and stick together. Rushing out there without thinking will only-"

"Only what?" Jace interrupts, his gaze sweeping over the huddled group. "Keep us safe? Because that's working out so well." He gestures to the fractured walls, the debris littering the floor.

Maya opens her mouth to respond, but the words stick in her throat. She sees the fear in the others' eyes, the way some of them look to Jace with a desperate kind of hope.

"We can't just wait for rescue," Jace continues, his voice growing stronger, more persuasive. "We need to take control of our own survival. Find supplies, secure our own shelter. I can lead us to safety, but we have to act now."

Maya's heart sinks as she watches a few students nod in agreement, their trust in her leadership eroding with each passing second. She wants to argue, to make them see reason, but a small, insidious voice whispers in the back of her mind.

What if Jace is right? What if her caution is only delaying the inevitable?

She shakes her head, forcing the thought away. No, she has to believe in the power of unity, of working together. Even as the ground shifts beneath her feet and the walls crumble around her, Maya knows she can't let fear tear them apart.

But as Jace's influence grows, as more eyes turn to him in the shadowed room, Maya feels the weight of leadership bearing down on her shoulders, heavier than any fallen stone.

Maya takes a deep breath, steadying herself against the tremors that shake the very foundation of their shelter. She steps forward, meeting Jace's challenging gaze with a quiet determination.

"We can't just rush out there without a plan," she says, her voice clear despite the quaver of fear she feels inside. "We need to think this through, work together. Splitting up now will only make us more vulnerable."

Jace scoffs, a harsh sound that cuts through the tense silence. "Vulnerable? Look around you, Maya. We're already vulnerable. Waiting for rescue that may never come is just a slower way to die."

His words hang in the air, heavy with the unspoken fear they all share. Maya sees it reflected in the faces of her classmates, the way some of them shift closer to Jace, drawn to his boldness in the face of their bleak reality.

"I know you're scared," Maya says, addressing the group as a whole. "I am too. But we have to remember what's important. We have each other. If we start turning on one another now, we've already lost."

She searches their faces, looking for a glimmer of the unity they once shared. Some meet her gaze with uncertainty, others with a flicker of hope. But too many eyes slide away, finding solace in Jace's confident stance.

Maya's heart aches with the realization that her grip on the group is slipping. She wants to reach out, to pull them back together, but the chasm between them feels wider with each passing moment.

In the shadows of the crumbling room, Jace's smile takes on a sharp edge. He leans in closer to those nearest to him, his voice low and conspiratorial. "Maya's way will get us killed. We need to be proactive, take what we need to survive. I have a plan, but I need your support."

Maya watches helplessly as more students gravitate towards Jace, their fear overriding their sense of community. She feels like she's standing on a precipice, the ground crumbling beneath her feet.

But even as despair threatens to engulf her, Maya clings to the belief that hope is not lost. She may have lost ground tonight, but she refuses to give up on the power of unity.

In the flickering light of their fading flashlights, Maya meets Riley's gaze across the room. In her friend's eyes, she finds a glimmer of unwavering support, a silent promise that she's not alone in this fight.

Maya draws strength from that connection, from the knowledge that there are still those who believe in the importance of staying human, even in the darkest of times.

As the aftershocks continue to rattle the city outside and Jace's influence grows like a shadow within their group, Maya silently vows to find a way to keep them together.

No matter what it takes.

The flickering light of a small fire illuminates the tense faces huddled in the warehouse, casting long shadows on the cracked walls. Maya watches as students break off into smaller groups, their hushed conversations punctuated by the occasional tremor that sends ripples of fear through the room.

"We can't just sit here and wait for help that may never come," a girl named Sarah argues, her voice sharp with frustration. "We need to find food, water, medical supplies. We need to survive."

"And what if we get lost out there? Or trapped in another collapse?" Riley counters, her brow furrowed with concern. "We don't know what the city looks like now. It's too risky."

Maya steps forward, her heart pounding as she feels the weight of every gaze upon her. "I know you're scared," she begins, her voice steady despite the churning in her gut. "But we have to stay calm and think this through. Rushing out into the unknown could put us in even more danger."

Jace scoffs, his eyes glinting in the firelight. "You think hiding in here like rats is the answer? We need to take control of our own fate."

Maya meets his challenging stare head-on, refusing to back down. "And what exactly is your plan, Jace? Lead us into a deathtrap? We need to be smart about this."

"Smart?" Jace laughs, a harsh, mocking sound. "Like your brilliant idea to wait for a rescue that's not coming? Face it, Maya. The world we knew is gone. It's time to adapt or die."

The group erupts into heated arguments, voices rising as fear and desperation take hold. Maya looks around at the faces of her classmates, seeing the cracks forming in their unity.

"Enough!" she shouts, her voice cutting through the chaos. Silence falls, all eyes turning to her once more. "Fighting among ourselves won't solve anything. We need to work together, now more than ever."

But even as she speaks the words, Maya feels a flicker of doubt. How long can she keep them together when the very ground beneath their feet is shifting?

As if in response to her thoughts, another tremor rocks the warehouse, dust raining down from the rafters. Maya watches as Sarah and a few others huddle closer to Jace, their eyes alight with a desperate hunger for action.

Maya's chest tightens with the realization that her grip on the group is slipping. She catches Riley's eye, seeing her own fears reflected back at her.

In that moment, Maya knows that the battle lines have been drawn. The aftershocks of the earthquake pale in comparison to the tremors of discord rippling through the group.

And she can only pray that when the dust settles, there will be something left to salvage.

Maya takes a deep breath, steadying herself as the aftershock subsides. The warehouse is quiet now, but the tension hangs thick in the air. She can feel the weight of everyone's gaze upon her, waiting for her next move.

"Listen," she begins, her voice calm but firm. "I know you're scared. I am too. But we can't let fear drive us apart. We're stronger together."

Jace scoffs, his arms crossed over his chest. "Stronger together? Look around you, Maya. The world's falling apart. It's every man for himself now."

A murmur of agreement ripples through his growing faction, their faces hardening with resolve. Maya's heart sinks as she realizes just how deep the cracks in their unity have become.

"And what happens when we run out of supplies?" she counters, holding Jace's gaze. "When we're out there on our own, with no one to watch our backs?"

"We take what we need," Jace retorts, his voice cold. "We adapt. We survive."

Maya shakes her head, frustration building in her chest. "At what cost? Our humanity? Our compassion? If we lose that, what's the point of surviving at all?"

The group falls silent, the weight of her words settling over them like a blanket. For a moment, Maya sees a flicker of doubt in some of their eyes, a glimmer of the unity they once shared.

But it's short-lived. Jace steps forward, his jaw set with determination. "You can cling to your ideals all you want, Maya. But when push comes to shove, it's the strong who will survive. And I intend to be one of them."

With that, he turns and strides away, his followers trailing behind him. Maya watches them go, a sense of helplessness washing over her.

Riley places a hand on her shoulder, squeezing gently. "You can't save everyone, Maya," she murmurs. "But you can't give up either. We need you."

Maya nods, swallowing past the lump in her throat. She knows Riley is right. She can't let Jace's words shake her resolve. She has to be strong, for herself and for those who still believe in her.

But as she looks out over the splintered remains of her group, Maya can't help but wonder how long that strength will last. The world they once knew is gone, and in its place is a harsh new reality where trust is a luxury they can no longer afford.

The night stretches on, the darkness broken only by the flickering light of their dwindling candles. Maya sits apart from the others, lost in thought as she tries to plan their next move.

But even as she weighs their options, she knows that the real battle lies ahead. Jace's faction may have left, but their influence lingers like a poison in the air.

And as the hours tick by, Maya can feel the walls closing in around her, the weight of responsibility crushing her from all sides.

She can only hope that when the sun rises, it will bring with it a new day and a new chance to hold her fractured group together. But deep down, she knows that the cracks are only growing wider, and the storm is far from over.

Maya's eyes sting with exhaustion as she stares into the dancing flame of the candle before her. The small circle of light feels like the only warmth left in a world turned cold and unforgiving. Around her, the remnants of her group huddle in small clusters, their whispers a constant reminder of the division that now plagues them.

She knows she should sleep, but her mind won't stop racing. Every decision she's made, every choice that's brought them to this point, plays out in an endless loop behind her eyes. The weight of it all presses down on her chest, making it hard to breathe.

"Maya?" Riley's voice breaks through her thoughts, soft and tentative. "Are you okay?"

Maya looks up, forcing a tired smile. "I'm fine. Just thinking."

Riley settles down beside her, the warmth of her presence a small comfort in the chilly night air. "You can't do this all on your own, you know. We're in this together."

Maya nods, but the words feel hollow. She knows Riley means well, but the truth is, she's never felt more alone. The responsibility of keeping them all alive rests squarely on her shoulders, and the burden is almost too much to bear.

"I just keep wondering if I'm doing the right thing," Maya admits, her voice barely above a whisper. "What if Jace is right? What if waiting here is just delaying the inevitable?"

Riley shakes her head firmly. "Jace is scared, just like the rest of us. But running off half-cocked isn't going to solve anything. We need to stick together, now more than ever."

Maya knows she's right, but the doubt lingers like a bitter taste in the back of her throat. She's seen the way some of the others look at her now, the uncertainty in their eyes. How long before they start to question her leadership too?

As if sensing her thoughts, Riley reaches out and takes her hand, giving it a reassuring squeeze. "We'll get through this, Maya. I know we will. And when we do, it'll be because of you."

Maya wants to believe her, wants to cling to that glimmer of hope like a lifeline. But as she looks out over the sea of frightened faces, the shadows of the night pressing in from all sides, she can't shake the feeling that this is only the beginning.

The ground trembles beneath them, another aftershock rippling through the ruined city. Maya feels it in her bones, a deep, unsettling vibration that seems to echo the turmoil inside her own heart.

She knows that come morning, she'll have to put on a brave face once more, to be the leader they all need her to be. But for now, in the quiet of the night, she allows herself a moment of vulnerability, a moment to feel the full weight of the impossible task ahead.

And as the candle flickers and dies, plunging them all into darkness, Maya closes her eyes and prays for the strength to see them through to the other side.

Maya's eyes fluttered open, the first rays of dawn filtering through the cracks in the warehouse walls. She'd barely slept, her mind churning with the events of the previous day and the challenges that lay ahead. Slowly, she sat up, her body stiff from the hard concrete floor.

Around her, the others began to stir, their faces etched with the same weariness and fear she felt in her own heart. Jace was already awake, his gaze hard as he surveyed the group. When his eyes met hers, Maya saw the challenge there, the unspoken question: What now?

She stood, squaring her shoulders as she faced them all. "Okay, everyone, listen up. We need to take stock of our supplies and figure out our next move. Jace, you and your group can search the east side of the warehouse. Riley and I will take the west. We'll meet back here in an hour to discuss what we've found."

Jace's lip curled in a smirk. "Sure thing, boss. But just remember, we're not your little soldiers to command. We're in this together, whether you like it or not."

Maya bristled at his tone, but she forced herself to remain calm. "I know that, Jace. But right now, we need to work together if we're going to survive. Can you do that, or are you going to keep trying to undermine me at every turn?"

Jace held her gaze for a long moment, the tension between them palpable. Finally, he shrugged. "Fine. We'll play it your way, for now. But don't expect me to follow you blindly. I'll do what I think is best for the group, even if it means going against your orders."

With that, he turned and stalked away, his group falling in behind him. Maya watched them go, her heart heavy with the knowledge that this was only the beginning of their struggles.

As she and Riley began their search, Maya's mind raced with the implications of Jace's words. She knew he was right, in a way. They were all in this together, and she couldn't expect them to follow her without question. But at the same time, she knew that without some kind of leadership, they'd be lost.

"What are we going to do, Riley?" she murmured, her voice barely above a whisper. "I'm trying my best to keep everyone together, but Jace... he's not making it easy. And the others... I can see the doubt in their eyes. They're starting to wonder if I'm really cut out for this."

Riley paused in her search, turning to face Maya with a fierce determination in her eyes. "Don't let him get to you, Maya. You're doing everything you can to keep us safe. And the others... they're simply scared. They'll come around, once they see that you're the one who's going to get us through this."

Maya swallowed hard, wanting to believe her friend's words. But deep down, she couldn't shake the feeling that things were only going to get worse before they got better.

As they continued their search, Maya's thoughts turned to the future. What would happen if they couldn't find enough supplies? What if the aftershocks kept coming, wearing them down until they couldn't go on? What if Jace's influence continued to grow, until the group was divided beyond repair?

She shook her head, trying to banish the dark thoughts. She had to stay focused on the present, on the task at hand. But even as she rummaged through the debris, her mind kept circling back to the same question: What was the right thing to do?

Was it to maintain her values of unity and cooperation, even if it meant sacrificing their chances of survival? Or was it to embrace a more assertive stance, to do whatever it took to keep them alive, even if it meant compromising her morals?

Maya didn't know the answer. All she knew was that the weight of responsibility was crushing her, the fear of losing control and failing her friends an ever-present specter in her mind.

But she couldn't let them see her doubt, her fear. She had to be strong, for them. Even if it meant making the hard choices, the ones that kept her awake at night.

Because in the end, that was what leadership was all about. Not just making the decisions, but living with the consequences. And as Maya looked out over the ruined city, the rising sun casting long shadows across the rubble, she knew that those consequences were only just beginning.

Maya's hands trembled as she sifted through the rubble, her breath coming in short, sharp gasps. The aftershock had passed, but the fear still lingered, a suffocating weight pressing down on her chest.

"Maya?" Riley's voice cut through the haze of panic, soft but insistent. "Are you okay?"

Maya looked up, meeting Riley's concerned gaze. She opened her mouth to respond, but the words stuck in her throat, choked by the tears she refused to let fall.

Riley moved closer, placing a gentle hand on Maya's shoulder. "Hey, it's alright. We're going to get through this, together."

Maya shook her head, a bitter laugh escaping her lips. "How can you be so sure? Look around us, Riley. Everything's falling apart."

"I know it seems that way," Riley said, her voice steady and calm. "But we can't give up hope. We have to believe that we'll find a way out of this."

Maya sighed, running a hand through her tangled hair. "I want to believe that, I really do. But Jace... he's not making it easy. He's undermining everything I'm trying to do, turning people against me."

Riley's eyes flashed with anger. "Jace is a fool. He thinks that rushing into dangerous situations is the answer, but it's not. It's reckless and irresponsible."

"But what if he's right?" Maya whispered, voicing the fear that had been gnawing at her for days. "What if I'm the one who's wrong? What if I'm leading us all to our deaths?"

Riley gripped Maya's shoulders, forcing her to meet her gaze. "Listen to me, Maya. You are not wrong. You're doing the best you can in an impossible situation. And I believe in you, even if Jace doesn't."

Maya felt a surge of gratitude, a warmth that pushed back against the icy fear in her veins. "Thank you, Riley. I don't know what I'd do without you."

Riley smiled, a glimmer of light in the darkness. "You'd figure it out. You're stronger than you think, Maya. And you're not alone. We're all in this together."

Maya nodded, drawing strength from Riley's words. She knew that the road ahead would be hard, that there would be more challenges and setbacks to come. But with Riley by her side, with the support of those who still believed in her, she felt a flicker of hope.

Maybe they could survive this, after all. Maybe they could find a way to build a new life from the ashes of the old. And maybe, just maybe, Maya could be the leader they needed her to be.

She took a deep breath, squaring her shoulders as she turned back to the task at hand. There was work to be done, and she couldn't afford to waste any more time on doubt and fear.

Because in the end, that was what survival was all about. Not just enduring the hardships, but finding the strength to keep going, no matter what. And as Maya looked out over the ruined city, the rising sun casting long shadows across the rubble, she knew that she would keep going, for as long as it took.

Maya's gaze drifted across the battered faces of her group, their eyes reflecting a mixture of fear and exhaustion. She caught sight of Jace, his jaw clenched as he surveyed the damage from the aftershock. Their eyes met briefly, and Maya saw the challenge in his stare, the unspoken accusation that she wasn't doing enough to protect them.

She tore her gaze away, focusing instead on the task at hand. "We need to check our supplies," she said, her voice steady despite the tremor of uncertainty she felt inside. "Make sure nothing was damaged in the quake."

Riley nodded, already moving to assess their meager stockpile. "On it. We should also see if there's anything useful in the rubble. Might be some supplies we missed earlier."

Maya agreed, grateful for Riley's practical approach. It helped ground her, reminding her that there were still things they could do, actions they could take to improve their situation.

As they worked, Maya's mind churned with the weight of her responsibilities. She knew that Jace was right, in a way. They couldn't just sit here and wait for rescue. They needed to be proactive, to find a way to secure their own survival.

But at what cost? How far was she willing to go to keep her people safe? The thought made her stomach twist with unease.

"You're doing the best you can," Riley said quietly, as if sensing Maya's inner turmoil. "Don't let Jace get in your head. He's just scared, like the rest of us."

Maya sighed, running a hand through her tangled hair. "I know. But he's not wrong, Riley. We can't just wait around and hope for the best. We need a plan."

"And we'll make one," Riley assured her. "But we can't just rush into things without thinking it through. That's how people get hurt."

Maya knew she was right, but the pressure was mounting. She could feel Jace's gaze boring into her back, could sense the growing unrest among the group.

They needed a leader, now more than ever. And whether she liked it or not, that leader was her.

She took a deep breath, squaring her shoulders as she turned to face the others. "Listen up," she said, her voice ringing out across the huddle of frightened faces. "I know you're scared. I am too. But we can't let fear control us. We need to work together, to find a way to survive this."

She met Jace's gaze head-on, refusing to back down. "We'll make a plan. But we'll do it the right way. No unnecessary risks, no reckless actions. We stick together, and we look out for each other. That's the only way we're going to make it through this."

There were murmurs of agreement, nods of approval from those who still believed in her. But Maya could feel the tension in the air, the growing divide between those who supported her and those who were swayed by Jace's bold promises.

She knew that the real test was still to come, that there would be harder choices ahead. But for now, she had to focus on the present, on getting her people through the next hour, the next day.

And with Riley by her side, with the strength of her convictions to guide her, Maya knew that she would keep fighting, no matter what challenges lay ahead.

Maya closed her eyes, trying to steady her racing heart. The aftershock had passed, but the fear lingered, a constant presence in the back of her mind. She couldn't afford to let it consume her, not when so many were counting on her to lead them through this nightmare.

As she took a deep breath, a memory surfaced, unbidden. She was twelve years old, at the park with her little brother, Ethan. He had wandered off while she was distracted, and when she found him, he was perched at the top of the tallest slide, his face pale with fear.

"I'm stuck," he had whimpered, his knuckles white as he gripped the sides of the slide. "I can't do it, Maya. I'm scared."

Maya had climbed up beside him, wrapping an arm around his trembling shoulders. "It's okay to be scared," she had told him. "But you're braver than you think. We'll do it together, okay?"

And they had, Maya going down first and catching Ethan at the bottom, both of them laughing with relief and exhilaration.

The memory faded, but the feeling remained—that fierce protectiveness, that unshakeable determination to keep her loved ones safe. It was the same feeling that had driven her to take charge when the earthquake hit, to step up and lead when no one else would.

Maya opened her eyes, her resolve hardening. She couldn't let fear hold her back, not when lives depended on her. She had to be strong, like she was for Ethan all those years ago.

She turned to Riley, her voice low but steady. "We need to take stock of our supplies, figure out how long we can last on what we have. And we need to start thinking about finding a more permanent shelter, somewhere safer than this."

Riley nodded, her expression grim but determined. "I'll take a small group to scout the area, see if we can find any other survivors or resources."

Maya hesitated, the thought of splitting up making her stomach clench with worry. But she knew Riley was right. They couldn't just sit and wait for rescue, not when help might never come.

"Be careful," she said, gripping Riley's hand tightly. "And come back safe."

As Riley gathered a few volunteers and set off into the rubble-strewn streets, Maya turned her attention back to the rest of the group, her mind already racing with plans and contingencies.

She knew it wouldn't be easy, that there would be setbacks and challenges at every turn. But she also knew that she would never stop fighting, never stop doing everything in her power to keep her people alive.

Because that was who she was—a protector, a leader, a beacon of hope in a world gone dark.

Jace sat on the cold, hard floor of the school gymnasium, his back pressed against the wall. The aftershock had settled, but the fear and tension in the room remained palpable. He watched as Maya moved among the other students, offering comfort and reassurance.

A bitter taste filled his mouth. He knew her type—the idealists who believed in the inherent goodness of people, who thought that cooperation and compassion would see them through any crisis. But Jace knew better.

His mind drifted back to that fateful day, the memory as vivid as if it had just happened...

The smell of smoke filled his nostrils, the sound of screams echoing in his ears. He was just a kid, barely ten years old, watching in horror as his family's apartment building burned. His mother clutched his baby sister, tears streaming down her face as she begged the firefighters to save them.

But the firefighters never came. The authorities, the people who were supposed to protect them, had abandoned them in their moment of need. Jace watched helplessly as the flames consumed everything he had ever known, his mother's screams fading into the roar of the inferno.

He survived, but a part of him died that day—the part that believed in the goodness of others, the part that trusted in the system to keep him safe.

Jace blinked, pulling himself back to the present. He looked around at the frightened, desperate faces of his classmates and knew that they were all in danger of suffering the same fate as his family.

Unless someone did something about it.

He stood up, his voice cutting through the murmurs of the crowd. "We can't just sit here and wait for rescue," he said, his tone harsh and uncompromising. "We need to take action, to do whatever it takes to survive."

Maya turned to face him, her expression wary. "And what exactly do you propose we do?" she asked, her voice calm but firm.

Jace met her gaze, his eyes hard and unyielding. "We need to secure our own resources, to make sure we have what we need to last until help arrives. And if that means taking from others, then so be it."

A murmur of unease rippled through the group, but Jace pressed on. "The world has changed. The old rules don't apply anymore. It's every man for himself now, and if we don't adapt, we'll die."

He could see the conflict in Maya's eyes, the struggle between her ideals and the harsh reality of their situation. But he knew she would never understand, never accept the truth that he had learned the hard way.

Survival required sacrifice, and Jace was willing to make those sacrifices, to do whatever it took to keep himself and those loyal to him alive.

Even if it meant leaving behind the weak and the naive, like Maya and her followers.

Jace turned away, his mind already racing with plans and strategies. He would gather those who shared his vision, those who understood that the only way to survive was to be ruthless and uncompromising.

And together, they would build a new world from the ashes of the old, a world where the strong ruled and the weak perished.

It was the only way forward, the only path to survival in this broken, shattered landscape.

And Jace would lead them there, no matter the cost.

Benji sat apart from the others, his back against the cold concrete wall of their makeshift shelter. The laughter and jokes from earlier in the evening had long since faded, replaced by a heavy silence punctuated only by the occasional sniffle or whispered conversation.

He had tried to keep the mood light, cracking jokes and making silly faces, but as the hours dragged on and the reality of their situation sank in, even his trademark humor had fallen flat.

Now, as he watched the group huddle together in small clusters, their faces etched with fear and uncertainty, Benji felt a growing sense of hopelessness wash over him.

"Hey, Benji," Maya called softly, making her way over to where he sat. "You okay?"

Benji forced a smile, but it felt stiff and unnatural on his face. "Yeah, I'm good. Just... thinking, you know?"

Maya nodded, settling down beside him. "It's a lot to process, isn't it? I keep expecting to wake up and find out this was all just a bad dream."

"If only," Benji muttered, his gaze fixed on the floor. "But this... this is real, isn't it? The earthquake, the destruction, all of it."

"I'm afraid so," Maya said, her voice heavy with sadness. "But we'll get through this, Benji. We have to."

Benji let out a short, humorless laugh. "Will we? Look around, Maya. We're just a bunch of scared kids trapped in a crumbling building with no food, no water, and no way out. How are we supposed to survive this?"

Maya was quiet for a moment, her brow furrowed in thought. "We'll find a way," she said at last, her voice firm with conviction. "We have to stick together, support each other. It's the only way."

Benji shook his head, his eyes stinging with unshed tears. "I want to believe that, Maya. I really do. But what if it's not enough? What if we're just delaying the inevitable?"

The words hung heavy in the air between them, a stark admission of the fear and doubt that had been growing in Benji's heart.

Maya reached out, placing a comforting hand on his shoulder. "We can't think like that, Benji. We have to hold on to hope, even when it feels impossible. We'll get through this, one day at a time."

Benji nodded, but the gesture felt hollow, a mere reflex rather than a true expression of agreement.

As Maya stood and made her way back to the others, Benji remained where he was, his mind churning with dark thoughts and bleak possibilities.

The world had changed, and with it, so had he. The carefree, lighthearted jokester was gone, replaced by a hardened survivor, his innocence and optimism stripped away by the harsh realities of their new existence.

Benji closed his eyes, letting the weight of his newfound cynicism settle over him like a heavy blanket.

There was no going back, no returning to the way things were before.

All they could do now was try to survive, and hope that somewhere along the way, they might find a reason to laugh again.

Tariq sat in a quiet corner of the shelter, his dark eyes scanning the room, taking in every detail, every interaction. He watched as Benji, once the group's lighthearted jester, retreated into himself, his shoulders slumped under the weight of their grim reality.

He observed the way Maya moved among the others, her voice steady and reassuring, even as her own fears flickered in the depths of her eyes. She was a natural leader, but Tariq could see the cracks beginning to form in her facade, the strain of holding everything together taking its toll.

His gaze drifted to Jace, who stood apart from the rest, his stance confident, almost defiant. There was a glint in his eye, a hunger for power that made Tariq uneasy. He could sense the shifting dynamics, the way some of the others were drawn to Jace's bold promises of action and survival.

Tariq's mind raced, analyzing each piece of the puzzle, trying to anticipate the next move. He knew that the divisions within the group would only grow deeper as time passed, as resources dwindled and desperation set in.

He had always been a loner, content to observe from the sidelines, but now, in this new world, he realized that isolation was a luxury he could no longer afford. Sooner or later, he would have to choose a side, to stake his claim in the battle for survival that loomed on the horizon.

Tariq's fingers tightened around the makeshift weapon he had fashioned from a broken pipe, the cold metal a reminder of the harsh realities they now faced. He had never been one for violence, but he knew that in this new world, he would do whatever it took to stay alive.

As the night wore on and the group settled into an uneasy silence, Tariq continued to watch, to plan, to prepare. He knew that the true test was still to come, and he would be ready to face it, no matter the cost.

Tariq's gaze drifted across the warehouse, taking in the huddled groups of survivors scattered throughout the cavernous space. The flickering light of the campfire cast long shadows across their faces, highlighting the fear and uncertainty etched into their features.

He watched as Maya moved among them, her voice low and reassuring as she checked on each person, offering words of comfort and encouragement. Despite the weight of leadership that rested on her shoulders, she remained calm and collected, a beacon of stability in the chaos.

But even as Maya worked to maintain unity, Tariq could see the cracks beginning to form. Jace's followers clustered together, their hushed conversations and furtive glances speaking volumes about their growing dissatisfaction with Maya's cautious approach.

Tariq's mind whirred with calculations, weighing the risks and rewards of each potential path forward. He knew that the decisions made in these early days would shape the course of their survival, and he was determined to be on the winning side.

As the night stretched on, Tariq found himself drawn to the perimeter of the warehouse, his restless energy driving him to pace the length of the building. He paused at a shattered window, peering out into the ruined landscape beyond.

The city lay in ruins, a twisted maze of crumbled buildings and debris-strewn streets. In the distance, the glow of fires lit up the night sky, a reminder of the destruction that had been wrought upon their world.

Tariq's hand tightened on the windowsill, his jaw clenching with resolve. He knew that out there, somewhere, lay the key to their survival - supplies, shelter, perhaps even other survivors. But to reach it, they would have to navigate the treacherous terrain of both the city and the fractured group dynamics within the warehouse.

As he turned back to the group, Tariq's gaze landed on Maya once more. She met his eyes across the room, her expression a mix of determination and exhaustion. In that moment, a flicker of understanding passed between them - a recognition of the challenges that lay ahead and the strength it would take to overcome them.

Tariq nodded almost imperceptibly, a silent acknowledgment of the unspoken alliance that had formed between them. He knew that in the days to come, he would need to choose his allies carefully, and Maya had proven herself to be a formidable leader, even in the face of adversity.

With a final glance at the ruined city beyond, Tariq made his way back to the group, his mind already racing with plans and possibilities. The road ahead would be long and treacherous, but he was ready to face whatever challenges lay in store. For now, all they could do was survive - one day at a time.

Maya's voice cut through the tense silence, her words measured but strained. "We need to focus on what we can control right now. Finding food, securing our shelter, taking care of each other."

She looked around at the faces of her classmates, some filled with fear, others with a growing desperation. The weight of their expectations pressed down on her, but she refused to let it crush her resolve.

"I know it's hard," she continued, her voice gaining strength. "But we can't give up hope. We have to believe that help is coming, that we'll make it through this together."

From the corner of her eye, she caught sight of Jace, his arms crossed and a skeptical expression on his face. She could practically hear his thoughts, the unspoken challenge to her leadership.

Ignoring him, Maya pressed on. "We'll take inventory of what supplies we have left, ration them carefully. And tomorrow, we'll send out a scouting party to search for more."

A murmur rippled through the group, a mix of uncertainty and tentative hope. Maya looked to Riley, seeking support, but found only a flicker of doubt in her friend's eyes.

As if on cue, Jace stepped forward, his voice cutting through the murmurs. "And what if there is no more help coming? What if this is all we have left?"

Maya felt a surge of frustration, but kept her voice steady. "We can't think like that. We have to hold on to hope, to the belief that we'll make it through this."

Jace scoffed, shaking his head. "Hope won't keep us alive, Maya. We need action, not pretty words."

The tension in the room thickened, the divide between them growing more palpable by the second. Maya could feel the eyes of the group on her, waiting for her response.

She took a deep breath, meeting Jace's gaze head-on. "We'll take action, but not at the cost of our humanity. We're not animals, Jace. We can't just turn on each other when things get tough."

Jace's eyes narrowed, a flicker of something dangerous in their depths. "We'll see about that," he muttered, turning away.

Maya watched him go, a sense of unease settling in the pit of her stomach. She knew that this was only the beginning, that the cracks in their group were widening with each passing hour.

But for now, all she could do was hold them together, one fraying thread at a time. She turned back to the group, mustering a smile that didn't quite reach her eyes.

"Let's get some rest," she said softly. "Tomorrow, we start rebuilding."

As the group began to disperse, seeking out what little comfort they could find, Maya felt a hand on her shoulder. She turned to find Riley, her expression a mix of concern and determination.

"I'm with you," Riley said quietly. "No matter what happens, I'm with you."

Maya nodded, grateful for the unwavering support. Together, they watched as the last of the students settled in for the night, the warehouse falling into an uneasy silence.

Outside, the ruined city loomed, a testament to the destruction that had brought them to this moment. But inside, the true battle was only just beginning - a battle for survival, for hope, and for the very soul of their group.

As Maya lay down on the hard concrete floor, staring up at the cracked ceiling, she couldn't shake the feeling that this was only the calm before the storm. The real test was still to come, and she could only pray that they would be strong enough to weather it.

Maya's eyes fluttered open, her brief moments of fitful sleep interrupted by the sounds of discontent echoing through the warehouse. She sat up slowly, her body aching from the hard floor, and surveyed the scene before her.

Clusters of students huddled together, their whispers sharp and urgent. Some cast furtive glances towards Jace, who stood at the edge of the group, his arms crossed and a smirk playing on his lips. Maya's heart sank as she realized the divide that had begun to form.

She pushed herself to her feet, wincing at the stiffness in her muscles. As she approached the group, the whispers died down, replaced by an expectant silence. Maya took a deep breath, her voice steady and calm.

"I know you're scared," she began, "and I know it feels like there's no hope. But we can't give in to despair. We have to stay united, work together, and trust that help will come."

A murmur rippled through the crowd, a mix of agreement and skepticism. Jace's voice cut through the din, his tone mocking.

"Trust? In what? In you?" He stepped forward, his eyes locked on Maya's. "We've been waiting for days, and nothing's changed. We need action, not empty promises."

Maya met his gaze unflinchingly. "Rushing out there without a plan is reckless. We need to be smart, conserve our resources, and—"

"And what? Wait for rescue that might never come?" Jace scoffed. "We need to take matters into our own hands, find our own way out of this mess."

A chorus of agreement rose from some of the students, their faces turning towards Jace with a mix of desperation and hope. Maya's stomach churned as she saw the balance of power shifting before her eyes.

"We can't just abandon each other," she argued, her voice rising. "We're stronger together, and we have a better chance of surviving if we stick together."

But even as the words left her mouth, Maya could see the doubt in their eyes. The seeds of division had been planted, and she could feel her grip on the group slipping.

Jace's voice was almost gentle as he replied, "Survival means making hard choices, Maya. It means doing whatever it takes to stay alive, even if it means leaving behind those who can't keep up."

Maya's fists clenched at her sides, anger and frustration burning in her chest. She wanted to argue, to make them see that Jace's way would only lead to more pain and suffering. But the words stuck in her throat, drowned out by the pounding of her own heart.

As the group began to splinter, some gravitating towards Jace while others remained uncertain, Maya felt a wave of exhaustion wash over her. She had fought so hard to keep them together, to be the leader they needed, but now it seemed like all her efforts had been for nothing.

She turned away, her shoulders sagging under the weight of her responsibilities. In the distance, she could hear Jace's voice, low and persuasive, as he continued to sway the others to his side.

Maya closed her eyes, taking a moment to steady herself. She knew the road ahead would be long and difficult, and there would be times when she would question her own decisions. But she also knew that she couldn't give up, couldn't let Jace's ruthless philosophy take hold.

With a deep breath, Maya squared her shoulders and turned back to face the group. She may have lost ground today, but the fight was far from over. She would find a way to keep them safe, to hold on to their humanity, no matter what challenges lay ahead.

For now, all she could do was take it one step at a time, one day at a time, and hope that her strength would be enough to see them through the darkness.

Maya sat down on a crumbling piece of concrete, her elbows resting on her knees as she stared out into the night. The aftershock had left everyone on edge, and she could feel the tension in the air, thick and suffocating. She knew that Jace was somewhere out there, plotting his next move, waiting for the right moment to strike.

But Maya refused to let him win. She had seen the way he manipulated people, preying on their fears and insecurities. She knew that his path would only lead to more pain and suffering, and she couldn't let that happen.

As she sat there, lost in thought, Riley approached and sat down beside her. "You okay?" she asked softly, her voice barely audible over the distant sound of settling rubble.

Maya shook her head. "I don't know anymore," she admitted, her voice raw with emotion. "I'm trying so hard to keep us together, but it feels like everything is falling apart."

Riley placed a comforting hand on Maya's shoulder. "You're doing the best you can," she said firmly. "We all are. And we're not going to let Jace tear us apart."

Maya nodded, drawing strength from Riley's words. She knew that as long as she had people like Riley by her side, she could face whatever challenges lay ahead.

With renewed determination, Maya stood up and faced the group. "Listen up, everyone," she called out, her voice steady and strong. "I know things are tough right now, but we can't let fear divide us. We need to stick together, now more than ever."

She looked around at the faces of her classmates, seeing the fear and uncertainty in their eyes. But she also saw something else - a glimmer of hope, a spark of resilience that refused to be extinguished.

"We're going to get through this," Maya continued, her voice growing stronger with each word. "But we have to do it together. We have to trust each other, support each other, and never give up on each other."

As she spoke, Maya could feel the mood shifting, the tension easing ever so slightly. She knew that it wouldn't be easy, that there would be more challenges to come. But for now, in this moment, she had given them something to hold onto - a sense of unity, a glimmer of hope in the darkness.

And as the night wore on, Maya knew that she would keep fighting, keep pushing forward, no matter what obstacles lay in her path. Because she believed in something greater than herself, something worth fighting for - the survival and the humanity of the group, the bonds that held them together even in the face of unimaginable adversity.

CHAPTER 4

Scarcity

The acrid smell of smoke burned Maya's nostrils as she led her group down the cracked asphalt of what used to be Main Street. Toppled buildings loomed on either side, their shattered windows gaping like hungry mouths. An eerie silence hung over the ruins, broken only by the crunch of rubble under their feet and the occasional groan of settling debris.

Maya's stomach clenched painfully, a stark reminder of how long it had been since their last meal. She glanced back at her followers, noting the fatigue etched on their faces. Riley caught her eye and gave a weak smile.

"We need to find water soon," Maya said, her voice hoarse. "And food. Anything that hasn't been picked clean already."

Riley nodded, wiping sweat from her brow. "Let's try that convenience store up ahead. Might still have some bottled water if we're lucky."

As they approached the store, Maya's heart sank. The windows were smashed, and shelves lay overturned inside. She pushed open the broken door, wincing at the screech of metal on concrete.

"Spread out," she instructed. "Check every corner. There might be something left."

The group dispersed, rummaging through the debris. Maya's fingers trembled as she lifted empty cardboard boxes, hoping against hope to find something—anything—that could sustain them.

We can't go on like this much longer, she thought, panic rising in her chest. What if we can't find enough? What if—

"Maya!" Riley's excited whisper cut through her spiraling thoughts. "Over here!"

Maya hurried to where Riley crouched behind the ruined counter. Her friend held up a dented can of beans, a triumphant gleam in her eyes.

"It's not much," Riley admitted, "but it's something."

Maya nodded, forcing a smile. "Good work. Let's see if there's any more."

As they searched, Maya's mind raced. One can of beans for a dozen hungry people. How long before desperation turns us against each other? How long before Jace's way starts to look like the only option?

A distant rumble shook the ground, sending a fresh wave of dust cascading from the ceiling. Riley stumbled, grabbing Maya's arm for support.

"Just an aftershock," Maya reassured her, even as her own heart pounded. "We should get back to the others. It's not safe here."

As they exited the store, the grim reality of their situation settled over Maya like a heavy cloak. The ruined city stretched before them, a maze of danger and scarcity. And somewhere out there, Jace and his followers were searching too, growing stronger while her own group weakened.

"What now?" Riley asked, her voice barely above a whisper.

Maya squared her shoulders, pushing down her fear. "We keep looking. We don't give up. It's the only way we'll survive this."

But as they trudged onward, the gnawing in Maya's stomach seemed to echo the doubts in her mind. How long could they hold onto hope in a world that seemed determined to crush it?

Maya's group trudged through the debris-strewn street, their footsteps crunching on broken glass and crumbled concrete. The oppressive silence was suddenly broken by a heated argument.

"We're wasting time!" shouted Jeremy, one of the younger students. "We should be checking the high-rises. That's where the real supplies will be!"

"Are you crazy?" Riley shot back. "Those buildings could collapse any second. We need to stick to safer ground."

Maya felt the weight of their expectant gazes. She took a deep breath, trying to steady her racing thoughts. "Both of you have valid points," she began, her voice calm despite the tension coiling in her stomach. "But we need to think this through carefully."

God, I wish I had all the answers, she thought. One wrong move and people could die.

"Carefully?" Jeremy scoffed. "While we're being 'careful,' Jace and his crew are probably scoring big. We need to take some risks!"

The mention of Jace sent a ripple of unease through the group. Maya clenched her fists, fighting to maintain her composure.

"Listen," she said firmly, "I understand the frustration. We're all hungry, we're all scared. But rushing into dangerous buildings isn't the answer. We'll focus on areas that are more stable, but also less likely to have been picked clean already."

She saw doubt flicker across some faces, and her heart sank. Before she could say more, a commotion erupted from around the corner. Jace's voice rang out, cocky and triumphant.

"Well, well," he drawled as his group came into view, arms laden with supplies. "Looks like the boy scouts are having a little disagreement. Having trouble keeping everyone in line, Maya?"

Maya felt her group tense around her, the earlier argument forgotten in the face of this new threat. She stepped forward, chin raised. "We're doing just fine, Jace. Glad to see you haven't gotten anyone killed yet with your reckless stunts."

Jace's eyes narrowed dangerously. "Reckless? I'd call it smart. While you're playing it safe, we're actually surviving. Face it, Maya. Your way is going to get everyone starved or worse."

He's right, a traitorous voice whispered in Maya's mind. Look at what they've found. She pushed the thought away, focusing on the present danger.

"And how many close calls did you have getting those supplies?" she challenged. "How long before your luck runs out?"

Jace smirked, stepping closer. "Maybe it's time you realized that in this new world, luck favors the bold. Your caution? It's just a slow death sentence."

Jace turned to address his followers, his voice carrying across the rubble-strewn street. "You see what I mean? While they debate and hesitate, we act. We survive." He gestured to the meager supplies in Maya's group. "Look at them. Hungry. Weak. Is that what you want to become?"

His followers murmured in agreement, their eyes glinting with a mix of fear and newfound resolve. Maya's stomach churned as she watched Jace's influence grow before her eyes.

"We can't keep playing it safe," Jace continued, his voice rising with passion. "The city's a war zone now. We need to start raiding nearby areas for real supplies. Yeah, it's risky, but what choice do we have?"

Maya stepped forward, her voice steady despite her racing heart. "Jace, you're talking about looting. That's dangerous, not to mention--"

"Not to mention what, Maya?" Jace cut her off. "Illegal? Wake up! The old rules don't apply anymore. It's survive or die now."

Maya felt the weight of everyone's stares. She knew her next words could determine who followed whom. "We can find another way. We just need to--"

"To what? Starve while we look for the moral high ground?" Jace sneered. He turned back to the group at large. "I say we hit the warehouse district. Tonight. Who's with me?"

A chorus of agreement rose from Jace's followers. Maya watched in dismay as even a few from her own group nodded hesitantly.

This is it, Maya thought. I'm losing them. But if I let this happen...

She opened her mouth to object, but the words died in her throat. The harsh reality of their situation pressed down on her like a physical weight. Was Jace right? Was her caution dooming them all?

As the two factions began to separate, the divide between them more apparent than ever, Maya felt the enormity of the choice before her. Stand firm in her beliefs, or compromise to keep the group together? The future hung in the balance, and she knew her next move would shape it irrevocably.

Maya's heart raced as she watched more students gravitate toward Jace. His confident smirk grew wider with each new follower.

"Look," Jace called out, his voice carrying across the rubble-strewn plaza, "Maya's way might have worked in the old world. But now? We need action, not caution."

A murmur of agreement rippled through the crowd. Maya felt a knot form in her stomach as she saw the hope kindling in their eyes – hope that Jace's bold promises could save them.

"We can't just throw away everything we believe in," Maya countered, her voice wavering slightly. "There has to be a middle ground."

But even as the words left her mouth, Maya felt doubt creeping in. Their supplies were dwindling fast, and the haunted looks on her followers' faces spoke volumes.

Jace stepped closer, his blue eyes glinting. "Middle ground gets us nowhere. You know it, Maya. Deep down, you know I'm right."

Maya's mind raced. She couldn't deny the truth in his words, but the thought of abandoning her principles made her feel sick.

"We need time to think this through," she said, trying to inject confidence into her voice. "Rushing into danger could get us all killed."

But as she spoke, she saw more of her group drifting towards Jace. His faction stood taller now, emboldened by their growing numbers.

I'm losing them, Maya thought, panic rising in her chest. But if I give in to Jace's way, what will we become?

The weight of leadership had never felt so heavy. As the two groups continued to separate, Maya realized she was standing at a crossroads. Her next decision could change everything.

Maya's stomach clenched painfully, a stark reminder of their dire situation. She scanned the faces of her group, noting the sunken cheeks and dull eyes that stared back at her. The warehouse's cavernous interior seemed to amplify their misery, every labored breath and weak cough echoing off the concrete walls.

"We can't go on like this," Riley whispered, her voice cracking. She leaned heavily against a rusted shelf, her usual energy sapped. "Maya, we need to do something."

Maya nodded, swallowing hard. "I know. I'm trying to think of—"

"The river," Riley interrupted, a spark of her old determination flaring. "We should head for the river. There has to be water there, maybe even fish."

Maya's heart raced at the suggestion. The river was at least a day's journey through treacherous terrain. "It's risky, Riley. We'd be exposed, and who knows what—or who—we might encounter along the way."

"And staying here?" Riley gestured around the warehouse. "That's a death sentence. Look at us, Maya. We're barely hanging on."

Maya closed her eyes, the weight of the decision crushing down on her. She could feel the expectant gazes of her group, their desperation palpable.

"You're right," she finally said, opening her eyes. "We don't have a choice anymore. We'll leave at first light."

As she spoke the words, Maya felt a mix of relief and terror. Am I leading them to salvation or doom? she wondered. But the small murmur of hope that rippled through the group told her she'd made the right call.

"Get some rest, everyone," Maya announced, trying to infuse strength into her voice. "Tomorrow, we find water or die trying."

As the group settled in for the night, Maya caught Riley's eye. Her friend gave her a weak smile and a nod. It wasn't much, but it was enough. Together, they'd face whatever lay ahead.

The ruined streets stretched before them, a maze of crumbled concrete and twisted metal. Maya led the group forward, her eyes scanning constantly for danger. The air was thick with dust and the acrid smell of smoke, making each breath a struggle.

Benji's voice cut through the eerie silence. "Hey, guys, I've got a new one. Why did the earthquake go to therapy?" He paused, waiting for a response that didn't come. "Because it had too many fault lines!"

His laugh was forced, almost manic. A few group members managed weak smiles, but most just trudged on, their faces etched with exhaustion and fear.

Maya glanced back at Benji, noting the strain in his eyes despite his attempt at levity. He's trying so hard to keep our spirits up, she thought. But even he's starting to crack.

"Tough crowd," Benji muttered, kicking at a piece of debris. "Maybe I should stick to knock-knock jokes. At least then I'd get a 'who's there?'"

As they rounded a corner, they came face to face with a collapsed office building. Glass and steel littered the street, forcing them to pick their way carefully through the wreckage.

"Watch your step," Maya called out, her voice hoarse from thirst. "And keep an eye out for anything useful."

Tariq, bringing up the rear, said nothing. His dark eyes darted from person to person, lingering on those who stumbled or lagged behind. Maya caught his gaze, and a chill ran down her spine at the coldness she saw there.

What's going on in that head of his? she wondered. He's always been quiet, but this... this feels different.

Benji's voice broke through her thoughts again. "Hey, I've got another one. What did the building say to the earthquake? 'Stop shaking me up!'" His laugh was hollow, almost desperate.

Maya saw Tariq's eyes narrow at Benji, a look of calculation crossing his face. She felt a sudden urge to put herself between them, though she couldn't explain why.

"Benji," she said softly, "maybe we should focus on moving forward for now. Save your energy."

Benji's smile faltered, then disappeared entirely. "Yeah, sure. Whatever you say, fearless leader."

The bitterness in his tone made Maya flinch. We're falling apart, she realized. And I don't know how to hold us together.

A glint of metal caught Maya's eye, drawing her attention to a partially collapsed building across the street. Her heart raced as she spotted what looked like cans through a broken window.

"Over there," she whispered, gesturing to the others. "I think I see something."

They approached cautiously, debris crunching under their feet. Maya peered inside, her eyes widening as she confirmed her suspicion. A small stash of canned food and water bottles lay scattered among the rubble.

"We found supplies," she announced, relief washing over her.

As the group crowded around, the initial excitement quickly gave way to tension. Riley's voice cut through the murmurs. "It's not much. Definitely not enough for everyone."

Maya's stomach twisted as she surveyed the meager cache. She could already feel the weight of the decision pressing down on her.

Jace pushed his way to the front, his blue eyes gleaming. "Well, well. Looks like we've got a problem on our hands."

"We need to divide it equally," Maya said firmly, though her voice wavered slightly.

Jace scoffed. "Equal shares? That's your solution? Wake up, Maya. We're not in school anymore. This isn't about fairness; it's about survival."

Maya clenched her fists, fighting to keep her composure. He's wrong, she thought. We can't lose our humanity. Not now.

"We stick together," she insisted. "That's how we survive."

The group erupted into arguments, their voices rising. Maya caught fragments of desperate pleas and angry demands.

"I haven't eaten in two days!"

"The strongest should get more. We need to keep our fighters healthy."

"What about the injured? They need it more!"

Maya's head spun as she tried to process everyone's needs and concerns. How do I make this fair? How do I keep us from tearing each other apart?

She looked to Riley for support, but her friend's face was a mask of uncertainty. The rift between them seemed to widen with each passing moment.

As the shouting intensified, Maya knew she had to act. But the weight of the decision threatened to crush her. Whatever I choose, she realized, someone will suffer. And they'll all be looking to me.

Maya took a deep breath, steeling herself for what was to come. The meager pile of supplies seemed to mock her, a stark reminder of their dire situation.

"Listen to me, all of you!" she shouted, her voice cutting through the chaos. The group fell silent, all eyes turning to her. "We're going to divide these supplies equally. Every person gets the same share, no exceptions."

A chorus of protests erupted immediately. Maya raised her hand, silencing them once more.

"I know it's not enough," she continued, her voice softening. "But it's all we have right now. We survive together, or we don't survive at all."

Jace stepped forward, his tall frame towering over Maya. "And who made you queen?" he sneered. "Some of us have been doing the heavy lifting. We deserve more."

Maya felt her resolve waver, but she stood her ground. "No one's more important than anyone else here, Jace. We're all in this together."

As she began to divide the supplies, she could feel the tension in the air, thick enough to choke on. Am I doing the right thing? she wondered, her hands shaking slightly as she portioned out the meager rations.

"This is bullshit," one of Jace's followers spat, snatching his share roughly. "The weak are dragging us down."

Maya's heart sank as she saw the disappointment and anger on many faces. Even some of her own group looked dissatisfied.

"Maya," Riley whispered, coming to stand beside her. "Maybe we should reconsider-"

"No," Maya cut her off, more sharply than she intended. She softened her tone. "We can't start down that path, Riley. Once we decide some lives are worth more than others, where does it end?"

As the last of the supplies were distributed, Maya felt the weight of leadership more acutely than ever before. She watched as people clutched their meager rations, some with gratitude, others with resentment.

I've kept us together for now, she thought. But at what cost? The divide in the group seemed more pronounced than ever, and she couldn't shake the feeling that this decision would have far-reaching consequences.

Jace's eyes gleamed with a predatory light as he stepped forward, his voice carrying across the ruined plaza. "You call this leadership, Maya? Look around you. We're starving, and you're handing out crumbs like it's charity."

Maya felt her stomach clench, not just from hunger but from the weight of the moment. She could see heads turning, people listening intently to Jace's words.

"Survival isn't about being fair," Jace continued, his voice rising. "It's about being strong. About making the hard choices."

He's right about one thing, Maya thought. These are hard choices. But aloud, she said, "And what would you suggest, Jace? Let the weak die?"

Jace's smile was cold. "I'm saying we focus on keeping the strongest alive. The ones who can actually help us survive."

A murmur rippled through the group. Maya saw fear in some eyes, agreement in others. She stepped closer to Jace, her voice low but firm. "And who decides who's strong enough to live?"

"Nature decides," Jace shot back. "It always has. Your way of thinking is outdated, Maya. It belongs to a world that doesn't exist anymore."

Maya felt a chill run down her spine. She looked around at the faces of her group, saw the doubt creeping in. He's getting to them, she realized with a sinking feeling.

"We're not animals," she said, loud enough for everyone to hear. "We don't abandon our humanity just because things got tough."

But even as she spoke, she could see the impact Jace's words were having. In this broken world, surrounded by ruin and scarcity, his brutal logic was beginning to make a twisted kind of sense to some.

I'm losing them, Maya thought, her heart racing. How do I fight this?

Maya clenched her fists, her nails digging into her palms as she faced Jace. The tension in the air was palpable, thick as the dust settling around them.

"You think you have all the answers, don't you?" Jace sneered, his blue eyes flashing with contempt. "Wake up, Maya. Your fairy tale ideals are going to get us all killed."

A few of Jace's followers nodded in agreement, emboldened by his words. Maya felt a surge of anger, but she forced it down, keeping her voice steady.

"Unity isn't a fairy tale, Jace. It's our best chance at survival," she countered, her gaze sweeping over the group. "If we start turning on each other now, we're finished."

Jace laughed, a harsh sound that echoed off the crumbling walls around them. "Unity? Look around you! The world's falling apart, and you want to hold hands and sing kumbaya?"

Maya's heart raced as she saw more students gravitating towards Jace. His words were seductive in their simplicity, offering an easy solution to their fear and desperation.

I can't let this happen, she thought, her mind racing. If we lose our humanity, what's left to fight for?

"We're better than that," Maya insisted, her voice growing stronger. "We can survive without becoming monsters. It's not about being weak or strong – it's about working together, pooling our skills and resources."

She turned to face the entire group, her eyes blazing with determination. "Yes, we're in a harsh reality now. But fairness and cooperation aren't luxuries – they're necessities. They're what will keep us alive and sane in the long run."

As she spoke, Maya saw a flicker of hesitation in some eyes, a spark of hope rekindling. But Jace's faction stood firm, their faces set in grim determination.

The lines were drawn. The confrontation Maya had feared was now inevitable, and she knew the coming days would test not just their survival skills, but the very core of who they were as human beings.

The sun beat down mercilessly as Maya led her dwindling group through the devastated streets. Sweat trickled down her back, her ponytail plastered to her neck. Every step felt heavier than the last.

"There's gotta be something here," she muttered, more to herself than the others. Her eyes scanned the ruins desperately, searching for any sign of untouched supplies.

Behind her, she heard the shuffling feet and labored breathing of her followers. A voice, raspy with thirst, called out, "Maya, we've been at this for hours. There's nothing left."

She turned, facing the group. Exhaustion etched deep lines in their young faces. "We can't give up," she insisted, trying to infuse her voice with a confidence she didn't feel. "We just need to keep looking."

"And then what?" Another student stepped forward, eyes narrowed. "We find a few scraps and pretend it's enough? Jace's group is probably feasting right now."

Maya's stomach clenched at the mention of Jace. She could almost hear his mocking laughter. No, she thought fiercely. We're doing the right thing. We have to be.

"Listen," she began, but was cut off by a loud crash nearby. Everyone tensed, instinctively huddling closer.

"What if... what if we joined Jace?" someone whispered. The words hung in the air, giving voice to the thought Maya knew had been festering.

She looked at each face, seeing the doubt, the fear, the wavering loyalty. I'm losing them, she realized with a sinking heart. But I can't let go of what makes us human.

"We stick together," Maya said firmly, even as uncertainty gnawed at her. "That's how we survive. Now, let's keep moving. There has to be something we've missed."

As they trudged on, Maya's mind raced. How long can we hold out like this? What if Jace is right? She pushed the treacherous thoughts away, focusing on the next step, the next building to search. But with each passing moment, the divide in the group grew wider, a chasm she wasn't sure how to bridge.

Riley sidled up to Maya as they picked their way through a crumbling office building. The blonde girl's face was smudged with dirt, but her green eyes shone with determination.

"Hey," Riley said softly, nudging Maya's shoulder. "You're doing the right thing, you know."

Maya sighed, running a hand through her tangled ponytail. "Am I? Sometimes I wonder if—"

"Stop," Riley interrupted. "I know what you're thinking, but Jace's way isn't sustainable. Sure, he might find more food now, but at what cost?"

Maya paused, considering Riley's words. The weight of leadership pressed down on her shoulders, threatening to crush her resolve. "But what if—"

"What if nothing," Riley insisted. "Jace's methods might work short-term, but they'll destroy us in the end. You're keeping us human, Maya. That matters."

Maya's gaze swept over their ragtag group, noting the exhaustion etched on every face. She saw doubt, fear, but also a flicker of hope. Her voice was low when she finally spoke. "I can't give up on them, Riley. I won't."

"I know," Riley squeezed her arm. "That's why we follow you."

Maya squared her shoulders, a familiar determination settling over her. "We keep going. We stay together. No matter what Jace does, we don't compromise who we are."

As they moved deeper into the ruins, Maya's mind raced. Jace's influence is growing, she thought. But I won't let him win. Not like this. She knew the path ahead was fraught with danger, but she'd face it head-on. For her group. For their humanity.

The makeshift camp was a patchwork of salvaged tarps and broken furniture, a stark reminder of how far they'd fallen. Maya sat on a cracked concrete slab, her eyes tracing the jagged skyline of collapsed buildings. The setting sun painted the ruins in shades of orange and red, a deceptively beautiful backdrop to their dire situation.

"We need to talk about tomorrow," Benji said, his usual humor absent as he approached. "People are getting restless."

Maya nodded, her throat tight. "I know. We didn't find enough today."

She watched as the group settled in for the night, their movements sluggish with exhaustion and hunger. Jace's followers huddled together, whispering and casting furtive glances her way. The division was palpable, a chasm widening with each passing hour.

How did it come to this? Maya thought, her chest constricting. We were supposed to stick together.

"Maya?" Tariq's voice pulled her from her thoughts. "What's the plan?"

She met his gaze, seeing the unspoken question there. Are you still fit to lead us?

"We'll... we'll head towards the river at first light," Maya said, her voice steadier than she felt. "There might be supplies we missed, maybe even fish if we're lucky."

Tariq nodded, but his expression remained skeptical. As he walked away, Maya overheard snippets of conversation from nearby.

"...Jace says we should raid the warehouse district..."

"...at least he's doing something..."

"...can't keep waiting around to starve..."

Each word was a blow, chipping away at her resolve. Maya clenched her fists, nails digging into her palms. I'm losing them, she realized, the thought settling like a stone in her gut. Everything's falling apart, and I don't know how to stop it.

Maya's gaze drifted to Jace's group, their faces illuminated by a small fire. She watched as he leaned in, speaking in hushed tones, his followers hanging on every word. A pang of doubt pierced her heart.

Maybe he's right, she thought, her ideals wavering. Maybe we need to be more aggressive to survive.

She pictured herself leading a raid, taking what they needed by force. The image made her stomach churn, but the gnawing hunger in her belly argued otherwise.

"No," Maya whispered, shaking her head. "That's not who we are. That's not who I am."

Riley approached, concern etched on her face. "You okay?"

Maya forced a weak smile. "Just thinking."

"About Jace?"

"About everything," Maya admitted. "I keep wondering if I'm doing the right thing. If my way is going to get us all killed."

Riley squeezed her shoulder. "Your way is keeping us human."

Maya nodded, but doubt still gnawed at her. She stared into the darkness, her mind racing. What if being human isn't enough anymore?

As the camp settled into an uneasy sleep, Maya remained awake, her resolve hardening with each passing moment. She clenched her jaw, a fire igniting in her eyes.

I won't let this fall apart, she vowed silently. I'll face Jace if I have to, but I won't let him tear us apart. We're surviving this together, or not at all.

The night air grew colder as Maya huddled close to the dying embers of their campfire. Across the makeshift camp, shadowy figures moved in whispered conversation. Jace's followers, no longer even pretending to be part of the larger group.

Maya's eyes narrowed as she watched Jace gesticulate animatedly, his voice a low rumble she couldn't quite make out. The flickering light caught his piercing blue eyes, giving them an almost predatory gleam.

"They're not even trying to hide it anymore," Riley muttered, settling down beside Maya.

Maya nodded grimly. "It's like watching a storm gather on the horizon."

"What are we going to do?" Riley asked, her voice tinged with fear.

Maya clenched her fists, fighting back the wave of uncertainty threatening to drown her. "We stick to our principles. We show them that unity and compassion are strengths, not weaknesses."

A harsh laugh cut through the night, unmistakably Jace's. Maya flinched involuntarily.

"And if that's not enough?" Riley pressed.

Maya turned to her friend, her eyes blazing with determination. "Then we fight. Not with fists or weapons, but with everything that makes us human. We prove that survival doesn't have to mean losing our souls."

As if on cue, Jace's group began to move, setting up their sleeping areas distinctly separate from the others. The physical divide was now as clear as the ideological one.

Maya stood, her voice carrying across the camp. "Everyone, get some rest. Tomorrow, we face this together."

She caught Jace's eye as he looked up, his smirk a silent challenge. Maya held his gaze, refusing to back down. The battle lines were drawn, and come morning, she knew nothing would be the same.

Benji's hollow laughter pierced the tense silence of the makeshift camp. "Hey, guys, I've got a great one. What do you call a group of teenagers trapped in a post-apocalyptic wasteland?" He paused, his eyes darting around the group. "The Hunger Games: Budget Edition!"

The joke fell flat, met with uncomfortable silence and a few bitter chuckles. Maya watched Benji's face fall, his usual cheerful mask cracking to reveal the despair beneath.

"Come on, that was gold!" Benji insisted, his voice strained. "Tough crowd. Maybe you'll like this one better. Why did the survivor cross the road? To get to the other side... where there's probably no food either!"

Maya winced, feeling the weight of hopelessness settle over the group like a suffocating blanket. She caught Riley's eye, seeing her own concern mirrored there.

"Benji," Maya said softly, reaching out to touch his arm. "Maybe we should-"

"What? Stop joking around?" Benji snapped, jerking away from her touch. "Sorry if I'm not taking our impending doom seriously enough for you, Maya."

The bitterness in his voice made Maya recoil. She watched as Benji stomped away, kicking at a piece of rubble in frustration.

"This isn't working," someone muttered from the back of the group. "We're all going to die here."

"No, we're not," Maya said firmly, standing up. She could feel Jace's eyes on her from across the camp, watching her every move. "We've made it this far together, and we'll keep going."

"Together?" Another voice scoffed. "Look around, Maya. We're falling apart."

Maya's heart raced as she surveyed the group. Faces that once looked to her with hope now showed only doubt and anger. She took a deep breath, fighting to keep her voice steady.

"I know things look bleak," she began, "but giving up isn't an option. We have to-"

"Have to what?" Jace's voice cut through the air like a knife. He sauntered over, arms crossed, a smirk playing on his lips. "Keep playing nice while we starve? Face it, Maya. Your way isn't working."

Maya felt a surge of anger, mixed with a paralyzing fear. She knew this moment had been coming, but she wasn't ready. Not yet.

"And your way is better?" she challenged, meeting Jace's gaze. "Turning on each other, becoming no better than animals?"

Jace's eyes narrowed. "At least animals survive, Maya. Can you say the same for us right now?"

The silence that followed was deafening. Maya could feel the group's eyes darting between her and Jace, waiting to see who would break first.

"This isn't over," Maya said quietly, her voice barely above a whisper.

Jace leaned in close, his breath hot on her ear. "You're right. It's only just beginning."

As he walked away, Maya felt a chill run down her spine. She looked around at the fractured group, the lines clearly drawn. Unity was crumbling, replaced by fear and desperation.

In that moment, as the last light of day faded, Maya realized with crushing clarity that tomorrow would bring a battle – not just for resources, but for the very soul of their makeshift community. And she wasn't sure if she was ready to fight.

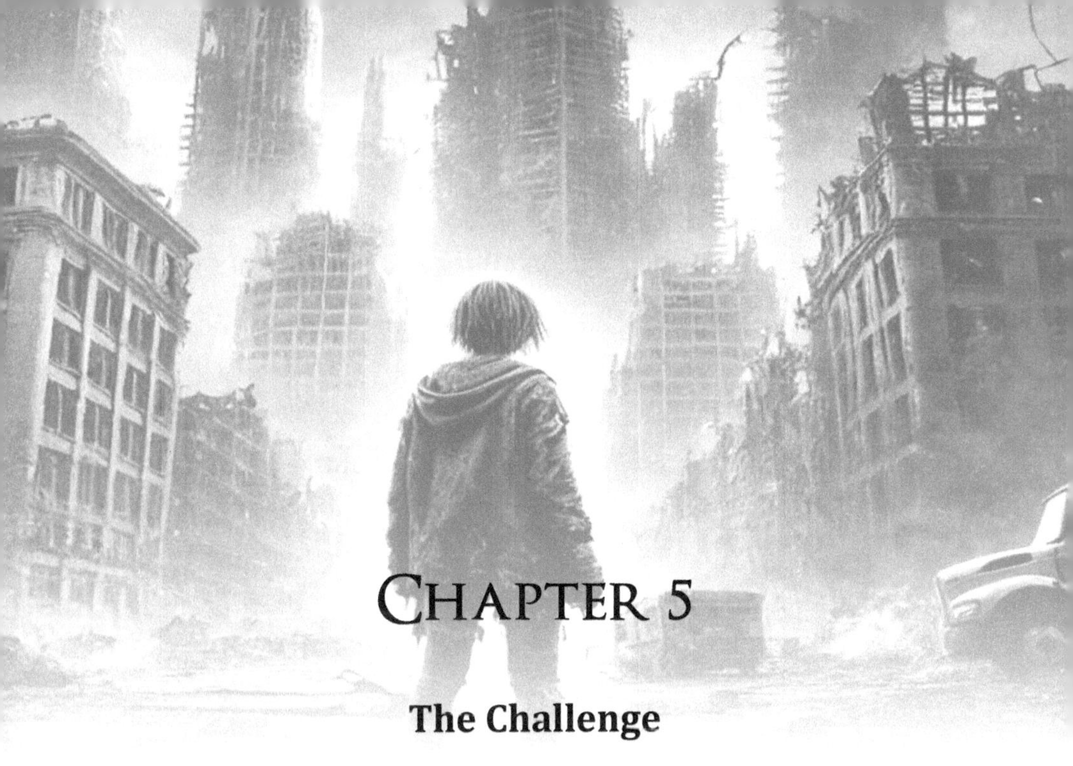

CHAPTER 5

The Challenge

Maya stood at the edge of the plaza, her eyes fixed on the looming silhouette of the warehouse across the wasteland. The air hung heavy with the acrid smell of smoke and decay, a constant reminder of the devastation that had torn their world apart. Her fingers traced the frayed edges of her once-pristine school blazer, now stained and tattered, a symbol of the innocence they'd all lost.

"We can't just let him have it all," Benji's voice cracked, desperation seeping through. "There are kids here who haven't eaten in days."

Maya's jaw clenched, her mind racing. The weight of leadership pressed down on her shoulders, threatening to crush her. She could feel the eyes of her group boring into her back, waiting, hoping for a solution.

"Maybe... maybe we can reason with him," she murmured, more to herself than the others. But even as the words left her lips, doubt gnawed at her insides. Jace wasn't known for his reasonableness.

Riley stepped closer, her voice low and urgent. "Maya, you know Jace. He'll see any attempt to negotiate as weakness. He'll use it against us."

Maya's hands balled into fists at her sides. She could picture Jace's smug face, that infuriating smirk as he lorded over the supplies they all desperately needed. The thought made her blood boil, but the idea of leading her people into a direct confrontation...

"What if we lose people?" she whispered, her voice barely audible over the distant rumble of another aftershock. "I can't... I can't be responsible for that."

She turned to face her group, taking in their gaunt faces and hollow eyes. They were looking to her for answers, for hope. But all she felt was the crushing weight of indecision.

"We need those supplies," Tariq spoke up, his usual quiet demeanor tinged with urgency. "Every day we wait, we get weaker. Jace knows that."

Maya closed her eyes, trying to shut out the world for just a moment. In the darkness behind her eyelids, she saw flashes of the life before – classrooms, laughter, the simple luxury of not having to make decisions that could mean life or death.

When she opened them again, her gaze was steely. "We... we need to be smart about this. Jace has the advantage right now, but maybe we can find a way to level the playing field."

She took a deep breath, her mind racing through possibilities. "I need time to think, to come up with a plan that doesn't put us all at risk."

The group shifted uneasily, murmurs of discontent rippling through them. Maya felt a pang of guilt – they needed action, not more deliberation. But the thought of leading them into a battle they might not win...

"Give me until nightfall," she said, her voice stronger now. "We'll make our move then, one way or another."

As the group dispersed, Maya turned back to face the warehouse. In the fading light, it looked like a fortress, impenetrable and forbidding. She squared her shoulders, steeling herself for what was to come.

"What are you going to do?" Riley asked softly, coming to stand beside her.

Maya's eyes never left the warehouse. "Whatever I have to," she replied, her voice barely above a whisper. "To keep us alive."

Maya's gaze lingered on the warehouse, its looming silhouette a stark reminder of everything they stood to lose. Her ideals of unity and cooperation, once so clear and unshakeable, now felt like fragile relics from a world that no longer existed.

"Riley," she murmured, her voice tight with tension, "do you ever wonder if we're fighting for something that doesn't matter anymore?"

Riley's brow furrowed. "What do you mean?"

Maya turned to face her friend, her eyes searching. "All this talk of working together, of maintaining our humanity... what if it's just slowing us down? What if Jace is right, and the only way to survive is to be ruthless?"

The words felt like ash in her mouth, but she couldn't deny the seed of doubt taking root in her heart. The constant struggle, the dwindling resources, the fractured group – it was all wearing her down, eroding her convictions.

Riley placed a hand on Maya's shoulder, her touch grounding. "Maya, listen to me. Those ideals are what make us who we are. The moment we abandon them, we lose something we can't get back."

Maya nodded, but the doubt lingered. "I know, I know. But at what cost? How many lives are we willing to risk for the sake of our principles?"

Riley's eyes softened with understanding. "What if we try a different approach? We could reach out to Jace, attempt to negotiate, but also prepare for the worst. Show strength through diplomacy, but be ready to defend ourselves if needed."

Maya considered this, feeling a glimmer of hope. "A middle ground... it could work. But Riley, what if it's not enough? What if we're just delaying the inevitable?"

"Then at least we'll know we tried," Riley said firmly. "And we'll be prepared for whatever comes next."

Maya took a deep breath, feeling some of the weight lift from her shoulders. Riley's pragmatism had given her a moment of clarity, a path forward. But as she looked back at the warehouse, the enormity of the challenge ahead crashed over her once more.

"Thank you, Riley," she said softly. "I don't know what I'd do without you."

Riley squeezed her shoulder. "You'd figure it out. You always do."

As they turned to rejoin the group, Maya felt the familiar burden of leadership settling back onto her shoulders. The road ahead was uncertain, fraught with danger and difficult choices. But for now, at least, she had a plan – and the strength to see it through.

The warehouse loomed before them, a hulking silhouette against the fading light. Maya's heart pounded as she led her group towards the entrance, the weight of their expectations pressing down on her like a physical force. As they approached, figures emerged from the shadows, their stances aggressive and weapons clearly visible.

"Well, well, well," a familiar voice rang out, dripping with mockery. "Look who finally decided to grace us with their presence."

Jace sauntered into view, his piercing blue eyes glinting with amusement. Maya's stomach clenched at the sight of him, so confident and in control.

"Jace," she acknowledged, fighting to keep her voice steady. "We've come to discuss—"

"Discuss?" Jace interrupted, his laugh echoing off the warehouse walls. "Oh, Maya. Always so diplomatic. Always so... weak."

Maya felt her followers shift uneasily behind her. She could almost hear their doubts growing.

"Strength isn't just about force," she countered, her mind racing. "It's about—"

"It's about survival," Jace cut in, his voice hardening. He gestured broadly at the warehouse. "And survival means having what you need. Food. Water. Medicine. Tell me, Maya, how many of your people have you lost because you were too busy trying to play nice?"

The words hit Maya like a physical blow. Images of those they'd lost flashed through her mind – the sick, the injured, the ones who'd simply given up hope.

"That's not fair," she managed, but her voice lacked conviction.

Jace's smirk widened. "Life isn't fair, princess. The sooner you learn that, the better chance your people have of making it through another day."

Maya felt a surge of anger, mingled with a treacherous whisper of doubt. Was Jace right? Had her attempts at unity and cooperation only led to more suffering?

"We don't have to be enemies," she said, forcing herself to meet Jace's gaze. "We could work together, share resources—"

Jace's laughter cut her off again, cruel and mocking. "Share? There's barely enough for one group to survive, let alone two. Face it, Maya. Your way doesn't work anymore. It's time to step aside and let someone who understands this new world take charge."

Maya felt the eyes of both groups on her, waiting to see how she'd respond. Her mind raced, searching for the right words, the right action. But as Jace's smug grin bore into her, she realized with a sinking feeling that she might have already lost this battle before it had truly begun.

Maya clenched her fists, her nails digging into her palms as she fought to maintain her composure. The warehouse loomed behind Jace, a fortress of survival that seemed to mock her ideals with every passing second.

"You think brutality is strength?" Maya challenged, her voice low but steady. "That's not leadership, Jace. That's tyranny."

Jace's eyes flashed dangerously. "Tyranny keeps people alive. Your soft touch?" He gestured dismissively at Maya's group. "It's a death sentence."

The words hung in the air, heavy and poisonous. Maya felt a flicker of doubt threatening to consume her. She glanced at her followers, seeing the uncertainty in their eyes, the hunger etched into their gaunt faces.

"My people are alive," Maya countered, but even to her own ears, the words sounded hollow.

Jace stepped closer, his voice dropping to a taunting whisper. "For now. But how long before your compassion gets them killed? How many more will starve because you're too weak to do what needs to be done?"

Maya's mind raced, grappling with the weight of leadership and the cost of her principles. She thought of the complex decisions ahead, the lines she might have to cross. For a moment, Jace's way seemed terrifyingly appealing in its simplicity.

"I won't become a monster to survive," Maya said finally, her voice barely above a whisper.

Jace's laugh was sharp and cruel. "Then you'll die a saint, and your people will follow you to the grave."

The tension between them crackled like electricity. Maya felt the eyes of both groups upon her, waiting to see how she'd respond. Her chest tightened as she realized that every word, every gesture now could determine not just her fate, but the fate of everyone who still believed in her.

Maya's gaze swept over her followers, their faces a mosaic of fear, doubt, and desperate hope. The warehouse loomed behind Jace, a fortress of survival that seemed to mock her ideals.

"We don't have to choose between being monsters or martyrs," Maya said, her voice stronger now. "There's another way."

A murmur rippled through the crowd. Maya caught sight of Lena, one of her most loyal supporters, stepping forward.

"Maybe... maybe Jace has a point," Lena said, her eyes downcast. "We're starving, Maya. How long can we hold out like this?"

Maya's heart sank. She could almost feel the group fracturing around her, loyalty crumbling like the ruins of their city.

"Jace offers security," another voice chimed in. "At least he has a plan."

Jace's smirk widened. He spread his arms wide, encompassing the warehouse. "My doors are open to those smart enough to choose survival. Who's ready to stop playing at democracy and start living?"

Several of Maya's group shifted uneasily, glancing between her and Jace. Maya's mind raced, searching for words that could stem the tide of doubt.

"And what happens when the supplies run out?" she challenged, her voice carried across the tense silence. "When Jace decides some of you aren't worth keeping around?"

Doubt flickered across a few faces, but Maya could see the hunger and fear winning out. She watched helplessly as three of her people crossed the invisible line, joining Jace's ranks.

"This isn't over," Maya thought, clenching her fists. "I have to find a way to keep us together, to prove there's strength in unity. But how?"

The group continued to splinter before her eyes, and Maya felt the crushing weight of failure pressing down on her shoulders.

Benji's harsh laugh cut through the air, drawing everyone's attention. His once-cheerful face was twisted into a bitter smirk. "Well, isn't this just peachy?" he said, his voice dripping with sarcasm. "Our fearless leader's grand plan is to starve together. How noble."

Maya felt a stab of betrayal. "Benji, we can figure this out if we stick together—"

"Stick together?" Benji interrupted, his eyes flashing. "Like those three who just walked away? Face it, Maya. Your kumbaya approach isn't cutting it anymore."

The remaining members of Maya's group shifted uncomfortably, murmuring amongst themselves. Maya's chest tightened as she saw doubt spreading like a virus.

"What do you suggest then, Benji?" she asked, struggling to keep her voice steady.

Benji shrugged, his cynicism palpable. "I'm saying maybe Jace has a point. At least he's not pretending this is summer camp."

Maya's mind raced. She could feel control slipping through her fingers like sand. Her gaze swept across the faces of her group—tired, hungry, scared. In the corner, she noticed Tariq, silent as always, watching the scene unfold with an unreadable expression.

"I've kept us alive this long," Maya said, her voice barely above a whisper. The weight of leadership felt heavier than ever, threatening to crush her. "I've tried to keep us human."

"And look where that's gotten us," Benji retorted.

Maya closed her eyes, wrestling with the torrent of emotions inside her. Was she being naive? Was her desire to maintain their humanity putting everyone at risk? The image of Jace's smug face flashed in her mind, and with it came a surge of anger and determination.

Opening her eyes, Maya squared her shoulders. "I hear you, Benji. All of you. But giving in to Jace isn't the answer. We need to be smart, not ruthless."

She paused, her mind working furiously. "Give me until sunrise. If I can't come up with a plan by then... we'll reconsider our options."

The group exchanged glances, some nodding reluctantly. Maya's heart raced as she realized how close she'd come to losing them entirely. As they dispersed to their makeshift shelters, she caught Tariq's eye. For a moment, she thought she saw a flicker of... something. Approval? Curiosity?

Alone with her thoughts, Maya slumped against a crumbling wall. "What am I going to do?" she whispered to herself, the enormity of her responsibility threatening to overwhelm her. The warehouse loomed in the distance, a stark reminder of what was at stake. She had until sunrise to prove her leadership or watch everything she'd fought for crumble away.

Jace's voice cut through the tense silence, a predatory grin spreading across his face. "Look who's come crawling back," he called out, his piercing blue eyes fixed on Maya's group. "Realized you can't make it on your own, huh?"

Maya's jaw clenched, her fingers curling into fists at her sides. She watched helplessly as several members of her group shuffled towards Jace, their eyes downcast but filled with desperate hope.

"That's right," Jace continued, his voice a seductive purr. "We've got food, water, and safety. All you have to do is pledge your loyalty to me." He gestured grandly towards the warehouse looming behind him, its steel walls gleaming in the harsh sunlight.

A young woman from Maya's group stepped forward hesitantly. "Is it true? You have enough for everyone?"

Jace's smile widened. "More than enough. Come, see for yourself."

Maya's heart raced as she watched more of her people gravitate towards Jace. She had to do something, say something. "Wait!" she called out, her voice cracking slightly. "Don't forget what we stand for. We can find another way-"

"Another way to starve?" Jace interrupted, his tone mocking. "Face it, Maya. Your way doesn't work anymore. It's time for real leadership."

Maya's mind reeled. She could feel control slipping through her fingers like sand. "This isn't about me," she said, trying to keep her voice steady. "It's about staying human, even when things are at their worst."

But as she spoke, she could see the doubt in her followers' eyes. The promise of immediate relief was too tempting, too real compared to her ideals.

Jace extended his hand, his voice now warm and inviting. "Come on, everyone. Let's get you some food and water. You must be exhausted."

Maya watched, a sinking feeling in her stomach, as more of her group crossed over to Jace's side. She caught Riley's eye, seeing her own fear and uncertainty reflected there.

"What do we do now?" Riley whispered.

Maya swallowed hard, her throat dry. "I don't know," she admitted, the weight of leadership bearing down on her like never before. "I really don't know."

Jace stood atop a stack of crates, his broad shoulders silhouetted against the dim light filtering through the warehouse's dusty windows. His voice boomed, filling the cavernous space with a potent mix of charisma and conviction.

"Look around you," he commanded, sweeping his arm in a wide arc. "This warehouse isn't just a building. It's our lifeline, our fortress against the chaos out there."

Maya's stomach churned as she watched her former followers hang on Jace's every word. His piercing blue eyes seemed to burn with an inner fire as he continued.

"We're not just survivors anymore. We're the ones who will rebuild this world, but only if we're strong enough to do what needs to be done."

A chorus of cheers erupted, and Maya felt each one like a physical blow. She clenched her fists, trying to quell the trembling in her hands.

"He's manipulating them," she thought bitterly. "Using their fear to turn them into something... harder."

Jace's voice dropped to a near-whisper, forcing everyone to lean in. "Maya wanted to play nice, to share with those who'd take everything from us. But I understand what it takes to survive. Who's with me?"

The response was deafening. Maya watched in horror as people she'd led, protected, and cared for raised their fists in support of Jace.

"We need to leave," Riley murmured urgently at her side. "This is getting dangerous."

But before Maya could respond, Jace's followers sprang into action. They began dragging heavy shelving units, creating a makeshift barricade near the warehouse entrance. Others brandished improvised weapons – pipes, broken boards, anything that could inflict damage.

"What are you doing?" Maya called out, her voice barely audible over the commotion.

Jace's smirk was cold as he replied, "Securing what's ours. Anyone who isn't with us is against us. And we'll defend what we've claimed… by any means necessary."

The finality in his tone sent a chill down Maya's spine. The warehouse, once a symbol of hope, had become a fortress of fear and division. As she backed away, Maya's mind raced.

"How did it come to this?" she thought, anguish and doubt threatening to overwhelm her. "And how can I possibly fight against it without becoming exactly what Jace wants me to be?"

Maya's heart raced as she stumbled away from the warehouse, the sounds of Jace's followers fortifying their position fading behind her. She grabbed Riley's arm, pulling her into a secluded alley between two crumbling buildings.

"We need to talk," Maya whispered, her voice strained. She glanced around, ensuring they were alone. "I don't know what to do, Riley. Everything's falling apart."

Riley's green eyes softened with concern. "Maya, you can't give up now. We need you."

Maya leaned against the cold brick wall, her shoulders slumping. "Do you really think that? Because from where I'm standing, it looks like everyone's chosen Jace."

"Not everyone," Riley insisted, placing a reassuring hand on Maya's shoulder. "Look, Jace is offering easy answers and quick solutions. But that's not sustainable. Your way – our way – it's harder, but it's right."

Maya closed her eyes, feeling the weight of responsibility crushing her. When she opened them again, they glistened with unshed tears. "But what if being right isn't enough? What if I can't protect them?"

Riley's voice hardened. "Then we adapt. We find a way. But we don't become like Jace."

Maya's mind raced, considering their dwindling options. The warehouse loomed in her thoughts, a fortress of supplies that could mean life or death for her people. She clenched her fists, fighting back the urge to simply give in to despair.

"I feel so alone in this, Riley," Maya admitted, her voice barely above a whisper. "Like I'm standing on the edge of a cliff, and one wrong move will send us all tumbling down."

Riley squeezed Maya's hand. "You're not alone. I'm here. And there are others who still believe in you. We just need to remind them why they chose to follow you in the first place."

Maya took a deep breath, steeling herself. "You're right. We can't let Jace win. Not like this. But how do we fight back without becoming exactly what he wants us to be?"

As they stood there, hidden in the shadows of a broken city, Maya felt a flicker of hope rekindling within her. She wasn't alone. And as long as that was true, there was still a chance to save not just their lives, but their humanity as well.

Maya's eyes scanned the faces of her group, huddled together in the dim light of their makeshift camp. The weight of their gazes felt heavier than ever, and she could sense the unspoken doubt hanging in the air. Even Benji, usually quick with a joke, wore a grim expression that spoke volumes.

"We need to make a decision," Tariq said, breaking the tense silence. "Jace's people are getting stronger by the hour."

Maya's heart sank as she noticed the nods of agreement. She swallowed hard, fighting to keep her voice steady. "I know you're all scared. I am too. But we can't abandon everything we've fought for just because times are tough."

"Tough?" someone scoffed from the back. "We're starving, Maya. Jace has food."

The murmurs of assent that followed felt like daggers in Maya's chest. She clenched her fists, struggling to find the right words.

"I get it," she said, her voice low. "I do. But at what cost? Jace's way... it's not living. It's just surviving."

"Maybe that's all we can hope for now," Benji muttered, not meeting her eyes.

Maya felt a surge of desperation. "No. I refuse to believe that. We're better than that. We have to be."

But as she looked around, she could see the resolve crumbling in their eyes. The ideals that had once united them seemed to be slipping away, replaced by the brutal calculus of survival.

In that moment, Maya felt the full weight of leadership crushing down on her. She thought of the Maya from before the quake – the girl who managed group projects and mediated conflicts. How naive that version of herself seemed now.

"We need to consider our options," Riley said, stepping forward. "Maybe there's a way to negotiate with Jace, find some middle ground."

Maya's stomach churned at the thought. Negotiating with Jace felt like a betrayal of everything she stood for. But as she looked at the tired, hungry faces around her, she knew she couldn't dismiss the idea outright.

"I... I'll think about it," she said, hating how uncertain she sounded. "We'll figure something out. Together."

But even as the words left her mouth, Maya could feel the fragile bonds holding their group together starting to fray. Jace's shadow loomed large, and she feared it would consume them all if she couldn't find a way to push back against the darkness.

Maya's heart raced as she watched her group splinter before her eyes. The abandoned parking lot where they had gathered felt like a pressure cooker, emotions boiling over in the fading light of day.

"We can't just sit here and starve!" Benji shouted, his usually jovial face twisted with frustration. "Jace has food, water – everything we need. We should at least try to talk to him!"

"Talk?" Tariq scoffed, his voice dripping with disdain. "You think that psycho will listen to reason? We need to take what's ours by force."

Maya's gaze darted between them, her mind reeling. How did it come to this? She clenched her fists, willing her voice not to shake as she spoke. "We're not animals. We can't just –"

"Can't what, Maya?" Benji interrupted, his eyes blazing. "Can't survive? Because that's what this is about now."

The words hit Maya like a physical blow. She'd always prided herself on being the voice of reason, the one who could find a peaceful solution. But now, faced with the harsh reality of their situation, she felt that certainty slipping away.

"Maybe..." she started, hating the waver in her voice. "Maybe we could send a small group to negotiate. See if there's any chance of –"

"And if he refuses?" Tariq cut in. "If he decides to make an example of our 'diplomats'? Then what?"

Maya's mind raced, trying to find an answer that wouldn't lead them down a path she feared they couldn't come back from. But before she could speak, another voice rang out.

"I say we take the fight to them!" someone shouted from the back of the group. "Show Jace we're not push-overs!"

A chorus of agreement rose up, and Maya felt her control slipping away. She looked around desperately, searching for any allies, any voice of reason in the growing chaos.

"Please," she said, her voice barely above a whisper. "We can't lose sight of who we are. If we do that, then what are we even fighting for?"

But as the argument raged on around her, Maya couldn't shake the sinking feeling that she was watching everything she had built crumble before her eyes. And in that moment, she realized that the true battle wasn't just for survival – it was for the very soul of their group.

Riley stepped forward, her green eyes flashing with determination. "Listen!" she shouted, her voice cutting through the din. "We've come this far together because of Maya's leadership. Remember how she got us out of the school when it collapsed? How she rationed our supplies to make them last?"

The crowd quieted, some nodding in reluctant agreement. Riley pressed on, her tone softening. "Unity is what's kept us alive. We can't throw that away now."

But her words seemed to ignite a new wave of frustration. Benji, his usual humor replaced by a bitter edge, spoke up. "Yeah, and look where that's gotten us. Starving, while Jace's crew feasts in that warehouse."

Murmurs of agreement rippled through the group. Maya felt a knot form in her stomach as she watched faces harden, doubt creeping into eyes that had once looked to her with trust.

"We need action, not more talk!" someone shouted.

Maya's mind raced. She knew she had to step in, to make a decision before the fractures in her group became irreparable. But as she opened her mouth to speak, the weight of leadership bore down on her like a physical force.

What if I choose wrong? she thought, her heart pounding. What if I lead them into danger... or worse?

She took a deep breath, steeling herself. The group fell silent, all eyes turning to her. In that moment, Maya felt the full weight of their expectations, their fear, their desperation.

"We can't rush into this," she began, fighting to keep her voice steady. "But we also can't sit back and do nothing. I propose…"

Maya paused, the tension in the air so thick she could almost taste it. Diplomacy or confrontation? The choice loomed before her, each path fraught with its own dangers.

Maya's eyes swept over her group, taking in their haggard faces and desperate expressions. The warehouse loomed in her mind, a fortress of survival that Jace had claimed. She clenched her fists, feeling the weight of her next words.

"We confront Jace," Maya declared, her voice stronger than she felt. "Negotiation isn't an option anymore."

A collective gasp rippled through the group. Some nodded in approval, while others shifted uneasily.

"Are you sure about this, Maya?" Riley asked, concern etching her features.

Maya met her friend's gaze, steeling herself. "We have to. Jace won't stop until he controls everything. If we don't act now, we'll lose any chance of unity."

And maybe I've already lost it, she thought, the doubt gnawing at her insides.

"What's the plan then?" someone called out.

Maya took a deep breath, her mind racing. "We approach the warehouse together. Show Jace we're not backing down. I'll speak with him directly."

"And if he doesn't listen?" Benji asked, his usual humor replaced by a hard edge.

Maya's stomach churned. "Then we're prepared for whatever comes next."

As the group began to gather what meager supplies they had, Maya turned away, her heart pounding. She stared in the direction of the warehouse, picturing Jace's smug face.

Am I doing the right thing? she wondered, fear and determination warring within her. Or am I leading us all to disaster?

But she knew there was no turning back now. The die was cast, and the future of their fractured community hung in the balance.

Maya's eyes swept across the faces of her followers, a mix of determination and fear reflected back at her. The weight of their expectations pressed down on her shoulders, threatening to crush her resolve. But she couldn't falter now.

"I know some of you are scared," she began, her voice steady despite the tremor in her hands. "I am too. But we can't let fear dictate our actions. We've come too far together to let Jace tear us apart."

A murmur rippled through the group. Maya caught sight of Benji, his usual smirk replaced by a skeptical frown. She pressed on.

"The warehouse isn't just about supplies. It's about our future. Our unity. If we let Jace control it all, we're giving up on everything we've built."

"And what if we fail?" someone called out. "What if Jace is too strong?"

Maya swallowed hard, fighting back the doubt that threatened to overwhelm her. "Then we fail together. But at least we'll know we stood for something."

She watched as her words settled over the group. Some nodded, a fire kindling in their eyes. Others looked away, uncertainty plain on their faces.

Am I leading them to their doom? The thought flashed through Maya's mind, but she pushed it aside. There was no room for doubt now.

"We move at dawn," she declared, injecting as much confidence into her voice as she could muster. "Get some rest. We'll need all our strength."

As the group dispersed, Maya felt a hand on her shoulder. She turned to find Riley, concern etched across her friend's face.

"Are you sure about this, Maya?" Riley asked softly.

Maya nodded, even as her stomach churned with uncertainty. "I have to be. For all of us."

As night fell, Maya retreated to the edge of their makeshift camp. She stared in the direction of the warehouse, picturing the confrontation to come. Despite the fear gnawing at her insides, she felt her resolve harden.

I won't let Jace win, she thought fiercely. Not without a fight.

The night air grew colder as Maya's group scavenged through the ruins of nearby buildings. Shadows danced across crumbling walls, cast by the flickering light of their makeshift torches.

Maya hefted a rusty metal pipe, testing its weight. "This'll have to do," she muttered, her voice tight with tension.

Riley approached, clutching a handful of glass bottles. "We can make Molotovs," she whispered, her eyes darting nervously. "It's not much, but..."

"It's something," Maya finished, forcing a smile. She glanced around at her ragtag group, armed with whatever they could find – broken chairs, pieces of rebar, even a few kitchen knives.

Is this really all we have? Maya thought, her stomach twisting. Are we walking into a massacre?

"Maya," Benji called out, his usual humor replaced by grim determination. "We've got movement at the warehouse. Jace's people are setting up barricades."

Maya's jaw clenched. "Of course they are," she said, more to herself than anyone else. Louder, she addressed the group: "Remember, we're not looking for a bloodbath. We just need to show Jace we won't be pushed around."

"And if he doesn't listen to reason?" someone asked, fear evident in their voice.

Maya paused, weighing her words carefully. "Then we do what we have to," she replied, hating how cold she sounded. "For our survival."

As they made their final preparations, Maya's gaze was drawn to the looming silhouette of the warehouse. In the darkness, she could make out figures moving, hear the distant sound of hammering.

Jace, she thought, a mix of anger and dread washing over her. What have you turned us into?

Maya took a deep breath, the cool night air filling her lungs. The warehouse loomed before them, a hulking shadow against the starless sky. Flickering lights from inside cast eerie, dancing shadows across the cracked pavement.

"This is it," she murmured, more to herself than to her followers. Her heart hammered in her chest, each beat a reminder of what was at stake. Our lives. Our future. Everything.

Riley appeared at her side, eyes dark with concern. "Maya, are you sure about this? We could still try to—"

"No," Maya cut her off, her voice steelier than she felt. "We're past negotiation. Jace made sure of that."

She turned to address her group, their faces a mix of determination and fear in the dim light. "Remember, we're fighting for more than just supplies. We're fighting for our right to exist, to have a say in our own destiny."

Am I really ready to lead them into this? The doubt gnawed at her, but she pushed it down. There was no room for hesitation now.

As if on cue, a figure emerged from the warehouse. Even at a distance, Maya recognized Jace's cocky stride.

"Well, well," his voice carried across the empty lot, dripping with mockery. "Looks like the princess finally grew a backbone."

Maya's fists clenched at her sides. "This doesn't have to end in violence, Jace," she called back, fighting to keep her voice steady. "We can still find a way to share—"

Jace's laughter cut through the night, harsh and cruel. "Share? In case you haven't noticed, sweetheart, the world doesn't work that way anymore. It's survival of the fittest now."

The air crackled with tension. Maya could feel her people shifting restlessly behind her, ready for action. She took a step forward, her resolve hardening.

"You're wrong, Jace," she said, her voice gaining strength. "And I'm going to prove it."

As the two factions faced off, the warehouse looming over them like a silent judge, Maya knew there was no turning back. Whatever happened next would shape not just their survival, but the very nature of the world they were fighting to rebuild.

CHAPTER 6

First Conflict

Maya's heart pounded as she led her group toward the warehouse, their footsteps echoing in the eerie pre-dawn stillness. The tension hung thick in the air, a palpable weight pressing down on them with each step. Maya's hands trembled slightly, and she clenched them into fists, trying to steady herself.

"Well, well, well. Look who finally decided to show up," Jace's mocking voice rang out from the barricades. He stood atop a makeshift wall of rubble and scrap metal, his followers gathered behind him like a pack of hungry wolves. "I was starting to think you'd chickened out, Maya."

Maya narrowed her eyes, her jaw tightening. She could feel the fear and anger radiating from her own group, their unease mingling with the determination in the air.

Jace leaped down from the barricade, sauntering toward them with a smirk. "I gotta hand it to you, Maya. You've got guts, coming here like this. But do you really think you have what it takes to do what needs to be done? To make the hard choices?"

His words were like barbs, designed to get under her skin. Maya took a deep breath, trying to steady the pounding of her heart. She couldn't let him get to her. Not now.

"We're not here to play your games, Jace," Maya said, her voice carrying across the empty space between them. "We're here to do what's right. For everyone."

Jace threw his head back and laughed, the sound harsh and grating. "Right, because you're such a saint, aren't you? Always trying to do the 'right thing.' Well, let me tell you something, Maya. In this world, there is no right thing. There's only survival. And you don't have the stomach for it."

His followers jeered and taunted from behind the barricades, their voices rising in a cacophony of mockery and aggression. Maya could feel her own group bristling, their anger and fear threatening to boil over.

She clenched her fists tighter, her nails digging into her palms. She couldn't let Jace's words get to her. She had to stay focused, stay strong. For her group. For herself.

But even as she stood there, facing down Jace and his followers, Maya could feel the doubts creeping in.

What if Jace was right? What if she didn't have what it takes to lead her people through this? What if her hesitation, her desire to cling to her humanity, was only going to get them all killed?

Maya shook her head, pushing those thoughts away. No. She had to believe in herself, in her choices. She had to believe that there was still a place for compassion and morality in this broken world.

Even if it meant fighting for it.

Maya's resolve wavered as she heard the murmurs of dissent rippling through her group.

"We can't just stand here and take this," Benji hissed, his usually jovial face contorted with anger. "We should charge in there and take what's ours!"

Others nodded in agreement, their hands tightening around their makeshift weapons. Maya could see the hunger in their eyes, the desperation for the supplies hidden within the warehouse walls.

But there were those who hung back, uncertainty etched across their faces. "We're not ready," Tariq murmured, his dark eyes flickering between Maya and the looming warehouse. "We need more time to prepare, to plan."

Maya's heart raced as she saw her group splintering before her eyes. Jace's taunts had found their mark, exploiting the cracks in their unity, the fears that lurked beneath the surface.

She had to act fast, had to find a way to bring them back together. Maya stepped forward, her voice ringing out above the rising tensions.

"Listen to me," she said, her tone firm but tinged with urgency. "I know you're scared. I know you're angry. But we cannot let Jace divide us. Not now, not when we've come this far together."

Maya's eyes swept over her group, meeting each of their gazes in turn. "Remember what we're fighting for. Not just for the supplies in that warehouse, but for each other. For the chance to build something better, something worth surviving for."

She could see some of the anger fading from their faces, replaced by a flicker of hope, of determination. But there were still those who shifted uneasily, their doubts written plainly across their features.

Maya took a deep breath, steeling herself for what was to come. She knew her words could only carry them so far. In the end, it would be their actions that defined them, that determined whether they would stand together or fall apart.

And as Jace's taunts echoed in her ears, as the weight of leadership pressed down upon her shoulders, Maya could only pray that she had the strength to lead them through the chaos to come.

The air was electric with tension as Maya's group stood at the edge of the warehouse lot, the imposing structure looming before them. Jace's words hung heavy in the air, his taunts and jeers still ringing in their ears.

Maya could feel the unease rippling through her people, the way they shifted and murmured, their eyes darting between her and the warehouse. She knew she had to act fast, had to find a way to steady them before the cracks in their resolve widened into chasms.

"I know you're afraid," Maya said, her voice cutting through the tense silence. "I am too. But we can't let that fear control us. We can't let Jace's words divide us."

She turned to face her group, her eyes blazing with a fierce determination. "We've come too far to turn back now. We've fought too hard to let them break us apart."

Maya's gaze settled on each of her followers in turn, from the nervous but steadfast Riley to the visibly shaken Benji. "Remember why we're here. Remember what we're fighting for. Not just for the supplies in that warehouse, but for each other. For the chance to build a better future, one where we don't have to live in fear."

She could see some of the tension easing from their shoulders, a flicker of hope rekindling in their eyes. But there were still those who looked uncertain, their hands trembling around their weapons.

Maya drew in a deep breath, her voice growing stronger, more resolute. "I believe in us. I believe in the strength we have when we stand together. And I know that if we hold on to that, if we trust in each other, there's nothing we can't overcome."

As she spoke, Maya could feel the weight of her own doubts pressing down on her, the fear that she might be leading them all to their doom. But she pushed those thoughts aside, focusing instead on the faces before her, on the fragile threads of unity that held them together.

She had to be strong for them. She had to be the leader they needed, even if it meant burying her own fears deep inside. Because in the end, it was their belief in each other that would see them through the trials to come.

And as Maya looked out over her group, as she saw the determination slowly overtaking the fear in their eyes, she knew that whatever challenges lay ahead, they would face them together. As one.

Maya's words hung in the air, a rallying cry that seemed to echo through the ruins around them. For a moment, the only sound was the distant whisper of the wind, the faint creaking of the warehouse's rusted walls.

Then, with a sudden burst of energy, Maya's group surged forward, their footsteps pounding against the cracked pavement. Maya led the charge, her heart hammering in her chest, adrenaline coursing through her veins.

As they neared the warehouse, Jace's faction emerged from the shadows, their faces hard and determined. They formed a wall before the entrance, brandishing their weapons, ready to defend their territory.

"Last chance to walk away," Jace called out, his voice cutting through the tension. "You don't want to do this, Maya."

Maya halted, her group fanning out behind her. She met Jace's gaze, saw the glint of challenge in his eyes. "We're not going anywhere," she said, her voice steady despite the fear churning in her gut. "This ends now."

Jace's lips curled into a sneer. "So be it."

And with those words, the two factions clashed, a violent collision of bodies and weapons. The air filled with shouts and grunts, the metallic clang of pipes against pipes.

Maya found herself in the thick of it, dodging blows, lashing out with her own makeshift club. She caught glimpses of her friends through the chaos - Riley fighting with a fierce determination, Benji's face twisted in a snarl as he grappled with one of Jace's followers.

But there was no time to focus on them, no time for anything but the next swing, the next dodge. Maya's world narrowed to the immediate threats, to the burning need to protect her people.

She spotted Jace across the fray, saw him taking down one of her group with a brutal blow. Rage surged through her, and she fought her way towards him, a cry tearing from her throat.

Jace turned to face her, his eyes wild, his face splattered with blood - whether his own or someone else's, Maya couldn't tell. "You should have walked away," he growled, raising his weapon.

Maya didn't respond. She launched herself at him, her club arcing through the air. Jace parried the blow, and then they were locked in a deadly dance, trading strikes, each seeking an opening.

Around them, the battle raged on, but Maya barely registered it. Her focus was entirely on Jace, on ending this threat once and for all. She poured all her fear, all her anger, into every swing, every step.

But Jace was strong, and he was fast. He matched her blow for blow, his face a mask of determination. Maya could feel her strength flagging, her muscles screaming with exhaustion.

And then, in a flash of movement, Jace's weapon connected with her side, sending a burst of pain rippling through her. Maya stumbled, her vision blurring, and in that moment of weakness, Jace pressed his advantage.

He drove forward, his weapon raised for a final, devastating blow. Maya's heart seized, time seeming to slow as she watched death approaching.

But before the strike could land, a figure barreled into Jace, knocking him off balance. Maya blinked, her vision clearing, and saw Riley standing over Jace, her face contorted with rage.

"Not her," Riley snarled. "You won't touch her."

Jace staggered to his feet, his eyes darting between Riley and Maya. For a moment, it seemed he might attack again.

But then, from the edges of the fight, a cry went up. "Enough! Stop!"

The cry cut through the chaos, and slowly, the fighting began to still. Maya looked around, her heart pounding, and saw Tariq standing atop a pile of rubble, his hands raised.

"Look at what we've become!" he shouted, his voice raw with emotion. "Is this what we want? To tear each other apart?"

Maya felt a wave of shame wash over her. She looked at her hands, bruised and bloodied, and then at the faces of her friends, twisted with pain and anger.

"He's right," she said softly, her voice trembling. "This isn't us. This isn't what we stand for."

Jace looked at her, his expression unreadable. For a moment, Maya thought he might argue, might urge his followers to keep fighting.

But instead, he lowered his weapon. "Fine," he said, his voice tight. "We'll stop. For now."

Maya nodded, relief flooding through her. She turned to her group, seeing the exhaustion and pain in their eyes.

"Let's go," she said. "We need to tend to our wounded."

As they began to retreat, Maya caught Riley's eye. Her friend gave her a small, tired smile, and Maya felt a surge of gratitude.

But even as they walked away, Maya couldn't shake the feeling that this was only the beginning. The fight had ended, but the divisions within the group were deeper than ever.

She knew that as a leader, it was her responsibility to find a way to heal these wounds, to bring them back together. But as she looked at the battered faces around her, she couldn't help but wonder if it was already too late.

The cost of survival, it seemed, might be higher than any of them had ever imagined. And as Maya led her limping, bleeding friends back to their shelter, she couldn't escape the nagging fear that in trying to save them, she might have lost them forever.

The warehouse felt cavernous and cold as Maya's group limped inside, the adrenaline of the fight fading into a bone-deep weariness. Benji and Tariq moved among the wounded, assessing injuries and offering what meager medical supplies they had. The air was heavy with the coppery scent of blood and the bitter tang of desperation.

Maya leaned against a wall, her breath coming in short, painful gasps. Every muscle in her body ached, and her mind reeled from the chaos of the battle. She watched as her friends tended to each other, their movements sluggish and their eyes haunted.

"We can't keep going like this," Riley said, coming to stand beside her. Her voice was low and strained. "We barely survived today. What happens next time?"

Maya closed her eyes, the weight of leadership pressing down on her. "I don't know," she admitted. "But we have to find a way. We have to stay together."

Riley was silent for a long moment. "Do we?" she asked finally. "Maybe... maybe Jace was right. Maybe the only way to survive is to be ruthless. To take what we need, no matter the cost."

Maya's eyes snapped open, and she turned to face her friend. "No," she said firmly. "That's not who we are. That's not who we want to be."

"But what if it's who we have to be?" Riley pressed. "What if it's the only way?"

Maya shook her head, even as doubt gnawed at her. She looked out at her group, at the pain and fear etched into their faces. They were looking to her for guidance, for strength. She couldn't let them down.

"We find another way," she said, her voice growing stronger. "We stay true to ourselves, to each other. We don't let this place, this situation, change us. That's how we survive. That's how we win."

Riley held her gaze for a long moment, then nodded slowly. "Okay," she said. "I'm with you."

Maya managed to have a small smile, gratitude welling up inside her. She knew the road ahead would be hard, that there would be more fights, more pain. But with her friends by her side, she knew they could face anything.

She pushed off the wall, ignoring the screaming protest of her muscles. "Let's get everyone patched up," she said. "And then we need to make a plan. We've got a lot of work to do."

As she moved among her group, offering comfort and support, Maya felt a flicker of hope amid the darkness. They had survived today. They would survive tomorrow. And no matter what challenges lay ahead, they would face them together.

Benji stumbled back, his shoulder slamming into the crumbling warehouse wall. His breath came in ragged gasps, eyes wide with fear and disbelief. The fight raged on around him, shouts and grunts echoing through the cavernous space.

He'd always been the jokester, the one to lighten the mood with a well-timed quip. But there was no humor in this, no punchline to diffuse the tension. This was raw, primal survival, and it terrified him.

A member of Jace's faction lunged at him, fists swinging. Benji ducked, muscle memory from playground scuffles kicking in. He lashed out, his own fist connecting with a sickening thud. The other boy fell back, surprise etched on his face.

Benji stared at his hand, knuckles already bruising. The cynicism that had been creeping in since the quake took root, hardening into something cold and bitter. This was his reality now. No more jokes. No more laughter. Just the grim business of staying alive.

Across the warehouse, Tariq watched the melee unfold, his dark eyes calculating. He stayed on the edges, intervening only when necessary. A strategic strike here, a well-timed shove there. He was a chess master, manipulating the board to his advantage.

But even as he played the game, Tariq couldn't fully commit. He saw the fractures forming in both factions, the way fear and desperation were twisting people he'd once known. This fight wasn't just about the warehouse. It was about the soul of their group, and Tariq wasn't sure either side deserved to win.

Maya's voice cut through the chaos, rallying her troops. Tariq's gaze snapped to her, taking in the determination in her stance, the fire in her eyes. She was a born leader, but leading in a world like this came with a heavy price. Tariq wondered how long she could bear the weight before it crushed her.

The fight began to turn, Maya's faction gaining ground. Tariq slipped back into the shadows, his mind already racing ahead. The warehouse was just the beginning. The real battle, he knew, would be for the hearts and minds of the survivors. And that was a battle he intended to win.

Benji slumped against the wall, exhaustion and adrenaline warring within him. The sounds of the fight were starting to fade, but he knew this was just a temporary reprieve. The joke was over. The punchline had fallen flat. All that was left was the grim reality of survival in this shattered world.

He looked up, catching Tariq's eye across the warehouse. An understanding passed between them, a recognition of the change that had been wrought. Nothing would ever be the same. They would adapt, or they would die.

The choice, Benji realized with a sinking feeling, was that simple. And that impossible.

Maya dodged a blow, her heart pounding in her chest. The fight was a blur of motion and noise, a desperate struggle for survival. She caught a glimpse of one of Jace's followers, injured and vulnerable. For a moment, time seemed to slow.

She could end it, right here. A quick strike, and they'd have the advantage. Maya's hand tightened on her weapon, the metal cold and heavy. One life, to save so many. Wasn't that the right choice?

But even as the thought formed, Maya recoiled from it. This wasn't her. She'd fought so hard to hold onto her humanity, to keep from becoming like Jace. If she did this, crossed this line, there'd be no going back.

The moment stretched, the noise of the battle fading to a dull roar. Maya's breath came in short gasps, her mind racing. The world had changed, but had she changed with it? Was survival worth the cost of her soul?

She looked at the injured opponent, saw the fear in their eyes. The same fear she'd seen in her own group, in herself. They were all scared kids, fighting for their lives in a world turned upside down.

Maya lowered her weapon, the decision made. She couldn't do it. Couldn't become the monster she feared. Even if it meant losing the warehouse, even if it meant putting her own life at risk. She had to hold onto her humanity, her compassion. It was all she had left.

The fight raged on around her, but Maya stood still, a calm settling over her. She'd made her choice, for better or worse. The consequences would come, but she'd face them as herself. As the leader she wanted to be, not the one this world was trying to force her to become.

Jace's voice rang out, mocking and triumphant. He'd seen her hesitation, and he was already using it against her. Maya's heart sank, but she stood tall. The battle for the warehouse was far from over, but the battle for her soul?

That, she'd won. And in the end, maybe that was the victory that mattered most.

Jace's laughter cut through the chaos like a knife. "Look at her!" he shouted, pointing at Maya with a sneer. "Your leader, the great Maya, showing mercy to the enemy. Is this who you want to follow? Someone who's too weak to do what's necessary?"

His words found their mark, sowing doubt among Maya's followers. She could see it in their eyes, the uncertainty, the fear. They were losing faith in her, just as Jace had intended.

"We fight to win!" Jace roared, his voice rising above the din of battle. "We take control, by any means necessary. That's the only way to survive in this world now."

His faction surged forward, emboldened by his words. They fought with a new ferocity, driven by desperation and the promise of power. Maya's group, already shaken, began to falter under the onslaught.

Maya's mind raced, searching for a way to turn the tide. But her moment of mercy had cost her dearly, and she knew it. The injured opponent she'd spared was already back on their feet, rejoining the fight with a vengeance.

"What have I done?" Maya thought, despair threatening to overwhelm her. "I've doomed us all, and for what? Some misguided sense of morality?"

But even as the doubts assailed her, Maya clung to her conviction. She'd made the right choice, the human choice. And if that meant losing the warehouse, so be it. She'd find another way to keep her group safe, another way to survive.

"Stand together!" Maya cried, rallying her fractured group. "We're stronger than this, stronger than him. We don't need to be monsters to survive. We just need each other."

Her words seemed small against the tide of violence, but Maya saw a flicker of hope in her followers' eyes. They were still with her, still willing to fight for what was right.

The battle raged on, the outcome uncertain. But Maya knew that whatever happened, she'd face it as herself. She'd face it with her humanity intact, and with the knowledge that some things were worth fighting for.

Even in a world torn apart, even in the face of brutality and despair, compassion could still be a strength. And Maya would cling to that truth, no matter the cost.

The battle ended as abruptly as it had begun, leaving behind a tableau of devastation. Bodies lay strewn across the warehouse floor, some moaning in pain, others ominously still. The air was thick with the coppery scent of blood and the acrid tang of sweat and fear.

Maya stood amidst the carnage, her chest heaving, her knuckles bruised and bloody. She looked around at her group, taking in their battered faces, their haunted eyes. They had survived, but at what cost?

Riley limped over to Maya, wincing with each step. "We held them off," she said, her voice raw. "But Jace still has the warehouse. And we lost... we lost so many."

Maya nodded, unable to speak past the lump in her throat. She saw Benji kneeling beside a fallen friend, his shoulders shaking with silent sobs. Tariq stood apart, his expression unreadable, but Maya could see the toll the fight had taken in the slump of his shoulders.

"What do we do now?" someone asked, their voice small and lost in the vastness of the warehouse.

Maya looked around, taking in the shattered windows, the blood-stained concrete. This place had been their hope, their chance at survival. And now it was just another battlefield, another scar on the landscape of their shattered world.

"We leave," Maya said finally, her voice heavy with exhaustion and grief. "We find somewhere else, somewhere safe. And we start again."

There were murmurs of dissent, of fear and anger. "How can we start again?" someone demanded. "Look at us! We're broken, we're—"

"We're alive," Maya interrupted, her voice growing stronger. "We're alive, and we're together. And as long as we have that, we have hope."

She looked around at her group, meeting each of their eyes in turn. "I know I've made mistakes. I know I've asked too much of you. But I still believe in us. I still believe in what we can be, if we just hold on to our humanity."

There was a long moment of silence, broken only by the distant sound of settling rubble. Then, slowly, one by one, Maya's group began to nod. They were still with her, still willing to follow her lead.

Maya felt a flicker of hope amid the despair. They had lost the warehouse, but they hadn't lost themselves. They were battered and bruised, but they were unbroken.

"Let's go," Maya said, leading the way out of the warehouse and into the uncertain future. "Let's find our way home."

As they walked, Maya felt the weight of leadership settling on her shoulders once more. But this time, it didn't feel quite so heavy. She had her group, her friends, her family. And together, they could face whatever the world had in store.

The road ahead would be hard, Maya knew. There would be more battles, more losses, more hard choices. But she also knew that as long as they held on to their humanity, as long as they held on to each other, they could find a way through.

In a world torn apart, compassion and unity were the most powerful weapons of all. And Maya would wield them with all the strength and courage she possessed.

The group disappeared into the ruins of the city, their footsteps echoing against the broken pavement. Behind them, the warehouse stood silent and empty, a monument to all they had lost and all they had yet to gain.

But ahead of them, the future stretched out, unknown and unwritten. And Maya knew that whatever it held, they would face it together.

Maya stumbled through the ruined warehouse, her breath coming in ragged gasps. The battle had drained her, both physically and emotionally. She looked down at her hands, still trembling from the adrenaline, and saw the blood and grime that covered them. Was this what leadership meant? Making choices that led to violence and pain?

Around her, the wounded lay on makeshift beds, their moans and cries echoing in the cavernous space. Riley moved among them, her face a mask of grim determination as she tended to their injuries. Maya watched her, feeling a surge of gratitude and guilt. Riley had always been there for her, always supported her, but now even she seemed to be buckling under the strain.

Maya closed her eyes, trying to block out the images that flashed through her mind. The clash of bodies, the sound of fists on flesh, the look of fear and anger on her friends' faces. She had led them into this fight, and now they were paying the price.

"Maya?" Riley's voice cut through her thoughts. Maya opened her eyes to see her friend standing before her, her hands stained with blood. "Are you okay?"

Maya shook her head. "I don't know," she admitted. "I keep wondering if I'm doing the right thing, if I'm leading us down the right path."

Riley sighed, sinking down beside her. "None of us know what the right path is anymore," she said. "We're just trying to survive."

"But at what cost?" Maya asked. "Look at what we've become, Riley. We're fighting each other, hurting each other. Is this really what we want?"

Riley was silent for a long moment. "I don't know," she said at last. "But I do know that we need you, Maya. We need your strength, your courage, your compassion. Without you, we'd be lost."

Maya felt tears pricking at her eyes. She reached out and took Riley's hand, squeezing it tightly. "I'm trying," she whispered. "I'm trying so hard."

Around them, the wounded continued to suffer, their pain a tangible presence in the air. Maya looked at them, feeling the weight of responsibility pressing down on her. She had to find a way to keep them safe, to keep them alive. But how could she do that when the world seemed to be tearing itself apart?

She took a deep breath, forcing herself to stand. "We need to get moving," she said. "We can't stay here. It's not safe."

Riley nodded, rising to join her. "Where will we go?"

Maya hesitated, her mind racing. "Somewhere far from here," she said at last. "Somewhere where we can start over, build something new."

She looked around at her group, at the faces she had come to know and love. They were battered and bruised, but they were unbroken.

The sun had barely risen over the ruined city when Jace's triumphant shouts echoed through the warehouse. Maya watched from a distance, her heart sinking as she saw the way his followers rallied around him, their faces alight with fierce joy.

"We have shown them our strength!" Jace cried, his voice ringing out over the cheers of his faction. "We have proven that we will not be broken, that we will not be beaten!"

He stood atop a pile of rubble, his tall frame silhouetted against the pale dawn sky. In the light of day, the wounds of the previous night's battle were starkly visible - the bruises, the cuts, the haunted eyes. But Jace seemed to feed off the pain, his grin widening with each new cheer.

Maya's hands clenched into fists at her sides. She could feel the eyes of her own group on her, could sense their growing unease. They had fought so hard, had risked so much, and yet the warehouse remained in Jace's control. What did that say about her leadership?

"We cannot let them win," she said softly, almost to herself. "We cannot let them take everything."

Beside her, Riley nodded grimly. "But how do we stop them? They're so strong, so ruthless..."

Maya didn't answer. She couldn't, not when she was asking herself the same questions.

Jace's voice rose again, cutting through her thoughts. "We are the survivors!" he shouted. "We are the ones who will rebuild this world in our image!"

His words were met with a roar of approval, and Maya felt a shiver run down her spine. She knew all too well the seductive power of

Jace's rhetoric, the way he could twist even the most heinous acts into something that seemed noble and necessary.

"We have to do something," she said, tearing her gaze away from the spectacle before her. "We can't let him keep control of the warehouse. It's too important."

"But what can we do?" Riley asked, her voice trembling slightly. "We're outnumbered, outmatched..."

Maya's jaw tightened. "We have to be smarter," she said. "We have to find a way to undermine him, to turn his own people against him."

It was a daunting prospect, but what choice did they have? Jace's power was only growing, and with each passing day, the chances of wresting control of the warehouse away from him seemed to dwindle.

Maya took a deep breath, forcing herself to stand tall. She couldn't afford to show weakness, not now. Her people needed her to be strong, to be the leader they deserved.

"Come on," she said, turning to face her group. "We have work to do."

As she led them away from the warehouse, Maya couldn't shake the feeling that they were walking into a storm. But whatever lay ahead, she knew one thing for certain - she would not let Jace win. Not without a fight.

Maya's group huddled together in the shadows of a crumbling building, their faces etched with fear and uncertainty. The sounds of Jace's victory speech echoed through the ruins, a haunting reminder of their recent defeat.

"I don't know if I can do this anymore," Benji muttered, his voice hollow. "Maybe Jace is right. Maybe we're just delaying the inevitable."

Maya's heart clenched at his words. She knew Benji's cynicism was a defense mechanism, but hearing him express doubts about her leadership stung.

"We can't give up," Maya said, trying to inject confidence into her voice. "If we do, Jace wins. And we all know what that means."

Tariq, ever the observer, spoke up. "Jace is strong, but he's not invincible. There must be a way to exploit his weaknesses."

Maya nodded, latching onto Tariq's words like a lifeline. "You're right. We need to find a way to turn his own tactics against him."

She began to pace, her mind racing. Jace's boldness had paid off in the short term, but could it also be his downfall? If they could find a way to use his aggression against him, to make his own people question his leadership...

"We need to be smart about this," Maya said, turning to face her group. "We can't beat Jace at his own game. We have to find another way."

Riley stepped forward, her eyes blazing with determination. "What if we could turn some of his people against him? Sow seeds of doubt?"

Maya considered the idea. It was risky, but it could work. If they could get even a few of Jace's followers to question his leadership, it could be the crack they needed to break his hold on the warehouse.

"It's worth a shot," Maya said. "But we have to be careful. If Jace catches wind of what we're doing..."

She didn't need to finish the thought. They all knew the consequences of crossing Jace.

As the group began to disperse, Maya caught a glimpse of Jace through the ruins. He was standing tall, his chest puffed out in victory. But there was something in his eyes, a flicker of doubt that vanished as quickly as it had appeared.

Maya felt a surge of hope. Jace was not invincible. He had weaknesses, just like anyone else. And if they could find a way to exploit them, they might just have a chance.

But as she turned away, Maya couldn't shake the feeling that they were running out of time. The pressure was mounting, and sooner or later, something would have to give. She just hoped that when it did, they would be ready.

Maya walked away from the group, her mind reeling from the events of the fight. She found a quiet spot amidst the rubble, a place where she could be alone with her thoughts. As she sat down on a crumbling wall, the weight of her decisions crashed over her like a suffocating wave.

She buried her face in her hands, her breath coming in short, ragged gasps. The images of the battle flashed through her mind—the shouts, the blood, the fear in her friends' eyes. She had led them into this. She had thought she was doing the right thing, but now...now she wasn't so sure.

"What have I done?" she whispered, her voice cracking with emotion. "I thought I could keep us together, keep us human. But look at what's happened. Look at what I've caused."

She thought back to the moment when she had hesitated, when she had chosen to spare that injured opponent. At the time, it had felt like the right thing to do. But now, seeing how Jace had used it against her, she wondered if it had been a mistake.

"I tried so hard to hold onto my principles," she said, her words punctuated by bitter laughter. "But what good are principles in a world like this? What good is mercy when it only gets you killed?"

She shook her head, tears stinging her eyes. She had always believed that there was a line she wouldn't cross, a moral code she would uphold no matter what. But now, faced with the brutality of this new reality, she couldn't help but question everything she had once held dear.

"Maybe Jace is right," she murmured, the words tasting like poison on her tongue. "Maybe the only way to survive is to be ruthless. Maybe I've been fooling myself all along."

She sat there for a long time, lost in her own dark thoughts. The sun dipped lower in the sky, casting long shadows across the ruins. And as the light faded, so too did Maya's hope. She had fought so hard to keep her group together, to lead them with compassion and understanding. But now, in the aftermath of the battle, she wondered if she had lost more than just the fight. She wondered if she had lost herself.

The sound of footsteps crunching on debris pulled Maya from her thoughts. She looked up to see Riley approaching, her face etched with concern. Riley sat down beside her, their shoulders nearly touching in the cramped space.

"You did what you thought was right," Riley said softly, her voice barely audible over the distant sounds of the city. "No one can fault you for that."

Maya shook her head, unable to meet Riley's gaze. "But what if I was wrong? What if I've been leading us down the wrong path this whole time?"

Riley was quiet for a moment, considering her words carefully. "You've always been the one to keep us together, Maya. You're the reason we've made it this far. The group looks to you for guidance, for hope."

"But I don't know if I can be that person anymore," Maya whispered, her voice cracking. "I don't know if I have any hope left to give."

Riley reached out, placing a hand on Maya's arm. Maya could feel the warmth of her touch even through the layers of her jacket. "You're not alone in this, Maya. We're all struggling. But we need you. The group needs you."

Maya finally met Riley's eyes, and she was surprised to see a flicker of doubt in their green depths. It was a look she had never seen on Riley's face before, and it made her heart sink.

"Do you really believe that?" Maya asked, her voice barely a whisper. "After everything that's happened, do you still have faith in me?"

Riley hesitated, and in that moment, Maya saw the truth. Even Riley, her most loyal friend, was starting to question her leadership. The realization hit her like a physical blow, and she felt the last shreds of her confidence crumble away.

"I don't know," Riley admitted, her voice heavy with emotion. "But I do know that we can't give up. We have to keep fighting, no matter what."

Maya nodded, but the words felt hollow. She knew that Riley was right, that they had no choice but to keep going. But she couldn't shake the feeling that she was leading them all to their doom.

As the two girls sat there in silence, the weight of the world pressing down on their shoulders, Maya couldn't help but wonder what the future held. She had always believed that they could find a way to survive, to rebuild what had been lost. But now, in the face of so much uncertainty and pain, she wasn't so sure.

All she knew was that she had to keep trying, even if it meant sacrificing everything she believed in. Because in this new world, there was no room for ideals or morality. There was only survival, by any means necessary.

Maya and Riley emerged from their quiet moment to a scene of barely controlled chaos. The group had retreated to their shelter, but it was clear that the fight had taken its toll. Wounded members lay on makeshift beds, their injuries hastily bandaged. Others paced restlessly, their faces etched with anger and fear.

Maya's eyes scanned the room, taking in the fractured and dispirited group. She could feel the tension crackling in the air, the unspoken accusations and doubts. It was as if the fight with Jace's faction had shattered not only their bodies but their very sense of unity.

Benji, usually the one to lighten the mood with a well-timed joke, sat in a corner, his eyes hollow and his fists clenched. The fight seemed to have stripped away his humor, leaving only a hardened shell behind.

Tariq, ever the quiet observer, watched the scene unfold with calculating eyes. Maya could almost see the gears turning in his head as he assessed the group's dynamics, weighing his options.

She knew she had to say something, to try to rally her fractured group. But the words stuck in her throat. How could she inspire them when she herself was so full of doubt?

"We need to regroup," she finally managed, her voice sounding small and uncertain even to her own ears. "We need to heal and come up with a new plan."

But even as she spoke, she could see the skepticism on their faces. The divide between her followers and Jace's faction had never felt wider, and trust was at an all-time low.

"And what good will that do?" Benji asked bitterly, his voice cutting through the tense silence. "Jace is out there, getting stronger every day. And we're here, licking our wounds like a bunch of beaten dogs."

Maya flinched at his words, feeling each one like a physical blow. She opened her mouth to respond, but no words came out.

Riley stepped forward, her voice calm but firm. "We can't give up now. We have to stick together, no matter what."

But even as she spoke, Maya could see the cracks in her loyal friend's facade. The fight had shaken them all to their core, and the road ahead seemed more uncertain than ever.

As the group continued to argue and voice their doubts, Maya felt a growing sense of despair. She had tried so hard to be the leader they needed, to hold on to her ideals in the face of so much darkness. But now, looking at the fractured and disillusioned faces around her, she couldn't help but wonder if it had all been for nothing.

The shelter, once a place of relative safety and comfort, now felt suffocating and claustrophobic. The wounds they had suffered, both physical and emotional, seemed to hang in the air like a thick fog.

Maya closed her eyes, trying to block out the pain and uncertainty. She knew that they couldn't stay here forever, that they would have to face Jace and his faction again. But for now, all she could do was try to hold her shattered group together, even as the cracks grew wider with each passing moment.

Benji's voice cut through the tense silence, his tone sharp and cynical. "Face it, Maya. We got our asses handed to us out there. Jace and his crew, they're not messing around. Maybe it's time we start playing by their rules."

Maya's eyes snapped open, fixing on Benji with a mix of surprise and disappointment. The once carefree jokester now stood before her, his face hardened and his eyes filled with a bitter resolve.

"You can't be serious, Benji," Maya said, her voice strained. "We can't stoop to their level. We have to be better than that."

Benji scoffed, shaking his head. "Better? Look around you, Maya. We're broken, beaten. Being 'better' isn't going to keep us alive."

The group shifted uncomfortably, some nodding in agreement with Benji's words, others looking away in shame. Maya felt her heart sink as she realized just how far they had fallen.

Tariq, who had been silently observing the exchange, finally spoke up. "Benji has a point," he said, his voice quiet but firm. "Jace's methods, while brutal, have kept his group safe and in control of the warehouse. We can't ignore that."

Maya looked at Tariq, searching his face for any sign of the quiet, strategic ally she had come to rely on. But his expression was unreadable, his eyes filled with a cold pragmatism that chilled her to the bone.

"So, what are you saying?" Maya asked, her voice barely above a whisper. "That we should just give up, join Jace's faction?"

Benji shrugged, a bitter smile playing at the corners of his mouth. "Maybe. At least then we'd have a fighting chance."

Maya felt the weight of their words crushing down on her, the last vestiges of hope slipping through her fingers. She looked around at the faces of her once-loyal followers, seeing the doubt and disillusionment etched into every line.

She wanted to argue, to rally them back to her side. But the words wouldn't come. The fight had taken something from all of them, and she wasn't sure if they would ever get it back.

As the group continued to murmur and debate, Maya felt a growing sense of isolation. The gulf between her and her followers had never felt wider, and she couldn't help but wonder if she had lost them for good.

Tariq's gaze met hers across the room, and for a moment, she thought she saw a flicker of sympathy in his dark eyes. But it was gone as quickly as it had appeared, replaced by the same cold detachment that had settled over all of them.

Maya closed her eyes again, trying to block out the pain and uncertainty. She knew that they couldn't stay here forever, that they would have to face Jace and his faction again. But for now, all she could do was try to hold the pieces of her shattered leadership together, even as they threatened to crumble in her hands.

Maya stepped outside, needing to escape the suffocating atmosphere in the shelter. The cool evening air hit her face, but it did little to soothe the turmoil within. She walked a short distance, finding a spot to sit among the rubble, and let her head fall into her hands.

The weight of her decisions pressed down on her, as heavy as the concrete slabs that littered the ground. Each choice she had made, each step that had led them to this point, played out in her mind like a twisted highlight reel. The lives lost, the trust broken, the innocence shattered—it all rested on her shoulders.

"I never asked for this," she whispered to herself, her voice barely audible above the distant sounds of the city. "I never wanted to be a leader."

But there was no escaping the role that had been thrust upon her. The earthquake had changed everything, and she had been forced to adapt. To make hard choices. To bear the burden of responsibility for the lives of others.

Even so, she couldn't help but question herself. Had she made the right calls? Could she have done something differently to avoid this conflict with Jace? Was there still a way to salvage what remained of her fractured group?

Maya looked up at the sky, the stars obscured by the haze of dust and smoke that seemed to perpetually hang over the city now. She searched for answers, for some sign that she was on the right path. But the heavens remained silent, offering no guidance.

She knew that the fight with Jace was far from over. That there would be more battles to come, both physical and mental. The very soul of their group hung in the balance, and she was the fulcrum upon which it all rested.

Maya took a deep breath, trying to center herself. She had to be strong, now more than ever. She had to find a way to lead, even if it meant making sacrifices. Even if it meant losing a part of herself in the process.

With a heavy heart, she stood, brushing the dust from her clothes. She turned back towards the shelter, towards the challenges that awaited her. Towards an uncertain future that she knew she must face, no matter the cost.

As she walked, a grim determination settled over her. She would not let Jace win. She would not let her group fall apart. She would find a way to lead them through this darkness, even if it meant walking through hell itself.

The road ahead was long and treacherous, but Maya knew there was no turning back. The fate of her friends, her family, rested in her hands. And she would not let them down. Not again. Not ever.

With a final steadying breath, she stepped back into the shelter, ready to face whatever lay ahead. Ready to be the leader they needed, even if it meant sacrificing everything she was. Even if it meant losing herself in the process.

Jace stood in the center of the warehouse, his eyes sweeping over the stockpiles of supplies that filled the cavernous space. The weight of his leadership hung heavy on his shoulders, but he refused to let it show. He had to be strong, had to be unshakable, if he was going to maintain control.

Around him, his followers worked to fortify their defenses, their faces grim and determined. They moved with a sense of urgency, knowing that another confrontation with Maya's group was inevitable. The tension in the air was palpable, a physical presence that pressed down on them all.

Jace clenched his fists, his mind racing with strategies and contingencies. He had to be prepared for anything, had to anticipate Maya's every move. He couldn't afford to show any weakness, not now, not when everything hung in the balance.

But even as he projected an image of unshakable confidence, Jace could feel the cracks beginning to form. The constant strain of leadership, the never-ending cycle of violence and retribution, was taking its toll. He could see it in the eyes of his followers, the flickers of doubt and uncertainty that they tried so hard to hide.

He shook his head, pushing those thoughts aside. He couldn't afford to indulge in self-doubt, not when so much depended on him. He had to be the leader they needed, the one who could guide them through this nightmare and out the other side.

"Jace, we need to talk." The voice belonged to one of his lieutenants, a wiry boy named Ethan. Jace turned to face him, his expression carefully neutral.

"What is it?" he asked, his voice steady and controlled.

Ethan hesitated, his eyes darting around the warehouse. "Some of the others, they're starting to have doubts. They're wondering if this fight with Maya is really worth it, if we shouldn't just try to find a way to coexist."

Jace's jaw tightened, a flash of anger surging through him. "Coexist? With Maya and her band of bleeding hearts? You know that's not possible. They're weak, and in this world, weakness is a death sentence."

Ethan flinched at the harshness in Jace's tone, but he pressed on. "Maybe, but if we keep fighting like this, we're going to destroy ourselves. We've already lost so much, Jace. How much more are we willing to sacrifice?"

Jace stepped forward, his eyes boring into Ethan's. "As much as it takes," he growled. "We don't have the luxury of mercy, not anymore. It's kill or be killed out here, and I'll be damned if I let Maya and her group destroy everything we've fought for."

Ethan held Jace's gaze for a long moment, then nodded slowly. "I understand," he said quietly. "I'll make sure the others fall in line."

Jace watched him go, a bitter taste in his mouth. He knew Ethan was right, knew that the constant fighting was taking a toll on all of them. But what choice did they have? In a world where the strong survived and the weak perished, there was no room for compromise, no room for mercy.

He turned back to the stockpiles of supplies, his resolve hardening. He would do whatever it took to protect what was his, to ensure his group's survival. Even if it meant sacrificing his own humanity in the process.

As the sun began to set over the ruined city, the two factions prepared for the coming storm. The wounds of the first battle were still raw, the scars still fresh. But both sides knew that this was only the beginning, that the true test of their resolve was yet to come.

In the gathering darkness, Jace and Maya stood on opposite sides of a divide that seemed insurmountable. They were two leaders, two visions of the future, locked in a struggle that could only end in blood and tears.

And as the night closed in around them, they both knew that there would be no turning back, no quarter given or asked. The die had been cast, and the fate of their world would be decided in the battles to come.

CHAPTER 7

Lines in the Dust

Maya's eyes traced the jagged line scratched into the dusty asphalt, her heart sinking with each step. The crude boundary stretched before her, a physical manifestation of their failure. Behind it loomed the warehouse, its corrugated metal walls gleaming in the harsh sunlight, a fortress now lost to them.

"We should never have tried to take it back," muttered a voice from the crowd gathered behind her. "Look where it's gotten us."

Maya's jaw clenched, but she didn't turn. She could feel the weight of their stares, the doubt radiating from her once-loyal followers. The warehouse stood as a stark reminder of everything they'd lost – not just supplies, but unity, hope, and faith in her leadership.

"Maya," another voice called out, louder this time. "What are we going to do now? We can't keep going on like this."

She closed her eyes, inhaling deeply. The air was thick with tension, almost suffocating. When she opened them again, she turned to face the group, her expression carefully composed.

"I know you're all scared," she began, her voice steady despite the tremor in her hands. "I am too. But we can't give up now."

A chorus of frustrated sighs and muttered disagreements rippled through the crowd. Maya felt a twinge of desperation. How could she make them understand?

"We lost the warehouse, yes," she continued, her words growing more urgent. "But we haven't lost everything. We still have each other, and that's—"

"That's not enough!" someone interrupted. "We need food and water. We need shelter. Your pretty words won't keep us alive, Maya."

The accusation stung, but Maya pushed through. "I know it's not enough. But if we turn on each other now, if we lose sight of who we are, then we've truly lost everything."

As she spoke, Maya's mind raced. She knew her words were falling short, that the growing doubt was threatening to consume them all. The weight of leadership pressed down on her shoulders, heavier than ever before.

I can't let them see how scared I am, she thought. If I falter now, we're finished.

"Look," she said, gesturing towards the warehouse. "Jace may have won this battle, but the war isn't over. We'll find another way. We'll—"

"And how many more of us will die while you figure it out?" The sharp question cut through the air, silencing the group.

Maya felt her resolve wavering. The faces before her, once filled with trust and hope, now showed only fear and resentment. She opened her mouth to respond, but the words wouldn't come.

In that moment of silence, the magnitude of their situation crashed over her. The loss of the warehouse wasn't just about supplies – it was about the fracturing of their community, the erosion of everything they'd built together.

As she stood there, struggling to find the right words, Maya realized that the line in the dust wasn't just a boundary between territories. It was a divide between who they were and who they might become in this harsh new world. And as their leader, she stood at the center of that divide, desperately trying to hold both sides together.

Riley stepped forward, her green eyes flashing with determination. She placed a hand on Maya's shoulder, squeezing gently. "We're not finished," she said, her voice clear and strong. "Maya's right. We'll find another way."

The group shifted uneasily, murmurs of dissent rippling through the crowd. Riley pressed on, her words tinged with a desperation she couldn't quite hide. "We've come this far together. We can't give up now. We need to—"

"Need to what?" Benji's voice cut through the air, cold and sharp. He pushed his way to the front, his once-friendly face now hard and lined with exhaustion. "Keep playing by rules that don't exist anymore?"

Maya felt her stomach clench. Benji had always been their voice of reason, their source of levity in dark times. But now, as she looked into his eyes, she saw only a reflection of the harsh world around them.

"Benji," she started, but he cut her off with a wave of his hand.

"No, Maya. It's time we faced facts. Jace has food, water, shelter. What do we have? Good intentions?" He laughed, a bitter sound that sent chills down Maya's spine. "If we want to survive, we need to start thinking like him."

The crowd's murmurs grew louder, some nodding in agreement. Maya felt the ground shifting beneath her feet, the fragile unity of their group crumbling.

This can't be happening, she thought, panic rising in her chest. We can't become like Jace. We can't lose our humanity.

But as she looked around at the tired, hungry faces of her friends, she wondered if they had any choice left at all.

Tariq watched from the shadows, his dark eyes taking in every detail of the unfolding scene. He'd always been content to observe, to analyze, but now he felt a restless energy coiling within him. The air was thick with tension, and he could sense the group teetering on the edge of collapse.

Maya's voice, once strong and sure, now wavered as she tried to rally her followers. "We're better than this," she pleaded, her eyes darting from face to face. "We can find another way."

Tariq's gaze shifted to Jace's camp in the distance, where figures moved with purpose, fortifying their position. He narrowed his eyes, weighing the stark contrast between the two groups.

Neither of them has the answer, he thought, his mind racing. Maya's idealism is crumbling, and Jace's brutality will only lead to more suffering.

He stepped forward, surprising even himself. "Maybe we're asking the wrong questions," Tariq said, his quiet voice cutting through the argument.

All eyes turned to him, shock evident on their faces. Tariq rarely spoke, let alone inserted himself into conflicts.

"What do you mean?" Maya asked, hope and wariness mingling in her tone.

Tariq took a deep breath, choosing his words carefully. "We're so focused on who's right and who's wrong, we've forgotten to ask what's actually possible. Both sides are flawed."

He gestured towards Jace's camp. "They have resources but no compassion." Then he turned to Maya. "We have ideals but no plan. Neither path leads to true survival."

Maya's brow furrowed, conflict clear in her eyes. "So, what are you suggesting?"

Tariq shook his head. "I don't have all the answers. But I think we need to start looking beyond just these two options."

As he spoke, Tariq could feel the weight of everyone's attention. For the first time, he wasn't just a silent observer. He was actively shaping the conversation, and the realization both thrilled and terrified him.

This changes everything, he thought, his mind already racing ahead to the potential consequences of his words. But someone had to say it.

Tariq's words hung in the air, heavy with implication. He retreated back to the edge of the group, his dark eyes scanning the faces around him. Some looked thoughtful, others confused, and a few seemed almost angry at his intervention.

Maya approached him, her voice low. "Tariq, I appreciate your input, but we need to be careful about sowing more doubt."

He met her gaze steadily. "Sometimes doubt is necessary for growth," he replied, his tone measured.

As Maya walked away, visibly troubled, Tariq noticed Benji watching him with newfound interest. The once-jovial boy, now hardened by their circumstances, gave Tariq a slight nod before turning back to his makeshift weapon.

Tariq moved quietly through the camp, listening intently to the whispered conversations his words had sparked. Near the dwindling food supply, he overheard two girls debating.

"Maybe Tariq's right," one said. "What if there's another way?"

"But what choice do we have?" the other countered. "It's Maya or Jace."

Tariq's mind raced. They're all so fixated on this false dichotomy, he thought. But there might be other options we haven't considered.

As the sun began to set, casting long shadows across their makeshift shelter, Tariq found a quiet corner to sit and observe. He watched as Riley tried to rally support for Maya, her usual enthusiasm somewhat dimmed. Meanwhile, others huddled in small groups, their loyalty clearly wavering.

This group is fracturing, Tariq realized, a chill running down his spine. And neither Maya nor Jace seems equipped to hold it together. But who am I to step into that void?

The question haunted him as night fell, bringing with it the eerie quiet of a city devoid of its usual bustle. Tariq knew that tomorrow would bring new challenges, and he had to be ready. For the first time since the earthquake, he felt the weight of responsibility settling on his shoulders. The game had changed, and he was no longer content to be just a pawn.

Maya stood at the edge of the plaza, her eyes fixed on the crude line drawn in the dust. The once-bustling square now served as a stark reminder of their division. She clenched her fists, feeling the weight of her group's disillusionment pressing down on her shoulders.

"Maya," a voice called out, tinged with frustration. "We can't keep going on like this."

She turned to face Jason, one of her most vocal critics lately. His gaunt face and sunken eyes mirrored the desperation that had taken hold of their group.

"What do you suggest we do, Jason?" Maya asked, her voice calm despite the turmoil inside her.

"Look at them," Jason said, gesturing towards Jace's territory. "They have food, water, shelter. We're barely surviving out here."

Maya's gaze followed his hand, taking in the fortified warehouse and the armed guards patrolling its perimeter. She felt a pang of envy, quickly followed by shame.

"We can't abandon our principles," she argued, but her words lacked their usual conviction.

"Principles won't keep us alive," Jason retorted. "More and more of us are wondering if Jace has the right idea. At least he can provide for his people."

As Jason walked away, Maya's mind raced. She could see the doubt in the eyes of her followers, hear the whispers of discontent. The line in the dust seemed to mock her, a physical manifestation of her failure to keep the group united.

How did it come to this? she thought, her heart heavy. I wanted to lead with compassion, but am I just leading them to their doom?

She watched as a small group gathered near the boundary, their faces turned longingly towards Jace's stronghold. The sight made her stomach churn.

"We can't give up," she whispered to herself, trying to summon the strength to face another day of challenges. But as the cool autumn wind whipped through the plaza, Maya couldn't shake the feeling that her grip on leadership was slipping away, just like the leaves falling from the trees around them.

Maya found herself alone at the edge of their makeshift camp, her eyes fixed on the distant warehouse. The setting sun cast long shadows across the rubble-strewn landscape, mirroring the darkness creeping into her thoughts.

"What if I'm wrong?" she murmured, her voice barely audible. The question had been gnawing at her for days, growing louder with each passing hour. She clenched her fists, feeling the weight of her responsibility crushing down on her.

Riley approached; her footsteps hesitant. "Maya? The others are asking about our next move."

Maya turned, forcing a smile that didn't reach her eyes. "I'm working on it, Riley. We'll figure something out."

As Riley nodded and walked away, Maya's facade crumbled. She slumped against a crumbling wall, her head in her hands. The guilt of their failed assault on the warehouse washed over her anew.

"Maybe Jace is right," she whispered, the words tasting like ash in her mouth. "Maybe in this world, brutality is the only way to survive."

The thought terrified her, but she couldn't shake it. She glanced at her group, huddled around meager fires, their faces gaunt and weary. The isolation she felt was palpable, a chasm growing between her and even her most loyal supporters.

"I can't let them down," Maya said, her voice cracking. "But how can I lead when I don't even know if I'm on the right path anymore?"

As night fell, Maya remained apart, the weight of leadership and the specter of failure pushing her towards the brink of despair.

Maya's stomach growled, a painful reminder of their dire situation. She pressed a hand against her abdomen, wincing as she surveyed the group's dwindling supplies. A few cans of beans, half a bottle of water, and a handful of stale crackers were all that remained.

"We need to do something," Riley whispered, her voice hoarse from thirst. "People are getting desperate."

Maya nodded, her eyes scanning the haggard faces of her group. Sunken cheeks and dull eyes met her gaze, a stark contrast to the hope that had once burned within them.

"I know," Maya replied, her voice barely audible. "But what options do we have left?"

She watched as an elderly man stumbled, caught by two teenagers before he could fall. The sight sent a jolt of panic through her.

"We can't go on like this," Maya thought, her heart racing. "Every hour that passes, we grow weaker. But if we make the wrong move..."

Her thoughts were interrupted by a fit of coughing from nearby. A young girl, no more than twelve, doubled over, her small frame wracked with each painful hack.

"Do we have any medicine left?" Maya asked, already knowing the answer.

Riley shook her head, her eyes glistening with unshed tears. "We used the last of it two days ago."

Maya's chest tightened, the weight of their predicament crushing down on her. She closed her eyes, trying to steady her breathing.

"Maybe if we..." she began, but the words died in her throat. Every plan seemed futile, every option a dead end.

"Maya," Riley's voice cut through her spiral of despair. "They need you to be strong. We all do."

Maya opened her eyes, meeting Riley's gaze. She saw the fear there, barely masked by determination.

"I'm trying," Maya whispered, her voice cracking. "But I don't know how much longer I can keep this up. How much longer any of us can."

As if to punctuate her words, another aftershock rumbled through the ruins, sending loose debris clattering to the ground. The group huddled closer together, their faces etched with exhaustion and fear.

Maya stood, her legs shaky but her resolve strengthening. "We need to move," she announced, her voice carrying across the makeshift camp. "There has to be something out there. Food, water, medicine. We just have to find it."

As the group began to stir, preparing for yet another desperate search, Maya caught sight of her reflection in a shard of broken glass. The face that stared back at her was a stranger - gaunt, haunted, but still standing.

"We're not done yet," she thought, clenching her fists. "As long as we're breathing, we keep fighting."

But even as she rallied her group, the gnawing emptiness in her stomach and the dryness in her throat reminded her of the harsh truth - their time was running out.

The sun hung low in the smog-filled sky, casting an eerie orange glow over the ruined cityscape. Maya's stomach clenched painfully, a constant reminder of their dire situation. She watched as her group huddled around their meager food supply - a few cans of beans and a half-empty bottle of water.

"We can't go on like this," growled Ethan, a lanky teen with sunken eyes. "We need to hit Jace's warehouse. Now."

Maya's heart raced. "That's suicide," she countered, her voice strained. "We're not strong enough-"

"And we never will be if we keep starving!" Lisa interjected, her normally quiet demeanor shattered by desperation.

Chaos erupted as voices clashed, fear and hunger fueling the argument.

"Jace will kill us all!"

"We'll die anyway if we don't eat!"

"There has to be other places to look!"

Maya's head spun, the cacophony of voices overwhelming her. She caught Riley's eye, silently pleading for help.

Riley stepped forward, her voice cutting through the noise. "Hey! Listen up, everyone!" The group fell silent, all eyes turning to her. "Fighting amongst ourselves won't solve anything. We need to stick together, that's our only chance."

Maya felt a surge of gratitude, but it was short-lived. Ethan scoffed, "Unity? That's what got us into this mess. Maybe Jace had the right idea all along."

A murmur of agreement rippled through the group. Maya's chest tightened, panic rising within her. She's losing them, she realized. Everything she'd fought for was slipping away.

"We can't become like Jace," Maya said, her voice barely above a whisper. But as she looked around at the gaunt faces of her friends, she saw the doubt in their eyes. The faith they once had in her was fading, replaced by a primal need to survive at any cost.

Riley tried again, "Maya's right. If we lose our humanity, what are we even fighting for?"

But her words seemed to fall on deaf ears. The group had already begun to splinter, small factions forming as they debated their next move. Maya watched helplessly as the fragile bonds that held them together began to unravel.

I'm failing them, she thought, her throat tight with unshed tears. How can I lead when I don't even know if I'm doing the right thing anymore?

As the group dispersed, Maya noticed Benji lingering near the edge of their makeshift camp. His once-cheerful demeanor had hardened into something unrecognizable. She approached him cautiously, her heart heavy.

"Benji?" Maya called softly.

He turned, his eyes glinting with a newfound intensity. "Maya," he acknowledged, his voice lacking its usual warmth.

"What are you thinking?" she asked, searching his face for any trace of the jokester she once knew.

Benji's jaw clenched. "I'm thinking we can't keep going on like this. Starving, waiting for a rescue that's never coming."

A chill ran down Maya's spine. "What are you suggesting?"

"We need to be smart. Tactical." Benji's voice grew stronger, drawing the attention of nearby group members. "Look at Jace. He's got food, water, shelter. His people aren't wasting away."

Maya felt the eyes of the others on them, hungry for direction. "But at what cost, Benji? We can't abandon our principles-"

"Principles won't fill our stomachs," Benji cut her off, his words sharp. "We need to start thinking like survivors, not scared kids."

Maya's mind raced. She knew Benji's words were resonating with the group. She could see it in their eyes – a spark of hope, however grim.

"There has to be another way," Maya insisted, but her voice wavered.

Benji stepped closer, his voice low. "Maybe there isn't. Maybe it's time we stop pretending and face reality."

As he walked away, Maya noticed several others following him, hanging on his every word. She stood alone, the weight of her dwindling influence crushing her chest.

What have we become? she thought, watching as Benji's pragmatism began to overshadow her idealism. And how do I stop us from losing ourselves completely?

Maya clenched her fists, her nails digging into her palms as she watched Benji's retreating back. The group that had gathered around him was growing, their whispers carrying on the cool autumn breeze.

"We can't just sit here and starve," one voice rose above the others.

"Maybe Benji's right," another chimed in. "We need to do something."

Maya's heart raced. She had to act now or risk losing everything she'd fought to build. Taking a deep breath, she strode towards the center of the group.

"Listen up, everyone!" Her voice cracked slightly, but she pushed on. "I know we're all scared and hungry. But becoming like Jace isn't the answer."

Benji turned, his once-friendly face now etched with cynicism. "Then what is, Maya? More waiting? More empty promises?"

She felt the weight of their stares, the desperation in their eyes. For a moment, she considered giving in, adopting Jace's ruthless tactics. It would be easier, wouldn't it?

No. She couldn't. She wouldn't.

"We find another way," Maya said, her voice growing stronger. "Tomorrow, we scout for new resources. Together."

"And if we don't find anything?" Benji challenged.

Maya hesitated, her mind racing. "Then... then we consider other options. But we do it as a group, not by becoming something we're not."

She saw doubt in some faces, hope in others. It wasn't a perfect solution, but it was something. As the group slowly dispersed, Maya's thoughts tumbled.

Have I done enough? Or am I just delaying the inevitable?

The line between survival and losing their humanity had never felt so thin.

Maya slipped away from the group, her feet carrying her to the edge of their makeshift camp. The cityscape sprawled before her, a jagged horizon of broken buildings and twisted metal. She perched on a chunk of concrete, her eyes scanning the desolation.

A lump formed in her throat as memories flooded back. The excitement of the field trip, the rumble that had shaken the earth, the screams that followed. It felt like a lifetime ago.

"We were so naive," she whispered to herself, her voice barely audible over the wind whistling through the ruins.

She closed her eyes, recalling those first days after the quake. The way they had huddled together, sharing stories and rationing their meager supplies. How Emma's jokes had lifted their spirits, how even Jace had seemed almost... human.

"We really thought help was coming," Maya murmured, opening her eyes to the harsh reality before her. No rescue helicopters dotted the sky, no aid workers sifted through the rubble. Just silence and dust.

She picked up a small stone, turning it over in her hands. "We were going to survive this together. All of us."

The sound of approaching footsteps made her tense. She turned to see Riley, her loyal friend's face etched with concern.

"Maya? You okay?" Riley asked, settling beside her.

Maya forced a smile. "Just... thinking."

Riley nodded, her eyes searching Maya's face. "About how things used to be?"

"Yeah," Maya admitted. "Remember how we used to take turns keeping watch? All of us, even Jace?"

Riley's laugh was tinged with sadness. "God, that feels like another lifetime."

They sat in silence for a moment, the weight of their lost innocence hanging between them.

"Do you think we can ever get back to that?" Maya asked, her voice small. "That... hope?"

Riley hesitated. "I don't know, Maya. But if anyone can lead us there, it's you."

Maya's chest tightened. She wanted to believe that, desperately. But as she looked out at the broken city, that hope felt as distant as the rescue they'd once dreamed of.

Maya's grip tightened on the stone, her knuckles turning white. "I'm not so sure about that anymore, Riley," she confessed, her voice barely above a whisper.

Riley's brow furrowed. "What do you mean?"

Maya's eyes welled with tears she refused to let fall. "I've failed them. All of them. We're starving, divided... I can't even keep us together, let alone safe."

She stood abruptly, pacing in tight circles. "Maybe... maybe someone else should lead. Someone stronger, someone who can make the hard choices."

"Maya, stop," Riley interjected, rising to her feet. "You're the reason we've made it this far."

Maya laughed bitterly. "Look around, Riley. How far is that, really?"

She paused, staring at the crumbling buildings in the distance. In her mind, she saw the faces of her group - tired, hungry, losing faith. The weight of their lives pressed down on her shoulders, threatening to crush her.

"I don't know if I can do this anymore," Maya admitted, her voice cracking.

Riley stepped closer, placing a hand on Maya's arm. "You can't give up. We need you."

Maya closed her eyes, taking a deep breath. When she opened them, there was a flicker of determination amidst the doubt.

"You're right," she said softly. "I can't give up. Not now, not ever."

She squared her shoulders, her jaw set. "We've come too far, been through too much. I won't let them down."

But even as the words left her mouth, uncertainty gnawed at her. How could she lead them through this? What if her decisions only made things worse?

"I just... I don't know how to do this, Riley," Maya confessed. "How do I keep us alive without losing who we are?"

Riley squeezed her arm. "We'll figure it out together. One step at a time."

Maya nodded, her resolve strengthening despite the doubt that still lingered. She may not have all the answers, but she knew one thing for certain - she wouldn't stop fighting for her people.

The warehouse loomed before them, a fortress of steel and concrete that seemed to mock their desperation. Jace stood atop a makeshift platform, his silhouette cutting a commanding figure against the setting sun. His voice carried across the yard, strong and assured.

"We have food! We have water! And most importantly, we have each other!" Jace's words rang out, met with cheers from his followers.

Maya watched from the shadows, her heart sinking. She could see the abundance that Jace's group enjoyed – crates of supplies stacked high, people moving with purpose rather than exhaustion.

Jace's eyes scanned the crowd, a hint of a smirk on his lips. "This is what survival looks like. This is what strength looks like. And I promise you, as long as you stand with me, we will not just survive – we will thrive!"

More cheers erupted. Maya clenched her fists, her nails digging into her palms.

"How does he do it?" she whispered, more to herself than anyone else. "How does he make them believe so completely?"

She watched as Jace descended from his platform, moving among his people with easy confidence. He clasped shoulders, offered encouraging words, his charisma palpable even from a distance.

"It's not just about the supplies," Maya realized, her voice barely audible. "It's about the hope he gives them. The certainty."

She turned away, unable to watch anymore. The stark contrast between Jace's thriving community and her own struggling group was too painful to bear.

"We have to do something," she murmured, her mind racing. "But what? How can we compete with... that?"

The weight of leadership pressed down on her once more, heavier than ever. As she walked away from the warehouse, Maya couldn't shake the feeling that with every passing day, Jace's control tightened – not just over his own people, but over the fate of them all.

Jace's voice cut through the air like a knife, harsh and unyielding. "Maya and her followers are weak," he declared, his piercing blue eyes scanning the crowd gathered in the warehouse. "They cling to outdated morals that have no place in this new world. And make no mistake – they will come for what we have."

A murmur of unease rippled through his followers. Jace raised his hand, silencing them instantly. "But we won't let that happen, will we?" His lips curved into a predatory smile. "We'll defend what's ours, by any means necessary."

As his words sank in, people began to nod, their faces hardening with resolve. Jace's charisma was palpable, his certainty infectious.

"Start reinforcing the perimeter," he ordered, pointing to a group of burly men. "I want those walls impenetrable. The rest of you inventory our weapons. We need to be ready for anything."

His followers sprang into action, a sense of purpose energizing them. Jace watched with satisfaction as they began fortifying the warehouse, his control over them tightening with each passing moment.

"What about Maya?" someone called out. "What if she tries to negotiate?"

Jace's eyes flashed dangerously. "Negotiation is for the weak. Maya had her chance to join us, to be strong. She chose weakness instead." He paused, his voice dropping to a menacing growl. "If she comes here again, we show no mercy. Is that understood?"

A chorus of agreement echoed through the warehouse. Jace nodded, a smirk playing on his lips. He thought to himself, 'This is how you lead. This is how you survive.' The divide between his group and Maya's was growing wider by the second, and he reveled in it.

As he surveyed his domain, Jace couldn't help but feel a thrill of power. The warehouse was more than just a stockpile of supplies – it was a fortress, a symbol of his strength. And he would defend it at all costs.

Maya stood at the edge of the abandoned plaza, her eyes scanning the desolate landscape. The overcast sky cast long shadows across the rubble-strewn ground, mirroring the darkness that had settled over her heart. She took a deep breath, steeling herself for what was to come.

"Everyone, gather around," she called out, her voice steady despite the tremor in her hands.

As the remaining loyal members of her group shuffled towards her, Maya noticed the weariness etched on their faces. Riley's once-bright eyes now held a haunted look, while Benji's sardonic smirk had morphed into a permanent scowl.

"I know we're struggling," Maya began, her gaze meeting each person's in turn. "But we can't give up. Not now."

"What's the point?" someone muttered from the back. "We're barely surviving as it is."

Maya swallowed hard, pushing down the despair threatening to overwhelm her. "The point is that we're still here. Still fighting. And I have a plan."

She paused, gauging their reactions. Some looked skeptical, others desperate for any glimmer of hope.

"We need resources," Maya continued, her voice gaining strength. "Food, water, medicine. I propose we split into small teams and scout the areas we haven't explored yet. The residential districts to the north, the old shopping center to the east."

Riley stepped forward, a flicker of her old determination returning. "It's risky, but it could work. We might find supplies others have overlooked."

Maya nodded gratefully at her friend's support. "Exactly. We'll be quick, quiet, and careful. No unnecessary risks."

Benji scoffed, crossing his arms. "And what if we run into Jace's people? Or worse?"

The group shifted uneasily at the mention of their rival faction. Maya felt a pang of guilt, remembering their failed attempt to reclaim the warehouse. She pushed the memory aside, focusing on the present.

"We avoid conflict at all costs," she said firmly. "This isn't about fighting. It's about survival."

As she outlined the details of her plan, Maya couldn't help but wonder if she was making the right choice. The weight of leadership pressed down on her, threatening to crush her resolve. But looking at the faces of those who still believed in her, she knew she had to try.

"We leave at first light," Maya concluded, her voice softer now. "Get some rest. Tomorrow, we fight for our future."

As the group dispersed, Maya turned away, her eyes fixed on the distant horizon. She whispered to herself, "I won't let you down. I can't."

Maya's gaze swept over the haggard faces of her group, their eyes sunken with hunger and desperation. The weight of their expectation pressed down on her shoulders like a physical burden. She took a deep breath, steeling herself for what she had to say next.

"Listen, everyone," she began, her voice low but steady. "I know we're all tired, hungry, and scared. But we need to face the reality of our situation."

She paused, swallowing hard. "Raiding Jace's warehouse... it might be our only option left."

A murmur rippled through the group. Maya held up her hand, silencing them.

"I'm not saying we do it now. It's a last resort, something we consider only if we find nothing else." Her eyes met each of theirs in turn. "But I want you to understand what's at stake here. It's not just about supplies."

Riley stepped forward, her brow furrowed. "What do you mean, Maya?"

Maya's voice grew passionate. "I mean our humanity. Our souls. If we become like Jace, if we resort to violence and theft without exhausting every other option, we lose something we can't get back. We become the very thing we're fighting against."

Benji scoffed, but Maya pressed on. "We've survived this long because we've stuck together, because we've helped each other. That's what makes us different from Jace's group. That's what makes us human."

She could see the conflict in their eyes, the battle between desperation and morality. Maya's heart raced, knowing how fragile this moment was.

"So, we'll search for supplies elsewhere first," she said firmly. "And if we have to consider raiding the warehouse, we do it as a last resort, and we do it without losing ourselves in the process."

There was a tense silence. Then, slowly, heads began to nod.

As the sun began to set, casting long shadows across the rubble-strewn street, Maya led her group forward. They moved cautiously, eyes darting to every darkened window and shadowy alley.

Maya's mind raced as they walked. 'Am I doing the right thing? Can I really keep them safe?' The doubt gnawed at her, but she pushed it aside, focusing on the path ahead.

The group's footsteps echoed in the eerie quiet of the devastated city. Every crunch of debris underfoot seemed to Maya like a beacon, announcing their presence to unseen threats.

As they rounded a corner, Riley fell into step beside Maya. "We're with you," she whispered, her voice barely audible. "No matter what."

Maya nodded, grateful for the support, but the knot in her stomach only tightened. The unity of the group felt as fragile as spun glass, ready to shatter at the slightest impact.

They pressed on into the gathering darkness, their determination tinged with fear. Maya knew that every step forward was a gamble, a desperate bid for survival that could either save them or tear them apart.

CHAPTER 8

The Fall

A frigid wind swept through the ruined city street, carrying with it the acrid scent of smoke and decay. Jace stood atop a crumbling wall, his eyes scanning the gray horizon. His dark hair whipped across his brow, but his gaze remained steady, searching for any signs of movement.

Below him, his followers huddled around makeshift fires, their faces gaunt and haunted. They looked to him for guidance, for the strength to survive in this shattered world. And he would not let them down.

Jace jumped down from the wall, his boots crunching on the rubble. He strode towards his inner circle, his most trusted lieutenants. They straightened as he approached, their eyes glinting with a mix of fear and respect.

"They're going to run," Jace said without preamble. "Maya and her little band of idealists. They think they can escape this hell."

"How do you know?" asked Thorn, a burly man with a jagged scar across his cheek.

Jace smirked. "Because it's what I would do, if I were in her position. Weak, desperate, clinging to some fantasy of a better life out there." He spat on the ground. "But there is no better life. There's only survival, and the strength to take what you need."

He turned to face his followers, his voice ringing out across the ruins. "I want scouts on every street, every rooftop. Eyes on the perimeter at all times. If they make a move, we'll be ready."

As his lieutenants dispersed to carry out his orders, Jace felt a surge of power coursing through his veins. This was his city now, his world to control. And he would crush anyone who dared to challenge him.

Maya, he thought, his lip curling. Do you think you can lead these people to some promised land? You're just a scared little girl playing at being a savior. And when you fall, I'll be there to pick up the pieces.

He looked out over the broken cityscape, the twisted metal and shattered glass glinting in the pale light. Somewhere out there, Maya was plotting her escape. But she would soon learn the truth that Jace had already embraced.

In this world, there was no escape. Only the strong survived, and the weak perished. And Jace was determined to be the strongest of them all.

Jace strode through the ruined streets, his boots crunching on the debris. The warehouse loomed ahead, a fortress of concrete and steel. Inside, his followers were preparing for the ambush, stockpiling weapons and fortifying defenses.

He entered the main hall, where a group of his most trusted lieutenants were gathered around a makeshift table, studying a map of the city. They looked up as he approached, their eyes filled with a mix of fear and respect.

"They'll make their move soon," Jace said, his voice echoing in the cavernous space. "Maya thinks she can slip away unnoticed, but we'll be ready for her."

"What if they try to fight their way out?" one of the lieutenants asked, nervously fingering the hilt of his knife.

Jace laughed, a harsh, mirthless sound. "Then we'll crush them like the insects they are. Maya's group is weak, broken. They don't have the stomach for a real fight."

He leaned over the map, tracing his finger along the routes Maya's group might take. "We'll set up choke points here, here, and here. When they try to pass, we'll cut them down."

The lieutenants nodded, their faces grim with determination. They knew the price of failure under Jace's command.

As they dispersed to make their preparations, Jace felt a flicker of doubt. Maya had proven resourceful in the past, and her group was desperate. Desperate people were unpredictable.

No, he thought, pushing the doubt aside. I am in control. This is my city, my world. And I will not let anyone take it from me.

He looked around the warehouse, taking in the stacks of supplies, the weapons, the hard-eyed men and women who followed him. This was power, the only thing that mattered in this broken world.

And yet, as he stood there, Jace couldn't shake the feeling that a reckoning was coming. Maya would not go quietly. She would fight, with every ounce of strength and will she had left.

Let her come, he thought, his fists clenching. Let her bring her righteous anger and her naive ideals. I'll be waiting, and I will show her what true strength looks like.

The die was cast, the pieces in motion. The ambush was set, and soon, the streets would run with blood. Jace smiled, a cold, predatory grin. The game was on, and he was determined to win, no matter the cost.

The grey light of dawn seeped through the cracks in the rubble, casting long shadows across the ruined cityscape. Maya crouched behind a collapsed wall, her heart pounding in her chest as she surveyed the path ahead. Behind her, the remnants of her group huddled together, their faces drawn and pale in the dim light.

"We move quickly and quietly," Maya whispered, her voice tight with tension. "Stay low, stay together, and if you see any of Jace's patrols, don't engage. We're not looking for a fight."

Riley nodded, her hand gripping a makeshift spear. "What if they spot us?"

Maya met her gaze, her eyes hard. "Then we run. We run and we don't look back."

They set out, picking their way through the debris-strewn streets. Every footfall seemed to echo in the eerie silence, every shifting stone a potential alarm. Maya led the way, her senses straining for any sign of danger.

This is insane, a voice whispered in her head. You're leading them to their deaths. But what choice did she have? To stay in the city was to be trapped under Jace's iron fist, to watch her people starve and suffer. At least out here, they had a chance.

The city was a maze of shattered buildings and blocked roads, and Maya soon found herself disoriented. The landmarks she once knew were gone, replaced by an alien landscape of destruction.

Where are the patrols? she wondered, unease prickling along her spine. Jace wasn't one to leave his territory unguarded. The silence felt wrong, heavy with anticipation.

Suddenly, a figure emerged from the shadows ahead. Maya froze, her hand signaling her group to halt. The figure stepped into a shaft of light, revealing the hard lines of Jace's lieutenant, a cruel smile on his face.

"Well, well," he said, his voice carrying in the stillness. "What do we have here?"

Maya's heart sank as more of Jace's followers emerged, surrounding them. They were heavily armed, their faces eager for violence.

He knew, Maya realized with a sickening lurch. He knew we were coming.

The lieutenant stepped forward, his eyes glinting. "Jace sends his regards," he said. "And a message. There is no escape. This city is his, and you... you belong to him now."

Maya's hand tightened on her weapon, anger and despair warring in her chest. Behind her, she could feel her group's fear, their fragile hope shattering.

I've failed them, she thought, despair threatening to overwhelm her. I've led them straight into a trap.

But even as the thought formed, Maya felt a flicker of defiance. No, she would not let it end like this. If Jace wanted a fight, then she would give him one. She would go down swinging, and she would make sure her people had a chance, however slim.

"We belong to no one," she said, her voice ringing out in the silence. "Least of all to Jace."

And with that, she charged forward, a battle cry on her lips, her group surging behind her. The clash of metal on metal filled the air as the two sides met, and the ruined city erupted into chaos once more.

The city loomed before them, a labyrinth of twisted metal and shattered concrete. Maya led her group through the winding streets, every step careful, every breath measured. The silence was oppressive, broken only by the distant groans of settling rubble and the whisper of wind through empty windows.

"Stay close," Maya whispered, her voice barely audible. "And stay low."

They moved like ghosts, slipping from shadow to shadow, pressing themselves against crumbling walls whenever a sound echoed through the ruins. Every shifting stone, every creaking beam, sent a jolt of fear through Maya's veins.

What if he knows? The thought had been circling her mind like a vulture, growing louder with each passing minute. What if this is all part of his plan?

She tried to push the doubts aside, to focus on the path ahead, but they clung to her like cobwebs. She could feel the weight of her group's trust, their lives, bearing down on her shoulders. If she was wrong, if she had misjudged...

No. She clenched her jaw, tightening her grip on her weapon. We have to try. We can't stay here, waiting for death or worse.

Behind her, Riley placed a hand on her shoulder, a silent show of support. Maya drew strength from the contact, from the knowledge that she wasn't alone.

They turned a corner, and Maya's heart seized. Ahead, the street was blocked by a wall of rubble, the buildings on either side leaning precariously inward. A dead end.

"We'll have to go around," she whispered, already scanning for another route. But every path looked the same - treacherous, uncertain, leading god-knows-where.

What if there is no way out? The thought whispered through her mind, insidious and cold. What if we're trapped here, in this city of the dead?

Maya closed her eyes for a moment, forcing herself to breathe. She couldn't afford to think like that. Not now. Not when they were so close.

"This way," she said, gesturing to a narrow alley. It was a risk, leading them into even tighter quarters, but it was the only option she could see.

As they slipped into the shadows, Maya sent up a silent prayer to whatever gods might be listening. Please, she thought, let this be the right path. Let us find our way out of this nightmare.

But even as the words formed, she could feel the doubt coiling in her gut, cold and heavy. The city seemed to press in around them, a living, malevolent thing, and Maya couldn't shake the feeling that they were walking straight into its jaws.

A sharp crack echoed through the alley, shattering the tense silence. Maya whirled around, heart pounding, searching for the source of the noise. Her eyes locked onto a figure perched on a crumbling balcony above them, a silhouette against the gray dawn sky.

"Well, well, well…" The voice was cold, mocking. "Look what we have here."

More shapes emerged from the shadows, blocking the alley's entrance and exit. Jace's followers, armed and menacing, their faces hard and unforgiving.

Maya's stomach dropped. They were surrounded.

"Jace warned us you might try something like this," the figure on the balcony continued, leaping down with feline grace. "Trying to run away? Abandon the city? Abandon us?" His voice dripped with accusation.

Maya's group huddled closer, eyes wide with fear. She could feel their gazes on her, looking to her for guidance, for a way out.

Think, Maya, think!

"We're not abandoning anyone," she said, surprised at the steadiness of her own voice. "We're just trying to find a safe place. For all of us."

The man laughed, a harsh, grating sound. "Safe? There's no such thing as safe anymore. Jace is the only one who can keep us safe. And you… you're a traitor for trying to leave."

Maya's mind raced, desperately seeking a way out, an escape route, anything. But the alley was narrow, the buildings high. They were rats in a trap.

This is all my fault, she thought, despair rising like bile in her throat. I led them here. I failed them.

"It doesn't have to be like this," she tried, fighting to keep her voice steady. "We can work together, find a way to survive..."

But even as the words left her mouth, she knew they were futile. The cold hard looks in the eyes of Jace's followers told her everything she needed to know.

There would be no negotiation, no compromise.

Only the swift, merciless reality of the ambush, closing in around them like the jaws of a steel trap, ready to snap shut.

Maya's heart pounded as she assessed their dire situation. Jace's group had them cornered, outnumbered, and outmatched. She glanced at her companions, their faces etched with fear and confusion. Riley met her gaze, a silent plea in her eyes.

I have to do something, Maya thought, desperation clawing at her chest. I can't let it end like this.

She stepped forward, hands raised in a placating gesture. "Listen, we don't want any trouble. Just let us go, and we'll leave the city. You'll never see us again."

The man sneered, his grip tightening on the makeshift club in his hand. "You don't get it, do you? There is no leaving. Jace owns this city now. And you... you're just a problem that needs to be dealt with."

He lunged forward, swinging the club in a vicious arc. Maya ducked, the weapon whistling past her head. Chaos erupted as her group scattered, trying to find cover in the narrow alley.

"Stay together!" Maya shouted, but her voice was lost in the din of shouts and the clash of metal on stone.

She grabbed a piece of rubble, using it to deflect another blow from her attacker. Out of the corner of her eye, she saw Riley grappling with a woman, both of them struggling for control of a knife.

This can't be happening, Maya thought, a sense of unreality washing over her even as she fought for her life. It wasn't supposed to be like this.

But there was no time for disbelief, no room for shock. Survival was the only thing that mattered now.

Maya lashed out with her improvised weapon, catching her opponent off guard. He stumbled back, cursing, blood dripping from a gash on his forehead.

"Fall back!" Maya yelled, trying to rally her group. "We have to get out of here!"

But even as she said it, she knew it was futile. Jace's followers pressed in from all sides, a tide of violence and chaos that threatened to overwhelm them.

I failed them, Maya thought, a bitter taste in her mouth. I led them into this trap. And now... now we'll pay the price.

The ambush raged on, a brutal, desperate struggle in the heart of the ruined city. And as Maya fought, a sinking feeling settled in her gut, the realization that her plan, her leadership, had led them to this moment.

A moment where hope seemed to flicker and fade, lost in the shadows of the unforgiving city.

A scream pierced through the chaos, a sound of pure agony that Maya knew she would never forget. She whirled around, her heart pounding, and saw one of her own, Liam, crumple to the ground, a jagged piece of metal protruding from his chest.

"No!" The cry tore from her throat, raw and desperate. She lunged towards him, but it was too late. Liam's eyes, once bright with determination, now stared blankly at the gray sky above.

Maya felt the world tilt beneath her feet. Liam, who had been with her from the beginning, who had believed in her even when she doubted herself... gone. Just like that.

"We have to go!" Riley grabbed Maya's arm, her voice cracking with urgency and grief. "Maya, we can't stay here. We have to run!"

But Maya couldn't move. She stared at Liam's body, at the blood pooling beneath him, and felt something inside her shatter.

I did this, she thought, the realization a lead weight in her chest. I led them here. I thought I could save them, but I... I only brought them to their deaths.

Around her, the fight continued, shouts and cries and the clang of metal on metal. But Maya barely heard it. All she could see was Liam, and the price of her failure etched in blood on the broken pavement.

"Maya!" Riley's voice cut through the haze, sharp and insistent. "We have to go. Now!"

Maya looked up, meeting Riley's gaze. In her friend's eyes, she saw the same pain, the same guilt, but also a flicker of something else. Determination. Resilience.

We have to survive, Maya realized. For Liam. For all of us.

She nodded, a single, sharp motion, and let Riley pull her to her feet. Together, they ran, leaving the ambush behind, leaving Liam behind, but carrying the weight of his loss with every step.

As they fled, Maya's mind raced, the gravity of what had happened sinking in like a stone. She had made a promise to keep them safe, to lead them to a better life. But now, with Liam gone and her plan in shambles, she wondered if she was worthy of that trust at all.

I have to be, she thought, even as doubt gnawed at her heart. They need me. I can't let them down again. I won't.

But even as she made that silent vow, Maya knew that nothing would ever be the same. The world had shifted, cracked open by loss and the harsh realities of survival.

And in that moment, as they ran through the ruins of the city, Maya felt the weight of leadership pressing down on her shoulders, heavier than ever before.

Maya's heart pounded in her chest as she led her group through the winding streets, their footsteps echoing off the crumbling buildings. The early morning light cast long shadows, making every corner feel like a potential threat. They moved quickly, urgently, but the weight of their loss hung over them like a shroud.

"We need to find shelter," Riley said, her voice low and tight. "Somewhere to regroup, to plan our next move."

Maya nodded, scanning the buildings around them. Her eyes locked on a partially collapsed storefront, its windows shattered but its structure mostly intact. "There," she said, pointing. "We can catch our breath, figure out what to do next."

They ducked inside, picking their way over broken glass and debris. Maya's mind raced as she surveyed her group, taking in their haggard faces, the fear and exhaustion etched into every line. This is my fault, she thought, the guilt twisting like a knife in her gut. I led them into this. I got Liam killed.

She closed her eyes, trying to push back the tide of emotion that threatened to overwhelm her. She couldn't afford to break down, not now, not when they needed her to be strong. But the image of Liam, lost in the chaos of the ambush, wouldn't leave her mind.

"Maya?" It was Benji, his voice uncharacteristically soft. "What do we do now?"

She opened her eyes, meeting his gaze. In that moment, she saw the doubt in his eyes, the unspoken question: Are you still fit to lead us?

Maya swallowed hard, her mouth dry. She knew she had to say something, to rally them somehow, but the words felt hollow on her tongue. "We keep going," she said finally, her voice rough. "We find a way out of the city, just like we planned."

"But how?" Tariq asked, his arms crossed over his chest. "Jace's people are everywhere. And now, with Liam..." He trailed off, looking away.

Liam. The name hung in the air, a reminder of their loss, of Maya's failure. She felt the weight of it pressing down on her, threatening to crush her.

"I don't know," she admitted, the words tasting like ash in her mouth. "But we can't give up. We have to keep trying, for Liam, for all of us."

She looked around at her group, at the faces of the people she had sworn to protect. They were broken, battered, but not defeated. Not yet.

"We'll find a way," she said, injecting as much conviction into her voice as she could muster. "We'll survive this, together."

But even as she spoke the words, Maya felt the doubt creeping in, the uncertainty that had plagued her since the earthquake. She had always been the one with the answers, the one who could fix anything.

But now, in the face of this loss, this failure, she wasn't sure of anything anymore. All she knew was that she had to keep going, to keep fighting, for the sake of her group.

I won't let them down again, she vowed silently. No matter what it takes, I'll get them out of this city, to safety.

But as she looked out at the ruined streets, at the desolation that stretched out before them, Maya couldn't shake the feeling that their journey was only just beginning, and that the worst was yet to come.

The crack of a gunshot shattered the tense silence, and Maya's heart leapt into her throat. Jace's group, armed and ready, emerged from the shadows of the crumbling buildings, their faces hard with determination.

"Did you really think it would be that easy?" Jace called out, his voice dripping with disdain. "That you could just walk away?"

Maya stepped forward, shielding her group with her body. "We're leaving, Jace. You can't stop us."

Jace laughed, a harsh, grating sound. "Oh, but I can. This is my city now, Maya. And nobody leaves without my permission."

His followers fanned out, surrounding Maya's group, weapons trained on them. Maya's mind raced, searching for a way out, but she knew they were trapped.

I led them into this, she thought, despair rising within her. I've failed them.

"Take them," Jace ordered, his eyes glinting with malice. "But leave Maya to me."

Rough hands seized Maya's arms, dragging her forward. She struggled, but it was useless. Jace's grip was iron-clad.

"You never should have challenged me," he hissed, his face inches from hers. "Now, you'll pay the price."

Maya's group, subdued and defeated, was herded back towards the heart of the city, their escape thwarted. Maya felt the weight of their disappointment, their fear, pressing down on her.

I'm sorry, she wanted to scream. I'm so sorry.

But the words stuck in her throat as Jace pulled her away, back into the depths of the city she had fought so hard to escape. The ruins closed in around her, a suffocating reminder of her failure.

This isn't over, Maya told herself, even as despair threatened to consume her. I'll find a way to get us out, to make this right.

But as Jace's laughter echoed in her ears, as the last glimpse of freedom disappeared behind the city's crumbling walls, Maya couldn't help but wonder if it was already too late.

Jace dragged Maya through the rubble-strewn streets, his grip unyielding. She stumbled, her feet catching on the debris, but he yanked her forward, uncaring.

"You thought you could outsmart me," he snarled, his voice dripping with contempt. "You thought you could take what's mine."

Maya remained silent, her mind racing. She had to find a way out of this, a way to save her group. But with each step, her hope dwindled.

They reached the central plaza, the once-bustling heart of the city now a desolate wasteland. Jace shoved Maya to the ground, towering over her.

"Look around you," he commanded, spreading his arms wide. "This is my city now. I control everything."

Maya lifted her head, defiance sparking in her eyes. "You control nothing but fear and violence."

Jace's face contorted with rage. He lashed out, his boot connecting with Maya's ribs. She gasped, pain exploding through her body.

"I control everything," he repeated, his voice low and dangerous. "And you? You're nothing. Just another piece of trash to be thrown away."

Maya struggled to her knees, her breath coming in ragged gasps. She looked up at Jace, at the madness swirling in his eyes, and realized the depth of his delusion.

He genuinely believes he's invincible, she thought, a chill running down her spine. He thinks he's a god in this ruined world.

Jace grabbed Maya's chin, forcing her to meet his gaze. "You'll never leave this city," he promised, his words dripping with venom. "You'll never escape me."

Maya held his stare, refusing to back down. "We'll see about that."

Jace laughed, a harsh, grating sound. He released her, stepping back. "Take her to the others," he ordered his followers. "Let them see what happens to those who defy me."

As they dragged her away, Maya caught a final glimpse of Jace, standing amid the ruins like a king surveying his kingdom. His arrogance, his hunger for power, radiated from him in waves.

He's lost himself, Maya realized, a wave of pity mixing with her fear. The city, the power... it's consumed him.

But even as the thought crossed her mind, Maya knew she couldn't afford to feel sorry for Jace. He was a threat, a danger to her group and to any hope of a future beyond these crumbling walls.

"I'll find a way," she vowed, even as they threw her into a makeshift cell with the others. I'll get us out of here, away from him.

But as the door slammed shut, as the darkness closed in, Maya couldn't help but wonder if Jace's victory was already complete.

The remnants of Maya's group huddled in the shadows of an abandoned building, their faces etched with grief and despair. The failed escape attempt, the loss of one of their own, weighed heavily on every mind.

Riley sat against a crumbling wall, her head in her hands. "We were so close," she whispered, her voice cracking. "We almost made it."

"Almost isn't good enough," Benji snapped, pacing the dusty floor. His eyes were hard, his jaw clenched. "We should've known better than to trust her."

Maya flinched at his words, but she couldn't argue. The guilt was a physical weight on her shoulders, pressing down until she thought she might crumble beneath it. She had led them into this, had promised them a way out. And now...

She looked around at the faces of her group, at the hopelessness and the fear. Tariq sat apart from the others, his expression unreadable. But even he couldn't hide the weariness in his eyes, the toll of one too many close calls.

"I'm sorry," Maya said, her voice barely above a whisper. "I thought... I thought we could make it."

"You thought wrong," Benji said, rounding on her. "And now we're right back where we started. Except now, Jace knows we tried to run. He'll be watching us even closer."

Maya closed her eyes, trying to block out the truth of his words. She had gambled everything on this escape, had risked their lives on the slim hope of freedom. And she had lost.

I don't know what to do, she admitted silently, despair clawing at her throat. I don't know how to fix this.

"We can't give up," Riley said, but even her eternal optimism sounded strained. "There has to be another way."

"Another way to what?" Benji demanded. "To get ourselves killed? To lose more people?"

The silence that followed was heavy, suffocating. Maya looked at each face, seeing the same hopelessness she felt reflected back at her.

I did this, she thought, the guilt a living thing inside her. I brought us to this point.

She knew she should say something, should offer some words of comfort or encouragement. But what could she say? What hope could she offer when she had none herself?

I'm sorry, she wanted to say again, but the words stuck in her throat. I'm so sorry.

In the distance, the sound of Jace's patrols echoed through the empty streets, a constant reminder of the net tightening around them. Maya shivered, feeling the walls of the city closing in, trapping them in this nightmare.

We have to find a way, she thought, even as despair threatened to swallow her whole. We have to keep fighting.

But as she looked at the broken faces of her group, at the shattered trust in their eyes, Maya couldn't help but wonder if the fight was already lost.

Maya slipped away from the group, finding a secluded corner among the ruins. She sank to the ground, drawing her knees to her chest, the weight of her failures crushing her.

I thought I could lead them, she thought, hot tears stinging her eyes. I thought I knew what was best. But look where it's gotten us.

The loss of their group member played over and over in her mind, a relentless loop of guilt and regret. She saw the fear in their eyes, heard their screams as Jace's ambush tore them apart.

I did this, she thought, her breath coming in ragged gasps. I led them into this. I'm responsible.

Around her, the city lay in ruins, a testament to the world they'd lost. The cold, damp stone pressed against her back, a physical reminder of the harshness of their reality.

Maybe Jace was right, a treacherous voice whispered in her mind. Maybe I'm not fit to lead. Maybe I never was.

Footsteps approached, and Maya hastily wiped at her tears. Riley appeared, her face etched with concern.

"Maya," she said softly, crouching down beside her. "It's not your fault."

Maya shook her head, unable to meet Riley's gaze. "Isn't it? I'm the one who pushed for the escape. I'm the one who led us into that ambush."

Riley was silent for a moment, the weight of Maya's words hanging between them. When she spoke, her voice was gentle but firm.

"You did what you thought was right. We all did. Jace is the one to blame, not you."

Maya wanted to believe her, wanted to cling to the absolution Riley offered. But the guilt was too heavy, the doubt too deep.

"I don't know if I can do this anymore," she whispered, her voice cracking. "I don't know if I'm strong enough."

Riley's hand found hers, squeezing tightly. "You are. You're the strongest person I know. And we need you, Maya. We can't do this without you."

Maya finally met Riley's gaze, seeing the unwavering faith there, the trust that somehow still remained. She drew in a shaky breath, trying to find the strength Riley seemed to see in her.

"What if I fail again? What if I lead us into something worse?"

"Then we'll face it together," Riley said, her jaw set with determination. "We're a team, Maya. We stand together, no matter what."

Maya nodded, letting Riley's words sink in, letting them bolster the fragile hope within her. She knew the road ahead would be hard, that there would be more challenges, more heartbreak. But with Riley by her side, with her group united, maybe they stood a chance.

We have to, she thought, steeling herself against the despair that threatened to consume her. We have to find a way.

She stood, Riley rising with her, their hands still clasped. Together, they made their way back to the group, back to the fight that lay ahead.

No matter what comes, Maya vowed silently, I won't let them down again.

Maya and Riley walked back to the group, their footsteps echoing in the cavernous warehouse. The others were huddled together, their faces etched with exhaustion and despair. As Maya approached, they looked up at her, their eyes filled with a mix of hope and doubt.

"I know you're all tired," Maya began, her voice steady despite the turmoil inside her. "I know you're scared. I am too. But we can't give up. We have to keep fighting."

"Fighting for what?" a voice called out from the back of the group. It was Liam, a boy who had always been quiet, always kept to himself. Now, he stood, his fists clenched at his sides. "We tried to escape, and look what happened. We lost Jenna. We almost lost everything."

Maya felt the weight of his words, the truth in them. But she couldn't let them sink in, couldn't let them take root. "I know," she said softly. "And I'm sorry. I'm so sorry for what happened to Jenna. But we can't let her death be in vain. We have to keep going, for her and for ourselves."

Murmurs rippled through the group, some nodding in agreement, others shaking their heads in disbelief. Maya could feel the fractures deepening, the cracks in their unity widening.

"Maybe Jace was right," someone murmured. "Maybe we should have stayed with him."

Maya's heart clenched at the words, at the thought of her group turning to Jace, to his cruelty and his thirst for power. "No," she said firmly, her voice rising. "Jace is not the answer. He's not our savior. He's just another tyrant, another person who wants to control us."

She looked around at the faces of her group, at the people she had come to know and care for. "We have to trust in each other," she said, her gaze locking with each of theirs in turn. "We have to believe in ourselves and in our ability to survive, to build something better than this."

Liam stepped forward, his face twisted with anger. "And what if we can't?" he demanded. "What if there's nothing better out there? What if this is all there is?"

Maya met his gaze unflinchingly. "Then we make it better," she said, her voice ringing with conviction. "We find a way to create something new, something worth living for. But we can't do that if we turn on each other, if we let fear and doubt consume us."

She reached out her hand to Liam, an offering of peace, of unity. "I know I've made mistakes," she said softly. "I know I've let you down. But I promise you, I will do everything in my power to keep us safe, to lead us to a better future. Will you stand with me?"

For a long moment, Liam hesitated, his eyes searching Maya's face. Then, slowly, he reached out and clasped her hand in his. "I'll stand with you," he said, his voice rough with emotion. "We all will."

Around them, the others nodded, their faces set with determination. Maya felt a surge of hope, of strength. They were broken, yes, but they were not defeated. They would rise again, stronger than before.

Together, she thought fiercely, we will survive. We will find a way.

Benji's voice cut through the moment of solidarity, sharp and bitter. "Are you kidding me?" He stepped forward, his eyes blazing with anger. "You think holding hands and making promises is going to fix this? We just lost everything, and it's all because of her." He jabbed a finger at Maya, his face twisted with resentment.

Maya flinched, feeling the weight of Benji's accusation like a physical blow. She opened her mouth to respond, but he barreled on, his voice rising with each word.

"You led us into this mess, and now you want us to trust you to get us out? I don't think so." Benji's gaze swept over the group, his expression hard. "We'd be better off with Jace. At least he knows how to keep his people safe."

The words hung in the air, heavy with implication. Maya felt a chill run down her spine, a sense of dread settling in her gut. She knew Benji was hurting, that he was lashing out from a place of fear and grief, but his words had power. She could see the doubt creeping into the faces of those around her, the uncertainty that had been simmering beneath the surface now brought to light.

Tariq stepped forward, his voice calm but firm. "Enough." He looked at Benji, his dark eyes unreadable. "We're all hurting. We're all scared. But turning on each other isn't going to solve anything."

He turned to face the group, his expression grave. "The truth is, I don't know if either Maya or Jace can lead us to safety. I don't know if anyone can. But I do know that we have a better chance of surviving if we stick together, if we watch each other's backs."

Maya felt a surge of gratitude towards Tariq, a glimmer of hope in the darkness. But even as she looked at him, she could see the doubt in his eyes, the hesitation that belied his words. She knew he was considering his own options, weighing the risks and rewards of striking out on his own.

The group fell silent, each lost in their own thoughts. Maya could feel the weight of their expectations, the burden of leadership that had never felt heavier. She knew she had to find a way to bring them back together, to restore their faith in each other and in themselves.

But as she looked out at the ruined city, at the desolation that stretched as far as the eye could see, she couldn't help but wonder if it was already too late. If the cracks that had formed in their fragile alliance had already grown too deep to mend.

We have to try, she thought fiercely, squaring her shoulders. We have to find a way to survive, to build something better from the ashes of what we've lost.

It was a daunting task, a seemingly impossible feat. But Maya knew they had no choice. They had to keep moving forward, one step at a time, no matter how difficult the path ahead might be.

Jace stood atop the warehouse roof, surveying the city with a keen eye. The failed escape attempt had only strengthened his resolve, his grip on power tightening like a vise.

He turned to his lieutenants, his voice cutting through the early morning silence. "Double the patrols. I want eyes on every street, every building. No one gets in or out without my say so."

They nodded, scurrying to carry out his orders. Jace allowed himself a small smile. This was his city now, his kingdom to rule as he saw fit.

He made his way down to the main floor, where his followers were already gathering supplies, stockpiling food and weapons. They worked with a fevered intensity, driven by fear and loyalty in equal measure.

Jace moved among them, his presence electrifying the air. "You see now, don't you?" he called out, his voice ringing with authority. "There is no escape from this reality. No way out except through strength, through power."

He paused, letting his words sink in. "And who has that power? Who has proven themselves worthy to lead, to make the hard choices necessary for survival?"

A chorus of voices rose up, chanting his name. "Jace! Jace! Jace!"

He basked in their adulation, feeling it fuel his ambition. "That's right," he said, his eyes glinting with a fierce light. "I am the only one who can guarantee your safety, your future. Those who oppose me, those who cling to their foolish ideals of cooperation and unity, they will fall. They will perish."

His tone turned ominous, a warning and a promise. "There is no room for weakness in this world. No place for those who cannot adapt, who cannot embrace the new order."

He thought of Maya then, of her stubborn refusal to bend to his will. She was a threat, a challenge to his authority that he could not allow to stand.

She will learn, he vowed silently. One way or another, she will learn the price of defiance.

Jace turned back to his followers, his expression hardening. "Get back to work," he snapped. "We have a city to secure, a future to build. And woe to anyone who stands in our way."

As they dispersed, Jace climbed back up to his perch, his gaze sweeping over the ruins of the once-great metropolis. It was a harsh and unforgiving world they inhabited now, a world where only the strong could hope to survive.

And he would make sure that he was the strongest of them all, no matter the cost. No matter who had to fall for him to rise.

This is my time, he thought, his fists clenching at his sides. My moment to seize control, to shape the future in my image.

The sun broke through the clouds, casting a pale light over the devastated landscape. And in that light, Jace saw only opportunity, only the promise of a new era dawning.

An era where he would reign supreme, unopposed and unquestioned. An era where the weak would serve and the strong would rule.

His lip curled in a smirk. Let them come, he thought. Let them try to challenge me.

In the end, they will all kneel before Jace, the lord and master of this brave new world.

Jace turned from the view, his mind already racing with plans and possibilities. He needed to consolidate his power, to make an example of those who dared to defy him.

And he knew just where to start.

He descended from his perch, his steps purposeful as he strode through the warehouse. His followers parted before him, their eyes filled with a mix of fear and awe.

Good. They were learning their place.

He found Benji in a corner, sorting through a pile of scavenged supplies. The boy looked up as Jace approached, his expression guarded.

"Benji," Jace said, his voice deceptively soft. "I have a special task for you."

Benji stood, dusting off his hands. "What is it?"

Jace smiled, but there was no warmth in it. "I need you to keep an eye on Maya's group. Report back to me on their movements, their plans."

Benji frowned. "You want me to spy on them?"

"I want you to be my eyes and ears," Jace said, laying a hand on Benji's shoulder. "You're clever, observant. I know I can trust you with this."

He could see the conflict in Benji's eyes, the wavering of his loyalty. But he also saw the hunger there, the desire to be seen, to be valued.

"I won't let you down," Benji said at last, his jaw set.

"I know you won't," Jace said, giving his shoulder a squeeze. "Because you understand what's at stake here. You understand that we need to be united, strong. That there can be no room for dissent or rebellion."

Benji nodded, his expression hardening. "I understand."

"Good." Jace released him. "Then go. And remember, Benji - I'm counting on you."

As Benji slipped away, Jace allowed himself a moment of satisfaction. Another piece falling into place, another strand of the web he was weaving.

But there was still much to be done. He needed to send a message, to make it clear that he was not to be trifled with.

And he knew just how to do it.

Maya sat alone in the dimly lit corner of the warehouse, her knees drawn up to her chest, her head bowed. The weight of the failed escape attempt, the loss of one of her own, pressed down on her like a physical burden.

She could still hear the echoes of the ambush ringing in her ears - the shouts, the chaos, the sickening crunch of bone. She could still see the look of terror on her follower's face in that final, fateful moment.

"I'm sorry," she whispered into the silence, her voice cracking. "I'm so sorry."

Tears slipped down her cheeks, leaving trails in the grime and dust. She had tried so hard to keep them safe, to lead them out of this nightmare. But she had failed. And now, one of them was gone, lost to Jace's brutality.

Maya's mind spun with doubts and recriminations. She had been so sure that escape was the answer, that getting out of the city was their only hope. But now, with the cold reality of their failure sinking in, she wondered if she had been wrong all along.

Maybe Benji was right. Maybe Jace was the only one who could keep them alive in this hellscape. Maybe her ideals of cooperation and unity were nothing more than a foolish dream.

She thought of her group, the ragtag band of survivors who had trusted her, followed her. How could she face them now? How could she ask them to put their faith in her again, when she had led them straight into a trap?

Maya buried her face in her hands, her shoulders shaking with silent sobs. She had never felt so alone, so utterly lost. The mantle of leadership, once a source of pride and purpose, now felt like a crushing burden.

From somewhere deep within the warehouse, she could hear the murmur of voices, the restless stirring of her group. They would be looking to her for guidance, for strength. But how could she give them what they needed when she had none left to give?

Maya took a shuddering breath, trying to steady herself. She knew she couldn't hide forever. She had to face them, had to find a way forward, even if every step felt like a journey into darkness.

Slowly, painfully, she pushed herself to her feet. Her legs felt weak, her heart heavy. But she forced herself to take a step, then another.

She had no idea what the future held, no clear path through the chaos and the horror. But she knew she had to keep going, had to keep fighting.

For her group. For the memory of the one they had lost.

And for the fading hope that somewhere, somehow, there was still a way out of this nightmare.

Maya stepped out into the main area of the warehouse, the weight of her thoughts bearing down on her like the crumbling city above. The remnants of her group huddled together, their faces etched with a mixture of fear, grief, and a dwindling hope that she knew reflected her own.

As she approached, Riley looked up, her eyes searching Maya's face for any sign of the strength and certainty that had once been her hallmark. But Maya knew she would find none.

"What do we do now?" Riley asked, her voice barely above a whisper.

Maya swallowed hard, the question echoing in the hollowness of her own heart. What could they do? Where could they go? Every path seemed to lead only to more pain, more loss.

"I don't know," she admitted, the words tasting like ash in her mouth. "I thought I could lead us out of this, but..." She trailed off, unable to give voice to the depth of her failure.

A heavy silence fell over the group, broken only by the distant groans of the settling ruins. Maya could feel their eyes on her, could sense the unspoken question that hung in the air between them.

Was she still fit to lead them? Could they still trust her to guide them through this hell?

Maya closed her eyes, the doubts and fears swirling in her mind like a maelstrom. She thought of all the choices she had made, all the lives she had risked in the name of survival. And for what? To lead them straight into Jace's clutches?

Perhaps it was time to step down, to let someone else bear the burden of leadership. Perhaps her ideals of cooperation and unity really had no place in this brutal new world.

But even as the thought crossed her mind, Maya knew she couldn't do it. She couldn't abandon her group, couldn't leave them to face the horrors of this city alone.

She opened her eyes, meeting the gazes of those around her. "We can't give up," she said, her voice growing stronger with each word. "Jace may have won this battle, but we can't let him win the war. We have to keep fighting, keep holding on to who we are."

Maya could see the flicker of hope reigniting in their eyes, the faint stirring of a renewed determination. It wasn't much, but it was something.

"We'll find another way out," she promised, even as the uncertainty of that vow twisted in her gut. "We'll keep searching until we do. And we'll do it together."

As the group began to nod, to murmur their agreement, Maya felt a small measure of the weight lift from her shoulders. It wasn't a solution, wasn't a guarantee of a brighter future.

But it was a start.

CHAPTER 9

Ashes of Hope

The warehouse loomed before them, a hulking silhouette against the ashen sky. Maya's eyes traced its jagged outline, her heart heavy as lead. The group huddled together in the shadow of a crumbling building, their faces etched with exhaustion and defeat.

"We should've never left," someone muttered, voice thick with despair.

Maya's chest tightened. She couldn't bring herself to look at her companions, couldn't bear to see the accusation in their eyes. The weight of their latest failure pressed down on her, threatening to crush what little resolve she had left.

"Maybe... maybe we could try talking to Jace again," another voice suggested timidly. "He might listen this time."

"Listen?" Riley scoffed, her usual optimism nowhere to be found. "He doesn't listen. He takes."

Maya's mind raced, searching for words of comfort, of hope. But how could she offer hope when she felt so utterly hopeless herself? The loss of Alex during their escape attempt replayed in her mind, a cruel reminder of the cost of her decisions.

"We can't give up," Maya finally managed, her voice barely above a whisper. "We have to keep trying."

But even as the words left her lips, she wondered if she honestly believed them anymore. The cities around them lay in ruins, a maze of broken dreams and shattered lives. And somewhere in that maze, Jace and his followers grew stronger while they grew weaker.

"And what happens when we run out of food?" Benji challenged, his eyes hard. "When the rain stops and we can't find clean water? What then, Maya?"

She had no answer. The silence stretched between them, as vast and unforgiving as the wasteland their home had become.

"I don't know," Maya admitted, the words tasting like ash in her mouth. "But we're still alive. That has to count for something."

A distant rumble of thunder rolled across the sky, as if nature itself was mocking their feeble hopes. Maya closed her eyes, fighting back tears. She had led them here, believing in unity and compassion. Now, as she looked at their haggard faces, she wondered if those ideals were nothing more than childish fantasies in this brutal new world.

"We should rest," Riley suggested softly, placing a hand on Maya's shoulder. "Maybe things will look better in the morning."

Maya nodded, not trusting herself to speak. As the group settled in for another restless night, she found herself staring at the warehouse in the distance. It stood as a monument to everything they had lost, everything Jace had taken from them.

And for the first time since the earthquake, Maya allowed herself to consider a terrifying thought: What if Jace had been right all along?

Maya's fingers traced the jagged crack running along the concrete wall, mirroring the fissure in her own resolve. She turned to face her group, huddled in the shadow of a crumbling apartment building. Their eyes, once bright with hope, now reflected only despair and exhaustion.

"I've failed you," Maya whispered, her voice barely audible over the distant rumble of aftershocks. "Every decision, every choice... it's led us here. To this." She gestured at their meager supplies, the haunted faces of her companions.

Riley stepped forward, her usual optimism wavering. "Maya, you can't blame yourself. We're all still—"

"Still what, Riley?" Maya interrupted, a bitter edge to her words. "Still alive? For how long? Look at us. We're barely surviving."

The weight of leadership pressed down on Maya's shoulders, threatening to crush her. She closed her eyes, memories of their failed escape flooding back. The screams, the chaos, the sickening realization that they'd lost someone. Someone she was responsible for.

"Maybe Jace was right," she murmured, more to herself than the others. "Maybe compassion has no place in this world anymore."

Riley's eyes widened. "You don't mean that. Maya, you're the reason we've made it this far. Your ideals—"

"My ideals?" Maya let out a hollow laugh. "My ideals are getting people killed, Riley. Unity? Compassion? They're luxuries we can't afford anymore."

She watched as Riley's face fell, the last embers of hope dying in her friend's eyes. It was like watching a part of herself crumble away.

"We can't give up," Riley said, but her voice lacked conviction. She turned to the group, forcing a smile that didn't reach her eyes. "Come on, guys. We've been through worse, right? We just need to stick together, and—"

"And what?" Benji cut in, his voice sharp. "Wait for another miracle? Face it, Riley. We're done."

Maya watched as Riley's shoulders slumped, the weight of their collective despair finally breaking through her friend's optimism. It was the final blow, seeing even Riley falter.

"I'm sorry," Maya whispered, her voice cracking. "I thought I could lead us to something better. I thought... I thought we could stay human through all of this. But maybe that's not possible anymore."

The silence that followed was deafening, broken only by the soft sobs of one of the younger members of their group. Maya looked at each of them in turn, these people who had trusted her, followed her. Now, she had led them to the brink of destruction.

"What do we do now?" someone asked, their voices small and afraid.

Maya's gaze drifted back to the warehouse in the distance, Jace's stronghold looming over them like a fortress of broken dreams. For a moment, she allowed herself to imagine surrendering, giving in to the ruthless pragmatism that had allowed Jace to thrive in this new world.

But even as the thought formed, she felt a flicker of something deep within her. A dying ember of the fire that had once driven her. She wasn't ready to let it go. Not yet.

"We survive," Maya said, her voice barely above a whisper. "Whatever it takes."

Maya's words hung in the air, heavy with unspoken implications. The group shifted uneasily, exchanging wary glances. The abandoned plaza around them, once a symbol of their unity, now felt like a battlefield of conflicting ideologies.

"Survive?" A bitter laugh cut through the tense silence. It was Alex, his face twisted with frustration. "Look around, Maya. We're barely hanging on as it is. How long before Jace decides to finish us off?"

Maya's throat tightened, but she forced herself to meet Alex's gaze. "We've made it this far—"

"And for what?" Alex interrupted, his voice rising. "To starve? To wait for the next aftershock to bury us alive?" He gestured wildly towards the warehouse. "At least Jace has food, shelter, protection."

Murmurs of agreement rippled through the group. Maya felt a cold dread settling in her stomach as she watched doubt spread across their faces.

"You can't seriously be considering joining him," she said, struggling to keep her voice steady. "After everything he's done?"

"What choice do we have?" This time it was Sarah who spoke, her eyes brimming with tears. "I'm tired, Maya. We're all tired. Maybe… maybe it's time to accept that we can't win this fight."

Maya's mind raced, searching for the right words to bring them back together. But as she looked at their worn, desperate faces, she realized with a sinking heart that her influence was slipping away. The ideals of compassion and unity that had once bound them now seemed like distant luxuries in a world that demanded ruthless pragmatism.

"We vote," Maya finally said, the words tasting like ash in her mouth. "Tomorrow morning, we decide. Stay and fight, or… or join Jace."

As the group dispersed, their whispered conversations a cacophony of fear and indecision, Maya found herself alone with her thoughts. She stared at the crumbling buildings around them, wondering if this were how humanity would end – not with a bang, but with a whimper of surrender to the darkness within.

Benji's voice cut through the tense silence, his words sharp and biting. "We're fooling ourselves if we think we can beat Jace," he said, eyes darting around the group. "Look at us. We're starving, we're weak, and we're divided. Jace has food, weapons, and people who actually follow orders."

Maya watched as Benji's words landed, seeing the impact ripple through the group. His once-friendly face was now hard, etched with lines of worry and cynicism. She opened her mouth to argue, but Benji pressed on.

"I'm not saying I like the guy, but he's proven he can keep people alive. And right now, that's what matters." Benji's fists clenched at his sides.

"We need to be pragmatic. Survival means aligning with strength, and face it – Jace is stronger than us."

"So, we just give up everything we've fought for?" Riley interjected, her voice quavering.

Benji laughed, a hollow sound. "Fought for what? The right to starve together? To watch more of us die?"

As the argument intensified, Maya's gaze drifted to Tariq. He stood apart from the others, his lean frame taut with tension. His dark eyes moved from person to person, assessing, calculating. Maya realized with a jolt that Tariq wasn't just watching the group – he was weighing his own options.

"Tariq," she said softly, approaching him. "What do you think?"

He met her gaze, his expression unreadable. "I think," he said slowly, "that both paths are fraught with danger."

Maya felt a chill run down her spine. "Both paths?"

Tariq's eyes flickered to the ruined cityscape beyond their shelter. "Staying. Going. Or..." he trailed off, leaving the third option unspoken.

As Benji's voice rose again, rallying support for his pragmatic approach, Maya found herself torn between addressing the group and probing Tariq's thoughts further. The future of their fragile community hung in the balance, and she could feel it slipping through her fingers like sand.

Maya turned away, her feet carrying her to the edge of their makeshift shelter. The cool autumn air bit at her skin as she stepped outside, seeking solitude. Behind her, the muffled voices of her group continued to argue, but they faded into the background as she focused on the desolate cityscape before her.

Crumbling buildings loomed like broken teeth against the overcast sky. A gust of wind stirred up debris, sending a discarded newspaper tumbling across the cracked pavement. Maya's eyes followed its path, her mind racing.

"What am I doing?" she whispered, wrapping her arms around herself. The weight of leadership pressed down on her shoulders, threatening to crush her.

She closed her eyes, memories of their recent losses flashing through her mind. Faces of those who had trusted her, followed her, and ultimately paid the price. Her chest tightened, guilt clawing at her insides.

"I can't do this anymore," Maya thought, her nails digging into her palms. "I'm leading them to their deaths."

A distant rumble of thunder echoed through the city, matching the turmoil in her heart. Maya opened her eyes, scanning the horizon. The warehouse – their goal, their salvation – stood in the distance, a fortress of hope and despair.

"Maya?" Riley's voice came from behind her, soft and hesitant.

Maya turned, forcing a smile she didn't feel. "Hey."

Riley stepped closer, concern etched on her face. "Are you okay? Things are getting pretty heated back there."

Maya's façade crumbled. "I don't know if I can do this, Riley. Every decision I make... people die. Maybe Benji's right. Maybe we should just..."

"Don't say that," Riley interrupted, grabbing Maya's hand. "You can't give up. We need you."

Maya pulled away, frustration bubbling up. "Need me for what? To lead you into another disaster? To watch more of us die?"

Her words hung in the air between them, heavy with the weight of unspoken fears. Riley's eyes widened, hurt flashing across her face.

"I'm sorry," Maya said quickly, regret washing over her. "I just... I don't know if I'm the right person for this. Maybe someone else should lead. Someone stronger, someone who can make the hard choices without..." she trailed off, unable to finish the thought.

Riley stepped forward, her voice firm. "Maya, look at me. You're the only one who can do this. You care about us, about keeping us human. That's why we follow you."

Maya met her friend's gaze, searching for the strength she desperately needed. "But at what cost, Riley? How many more lives am I willing to sacrifice for my ideals?"

The question hung between them, unanswered. In the distance, another rumble of thunder rolled across the sky, a reminder of the harsh world they now inhabited. Maya turned back to the cityscape, her mind racing with impossible choices and the lives that hung in the balance.

Maya's gaze lingered on the ruins of the city, her fingers tracing the cold metal of the railing. The weight of leadership pressed down on her shoulders, threatening to crush her resolve.

"Maybe Jace is right," she whispered, more to herself than to Riley. "Maybe compassion is a luxury we can't afford anymore."

Riley's sharp intake of breath cut through the silence. "You don't mean that."

Maya turned, her eyes hard. "Don't I? Look around us, Riley. Every time we've tried to do the right thing, to be kind, we've lost people. Maybe it's time we fight fire with fire."

She could see the shock on Riley's face, but a part of her relished it. It felt good to let the darkness out, to give voice to the cruel thoughts that had been gnawing at her.

"We could do it, you know," Maya continued, her voice low and intense. "We could be just as ruthless as Jace. Take what we need, eliminate threats before they become problems. Survive at any cost."

Riley stepped back, shaking her head. "Maya, listen to yourself. This isn't you."

"Maybe it is now," Maya shot back. But even as the words left her mouth, she felt a twist in her gut. The image of Jace's smirking face flashed in her mind, and suddenly, she saw herself wearing that same cruel expression.

The realization hit her like a physical blow. She stumbled, catching herself on the railing.

"Oh god," she whispered, horror creeping into her voice. "What am I saying?"

Riley was at her side in an instant, steadying her. "It's okay, Maya. You're only tired and scared. We all are."

Maya looked up, meeting Riley's concerned gaze. "But that's no excuse. If I start thinking like Jace, if I abandon everything we've fought for... what's left? What are we even surviving for?"

As she spoke the words aloud, Maya felt something shift inside her. The crushing weight of despair began to lift, replaced by a fierce determination.

"No," she said, straightening up. "We can't give up on who we are. Our humanity, our compassion – that's what makes us different from Jace. It's what makes us worth saving."

Riley's face broke into a relieved smile. "There's the Maya I know."

Maya nodded, her resolve growing stronger with each passing moment. "It won't be easy. We're outnumbered, outgunned, and the odds are stacked against us. But we have something Jace and his followers don't."

"What's that?" Riley asked.

"Hope," Maya replied, her voice steady and sure. "And each other. As long as we hold onto that, we have a chance."

The path ahead was still fraught with danger, but for the first time in days, Maya felt a flicker of genuine hope. They would face whatever came next together, holding fast to the values that defined them. In a world torn apart by disaster, humanity might just be their greatest strength.

Maya's eyes swept across the dimly lit room, taking in the haggard faces of her remaining followers. Their clothes were tattered, their bodies thin from rationed meals, but a spark of determination still flickered in their eyes. She took a deep breath, steeling herself for what was to come.

"Listen up, everyone," Maya said, her voice low but firm. "We're running out of options, and more importantly, we're running out of time."

She paused, watching as the group leaned in closer, their attention fixed on her words.

"The warehouse," Maya continued, her hands clenching at her sides. "It's our only chance. We need those supplies if we're going to survive, and we can't let Jace control them any longer."

A murmur rippled through the group. Maya could sense their fear, their uncertainty. She pressed on, her heart pounding.

"I know it's risky. I know we're outgunned. But we have something Jace doesn't – we have each other, and we have a cause worth fighting for."

As she spoke, Maya's mind raced. Images of the warehouse flashed before her eyes – its looming silhouette against the ruined skyline, the stockpile of food and water within its walls. She could almost taste the desperation that had driven Jace to seize control of it.

"What's the plan, Maya?" someone called out from the back.

Maya took a steadying breath. "We go in under cover of darkness. Small teams, coordinated strikes. We're not trying to overpower them – we're aiming to outmaneuver them."

She began to outline the details, her voice growing stronger with each word. As she spoke, Maya could feel the weight of leadership pressing down on her shoulders. But this time, instead of crushing her, it fueled her resolve.

This is it, she thought. Our last stand. If we fail here, we lose everything.

The thought sent a chill down her spine, but Maya pushed it aside. She couldn't afford doubt now. Not when so many lives depended on her.

As she finished explaining the plan, Maya looked around at her followers. Their faces were a mix of determination and fear, hope and resignation. She knew she was asking so much of them, perhaps too much.

But what choice did they have?

"I know I'm asking for a lot," Maya said softly, her voice thick with emotion. "But this isn't just about survival anymore. It's about what kind of world we want to live in. Jace's way – it's not living, it's just existing. We have to show there's another way."

She paused, swallowing hard. "I can't promise we'll all make it. But I can promise that if we stand together, we have a chance. A chance to build something better from the ashes of what we've lost."

The silence that followed was deafening. Maya held her breath, waiting for their response, knowing that everything hinged on this moment.

Riley stepped forward, her green eyes blazing with determination. "I'm with you, Maya. To the end." She turned to face the group, her voice steady and clear. "We've come too far to give up now. We owe it to ourselves and to those we've lost to see this through."

A murmur rippled through the gathered survivors. Maya could see the conflict in their eyes, the fear warring with desperation. She understood their hesitation; the weight of potential failure hung heavy in the air.

"It's a suicide mission," someone whispered, echoing the thought Maya had been pushing away.

She closed her eyes briefly, steeling herself. When she opened them, her gaze was resolute. "Maybe," she admitted. "But staying here, waiting for our supplies to run out or for Jace to find us – that's certain death. At least this way, we choose our fate."

Maya stepped forward, her hands slightly shaking as she gestured to the crude map she'd drawn of the warehouse. "The attack needs to be coordinated and swift," she explained, her voice growing stronger with each word. "We'll split into three groups. Team One will create a diversion at the main entrance. Team Two will infiltrate through the loading docks. Team Three will secure our escape route."

As she spoke, Maya could see a change coming over the group. The fear was still there, but something else was building – a spark of hope, of possibility.

"Every single one of us has a crucial role to play," Maya continued, her heart pounding. "This isn't just about taking back the warehouse. It's about taking back our future, our right to live as human beings, not just survivors scrambling for scraps."

She paused, looking each person in the eye. "I know I'm asking you to risk everything. But think about what we're fighting for – a chance to rebuild, to create a community based on compassion and cooperation, not fear and domination. This is our last chance to prove that Jacc's way isn't the only way forward."

Maya's voice cracked slightly as she finished, "We can do this. Together. But only if we're all in. So, I'm asking you now – are you with me?"

The silence that followed seemed to stretch for an eternity. Maya held her breath, acutely aware of the weight of this moment. In her mind, she could see all the possible outcomes – victory, defeat, or something in between. The uncertainty was almost unbearable.

But as she looked at the faces around her, she saw something change. Fear gave way to determination. Doubt transformed into resolve. One by one, heads began to nod. Whispers of agreement grew into a chorus of support.

Maya felt a lump form in her throat. They were with her. Against all odds, they were choosing to fight. The responsibility was overwhelming, but for the first time in days, she felt a flicker of real hope.

"Alright," she said, her voice thick with emotion. "Let's get to work. We move at nightfall."

The fragile unity Maya had managed to foster shattered like glass. Benji stepped forward, his once-cheerful face now etched with lines of worry and resentment. His eyes, usually bright with humor, were now dark with fear.

"This is madness," he spat, gesturing wildly. "We're not soldiers, we're kids! You're leading us to our deaths, Maya."

Maya felt her heart sink. She'd known Benji would be a hard sell, but the venom in his voice caught her off guard. "Benji, I understand you're scared—"

"Scared?" Benji laughed, a harsh, humorless sound. "I'm terrified. And you should be too. Jace has guns, supplies, people. We have... what? Desperation and a death wish?"

Murmurs of agreement rippled through the group. Maya's mind raced, searching for the right words to bring them back. But Benji wasn't finished.

"We need to face facts," he continued, his voice growing louder. "Jace has won. He controls the warehouse, he controls the city. Our best chance—our only chance—is to surrender. To join him."

"Join him?" Maya couldn't keep the shock from her voice. "After everything he's done?"

Benji's face hardened. "Pride won't keep us alive, Maya. Jace might be a bastard, but he's a bastard with food and protection. Sometimes you have to choose between your morals and your life."

The words hit Maya like a physical blow. She looked around, seeing the doubt spreading across faces she'd come to know so well. Friends who'd stood by her through hell were now wavering, Benji's words finding purchase in their fear.

This can't be happening, Maya thought, panic rising in her chest. After everything we've been through, everything we've fought for...

But she knew she couldn't let that panic show. Not now, when everything hung by a thread. She took a deep breath, steeling herself for the fight ahead. Because this, she realized, was where the real battle began. Not against Jace, but for the very soul of their group.

"Listen to me," she said, her voice low but intense. "All of you. I know you're scared. I'm scared too. But giving in to Jace isn't the answer..."

Riley stepped forward, her green eyes flashing with determination. "Maya's right," she said, her voice cutting through the murmurs of dissent. "Joining Jace isn't survival, it's surrender. We'd be trading one death for another—maybe slower, but just as certain."

Maya felt a surge of gratitude towards her friend, but it was tempered by the realization of just how divided the group had become. Some nodded along with Riley's words, while others shifted uncomfortably, exchanging uncertain glances.

"And what about the warehouse?" Riley continued, her tone growing more urgent. "It's not just about food and shelter. It's about hope. About having a future that's ours, not one dictated by Jace's twisted vision."

Benji scoffed, his once-cheerful face twisted into a bitter scowl. "Hope? Hope doesn't fill empty stomachs or heal broken bones."

The group erupted into heated debate, voices rising and falling like waves. Maya watched, her heart sinking as she saw the fractures deepen. This is it, she thought. This is where we either come together or fall apart completely.

Taking a deep breath, Maya raised her voice. "Enough!" The sharpness in her tone cut through the chaos, silencing the arguments. All eyes turned to her, a mix of expectation and wariness in their gazes.

"I hear you. All of you," Maya said, her voice softening but remaining firm. "I know what I'm asking isn't easy. But look around. Look at what we've built together, what we've survived. Are we really ready to throw that away?"

She paused, letting her words sink in. "I can't force anyone to follow me. If you believe surrendering to Jace is your best chance, I won't stop you. But I'm going to fight. For our home, for our future, for everything we've stood for."

Maya's heart raced as she looked at the faces around her. Some showed resolve, others fear, and still others a conflicted mix of emotions. She knew, with a certainty that both steeled and terrified her, that not everyone would stay. But she also knew she had to see this through, no matter the cost.

"So," she said, her voice barely above a whisper but carrying to every corner of the room, "who's with me?"

As the group dispersed, murmurs of uncertainty still rippling through the air, Maya felt a presence behind her. She turned to find Tariq, his tall frame looming in the dim light of their makeshift shelter. His dark eyes, usually so unreadable, seemed to hold a spark of... something. Not quite support, but not opposition either.

"Tariq," Maya said, her voice low and tired. "I didn't expect you to stick around."

He shifted, his lean body tense. "I'm not here to sing your praises, Maya," he replied, his tone as measured as ever. "But I'll fight."

Maya's eyebrows shot up in surprise. She hadn't anticipated this from the group's most distant member. "You will? Why?"

Tariq's gaze swept across the room, taking in the dwindling supplies and the weary faces of their companions. "Look around. We're running out of options. Jace, the warehouse... it's our only shot."

Maya nodded slowly, processing his words. She couldn't help but wonder about his true motivations. "So, it's just about survival for you?"

"Isn't that what it's always been about?" Tariq countered, his voice carrying a hint of challenge.

Maya felt a pang in her chest. Was that really all they'd been reduced to? Mere survival? She pushed the thought away, focusing on the present.

"Well, whatever your reasons, I'm glad to have you with us. We need every person we can get."

Tariq gave a curt nod, already turning to leave. "Don't mistake this for blind loyalty, Maya. I'm doing what I think gives me the best chance. Nothing more."

As he walked away, Maya watched his retreating form, a mix of gratitude and unease settling in her stomach. She couldn't shake the feeling that Tariq's decision, while helpful, was a stark reminder of how fragile their unity truly was.

Maya's eyes lingered on Tariq's back as he retreated to his corner of the room. The distance between them felt palpable, a chasm wider than the physical space separating them. She inhaled deeply, her chest tight with a cocktail of emotions—relief, uncertainty, and a gnawing sense of isolation.

"Tariq," she called out, her voice barely above a whisper. He paused, turning his head slightly but not fully facing her. Maya swallowed hard. "Thank you. I know this isn't easy for any of us."

He remained silent for a moment, then gave a barely perceptible nod. "Don't thank me yet. We haven't survived this."

As Tariq continued to his solitary spot, Maya's mind raced. She'd gained an ally, yes, but at what cost? The calculated nature of his decision gnawed at her. Was this what leadership had come to? Accepting help from those who saw her not as a guide, but merely as a means to an end?

She clenched her fists, nails digging into her palms. "We need everyone," she muttered to herself, "Even if they're not here for the reasons I'd hoped."

Across the room, Riley caught her eye, offering a supportive smile. Maya tried to return it, but knew it didn't reach her eyes. She turned away, facing the cracked window that looked out onto the devastated city.

"What would you do?" she whispered to her reflection, barely recognizing the tired, haunted face staring back at her. "Is this really the only way forward?"

The silence that followed was deafening.

Maya's reflection offered no answers, only the hollow stare of a leader pushed to her limits. She turned away, her gaze sweeping across the dimly lit room where her group huddled in small clusters, their faces etched with fear and determination.

"Alright," she called out, her voice steadier than she felt. "Let's get to work."

The room burst into a flurry of activity. Maya watched as Riley distributed makeshift weapons – pipes wrenched from walls, sharpened pieces of debris, and a few precious knives. The metallic clang of their arsenal sent a chill down her spine.

"We need to know what we're up against," Maya said, turning to Benji. "Can you scout the warehouse perimeter?"

Benji's eyes narrowed. "You're asking me to risk my neck before the fight even starts?"

Maya's jaw clenched. "I'm asking you to give us a fighting chance."

After a tense moment, Benji nodded curtly. "Fine. But don't expect any heroics."

As he slipped out, Maya's mind raced. How many of Jace's people would be there? How well-armed were they? The variables seemed endless, each one potentially fatal.

Riley approached; her freckled face tight with worry. "Maya, are you sure about this? We're barely holding it together as it is."

"We don't have a choice," Maya replied, her voice low. "That warehouse is our only shot at survival. Without those supplies..."

She left the sentence unfinished, the implications hanging heavy in the air.

Riley nodded, her expression hardening. "Then we better make this count."

As they huddled around a crudely drawn map of the area, Maya felt the weight of every eye upon her. She traced potential entry points, her finger trembling slightly.

"We'll need to split into three teams," she explained, her mind racing ahead to all the ways this could go wrong. "One for distraction, one for infiltration, and one for securing the supplies."

The group listened intently, their faces a mix of fear and resolve. Maya's heart pounded in her chest as she assigned roles, knowing full well that each decision could mean life or death.

As the final preparations were made, an eerie quiet settled over the room. Maya stood apart, her back against the wall, watching her people ready themselves for what could be their last stand.

"This is it," she thought, a lump forming in her throat. "Everything we've fought for comes down to this moment."

She closed her eyes, taking a deep breath to steady herself. When she opened them again, she saw not just survivors, but fighters – people who had endured the unthinkable and still stood tall.

"For our future," Maya whispered, more to herself than anyone else. "For our humanity."

With a nod to Riley, she stepped forward to lead her group into the uncertain night, the looming silhouette of the warehouse casting long shadows across their path.

Maya's gaze swept over the gathered faces, each one etched with a mixture of determination and fear. The weight of leadership pressed down on her shoulders, heavier than ever before. She swallowed hard, her throat dry as sandpaper.

"This is our last stand," she thought, her heart racing. "Everything we've endured, every sacrifice… it all comes down to this."

The warehouse loomed in the distance, a dark monolith against the overcast sky. Maya's fingers tightened around the makeshift weapon in her hand, her knuckles white with tension.

"Maya?" Riley's voice cut through her thoughts. "Can we talk for a moment?"

Maya nodded, following Riley to a quiet corner. The freckles on Riley's face stood out starkly against her pale skin, her green eyes filled with concern.

"Are you sure about this?" Riley asked softly, her voice barely above a whisper.

Maya hesitated, then replied, "We don't have a choice, Riley. If we don't take back the warehouse, we're as good as dead anyway."

Riley placed a hand on Maya's arm. "I know. I just... I want you to know that no matter what happens, you've done right by us. We've fought for what matters."

Maya felt a lump form in her throat. "Have we? Sometimes I wonder if I've just led everyone to their doom."

"No," Riley said firmly. "You've kept us human in a world that's trying to strip that away. That matters, Maya. It matters more than anything."

For a brief moment, Maya felt a flicker of peace wash over her. She nodded, grateful for Riley's unwavering support.

"Thank you," she whispered, her voice thick with emotion.

As they rejoined the group, Maya felt the tension settle back over her like a heavy cloak. The coming battle loomed before them, fraught with uncertainty and danger. But as she looked at the faces of those who had chosen to stand with her, she knew that giving up now would mean losing everything they had fought so hard to preserve.

With a deep breath, Maya steeled herself for what was to come. "It's time," she announced, her voice steady despite the turmoil within. "Remember why we're doing this. For our future, for our humanity. Let's move out."

The warehouse loomed before them, a hulking shadow against the darkening sky. Maya's group huddled in the nearby alley, their faces etched with a mix of fear and determination. The cool autumn air carried the scent of rain, matching the somber mood.

"This is it," Maya whispered, her eyes scanning the faces around her. "Any last words before we go?"

A heavy silence fell over the group. Then, unexpectedly, Tariq spoke up, his voice low and measured. "I want you all to know... whatever happens in there, I'm glad I'm not facing it alone."

Maya's eyebrows rose slightly. It was the most emotion she'd heard from Tariq in weeks. She nodded, a lump forming in her throat.

"We're in this together," Riley added, her green eyes shining with unshed tears. "To the end."

As the group murmured their agreement, Maya noticed a young girl named Zoe trembling slightly. She knelt beside her, placing a gentle hand on her shoulder. "You okay, Zoe?"

Zoe's voice quavered as she replied, "I'm scared, Maya. What if... what if we don't make it?"

Maya swallowed hard, her own fears threatening to surface. She pushed them down, forcing a small smile. "Then we'll have gone out fighting for what's right. But we're not going to think like that, okay? We're going to win this."

"How can you be so sure?" another member, Alex, asked, his tone bordering on desperation.

Maya stood, addressing the group. "Because we have to. Because the alternative is unthinkable. We've come too far to give up now."

As she spoke, Maya felt a familiar weight settling on her shoulders. The burden of leadership, of responsibility for these lives. But beneath it, a steely resolve took hold. They had to succeed. There was no other option.

The dim light of dusk filtered through the broken windows of their makeshift shelter, casting long shadows across the faces of Maya's group. In a corner, Benji sat hunched over, his usual smirk replaced by a furrowed brow. Maya approached him cautiously, noting the tension in his shoulders.

"Hey," she said softly, crouching beside him.

Benji looked up, his eyes uncharacteristically dull. "Hey yourself," he mumbled, attempting a weak smile that didn't reach his eyes.

Maya waited, sensing there was more. After a moment, Benji's facade crumbled.

"I'm scared, Maya," he whispered, his voice cracking. "I know I've been talking big about joining Jace, about how it's the smart move, but... the truth is, I'm terrified of what comes next."

Maya's heart clenched. This was Benji, the class clown, always ready with a joke to lighten the mood. Seeing him so vulnerable shook her.

"We all are," she admitted, placing a hand on his arm. "It's okay to be scared."

Benji shook his head, a bitter laugh escaping him. "Is it? Because I feel like a coward. All this time, I've been pushing for us to give up, to surrender. But it's not because I think Jace is right. It's because I'm too afraid to keep fighting."

Around them, the rest of the group was engaged in their own hushed conversations. Maya could hear snippets - words of encouragement, quiet goodbyes, promises to watch each other's backs.

"You're not a coward, Benji," Maya said firmly. "You're here, aren't you? Despite your fear, you're still with us."

Benji met her gaze, a glimmer of his old self shining through. "Yeah, well, someone's gotta keep you all from taking life too seriously, right?"

Maya smiled, squeezing his arm before standing. As she moved away, she heard Benji mutter, "Thanks, Maya. For everything."

She nodded, her throat tight with emotion. As she walked among her group, Maya felt the weight of their impending battle settling over them all. But beneath the fear and uncertainty, she sensed a newfound resolve. They might be scared, but they were in this together. And that, she realized, might just be enough to see them through.

Maya slipped away from the group, finding a quiet corner amidst the rubble. She leaned against a crumbling wall, her eyes scanning the ruined cityscape. The setting sun cast long shadows across the debris-strewn streets, a stark reminder of how much had changed since that fateful day.

"How did we get here?" she whispered to herself, her fingers tracing the rough concrete.

In her mind's eye, she saw flashes of the past - the initial chaos of the earthquake, the terrified faces of her classmates, the first tough decisions she'd had to make. Each memory was a step on the path that led to this moment.

"We were just kids on a field trip," Maya mused, a bitter smile playing on her lips. "Now look at us."

She closed her eyes, inhaling deeply. The air still carried the acrid scent of smoke and dust, a constant reminder of their harsh reality. When she opened them again, her gaze fell on her hands - once soft and clean, now calloused and dirt-streaked.

"I've changed," she realized, flexing her fingers. "We've all changed."

A flicker of movement caught her attention. Riley approached, her face etched with concern.

"Maya? Are you okay?" she asked softly.

Maya turned to her friend, seeing the same weariness and determination in Riley's eyes that she felt in her own heart.

"I'm... I don't know," Maya admitted. "I keep thinking about everything we've been through. How different we all are now."

Riley nodded, understanding in her gaze. "We've had to grow up fast. But you've led us this far, Maya. We wouldn't have survived without you."

Maya's throat tightened. "But at what cost? Look at what we're about to do. We're preparing for a battle, Riley. A real fight. Part of me wonders if we're any better than Jace now."

"Don't say that," Riley insisted, gripping Maya's arm. "We're fighting for our survival, yes, but we're also fighting for our humanity. That's what sets us apart."

Maya met Riley's gaze, seeing the unwavering faith there. It sparked a glimmer of hope in her chest, fragile but persistent.

"You really believe we can do this?" Maya asked, her voice barely above a whisper.

Riley's response was immediate. "I believe in you, Maya. We all do."

Maya took a deep breath, straightening her shoulders. The weight of leadership settled over her once more, but this time it felt less like a burden and more like armor.

"Then let's make it count," she said, her voice gaining strength. "For all of us."

As they walked back to the group, Maya's mind raced with possibilities - both hopeful and terrifying. The outcome of their stand against Jace was far from certain, but one thing was clear: win or lose, they would face it together.

Maya stood at the edge of the warehouse, her heart pounding in her chest. The looming structure cast long shadows in the fading twilight, a stark reminder of what they were about to face. She clenched her fists, feeling the roughness of her makeshift weapon against her palm.

"This is it," she murmured, more to herself than anyone else. "Everything we've been through, everything we've lost... it all comes down to this."

Riley appeared at her side, her face etched with determination. "We're ready, Maya. Just say the word."

Maya nodded, her eyes scanning the faces of her ragtag group. Some looked scared, others resolute. All of them were counting on her.

"Remember," she said, her voice low but firm, "we're not just fighting for supplies. We're fighting for our right to live with dignity, with compassion. Jace thinks brutality is the only way to survive, but we know better."

Benji, still skeptical, spoke up. "And if we lose? What then?"

Maya met his gaze unflinchingly. "Then we lose knowing we stood for something greater than ourselves."

She turned back to the warehouse, her mind racing with tactical considerations and moral quandaries. The weight of leadership had never felt heavier, but neither had her resolve been stronger.

"This is our last chance," she thought, steeling herself. "Our last stand against the darkness that's threatening to consume us all."

With a deep breath, Maya raised her hand, ready to give the signal. In that moment, she knew that whatever the outcome, they would face it together, holding onto their humanity in a world determined to strip it away.

CHAPTER 10

Ruins of Civilization

A sentry's shout pierced the tense silence. "Intruders!"

Chaos erupted as Maya's group charged forward, makeshift weapons raised. The once-quiet warehouse exploded into a battlefield of clashing bodies and desperate cries.

Maya gripped her heavy pipe, heart pounding as she ran. All around her, the sounds of struggle filled the air - grunts of effort, the clang of metal on metal, ragged breaths and shouts of pain. She could barely make out individual faces in the dim light, friend and foe blurring together in the frantic melee.

A figure lunged at her from the shadows. Maya swung her pipe, connecting with a sickening crunch. The attacker crumpled.

She caught a glimpse of Riley a few feet away, his features twisted in a snarl as he grappled with one of Jace's followers. For a split second, their eyes met - a moment of shared desperation and resolve. Then the tide of battle pulled them apart again.

Maya's thoughts raced as she fought. Was this truly the only way? Beating down other survivors, people just as scared and desperate as her own group? But Jace's cruelty left them no choice. They had to take the warehouse, secure the supplies. Survival demanded it.

She slammed her pipe into an opponent's ribs, wincing at his howl of agony. The brutality of it all threatened to overwhelm her, but she pushed the horror aside. Later there would be time for guilt, for mourning the loss of her ideals. Now, she had to lead.

"Push forward!" Maya yelled over the din. "We can do this! Stay together!"

Her group rallied at the sound of her voice, surging ahead with renewed determination. The battle raged on, the screams and clash of weapons echoing through the warehouse. Maya fought to hold onto her humanity amidst the swirling violence, praying she could lead them to victory before they all lost themselves.

Benji emerged from the fray, his face streaked with blood and sweat. "Maya!" he shouted, his voice hoarse. "We're gaining ground, but Tariq...I don't see him!"

Maya's heart clenched. She scanned the chaos, desperate for a glimpse of Tariq's familiar form. The thought of losing him, of losing any more of her people, was unbearable.

"There!" Riley pointed with his makeshift club, his other arm hanging limply at his side. "By the crates!"

Maya followed his gaze and spotted Tariq, cornered by two of Jace's fighters. He was holding his own, but barely, exhaustion clear in every movement.

"Cover me!" Maya ordered, already racing towards him.

She wove through the battle, dodging blows and lashing out when needed. The metallic scent of blood mixed with the dust and sweat, a sickening cocktail that coated her throat. But she pushed forward, driven by the need to reach Tariq.

Just as one of the fighters raised a jagged piece of metal to strike, Maya slammed into him from behind. They tumbled to the ground, grappling for control. Maya's world narrowed to the struggle, the press of bodies, the frantic need to come out on top.

With a final, desperate surge of strength, she pinned her opponent. Their eyes locked, and in that moment, Maya saw not an enemy, but a frightened boy, hardly older than herself.

"Stay down," she growled, her pipe pressed against his throat. "Please."

Something in her tone, or perhaps the flicker of empathy in her eyes, made him go still. Maya rolled off him, turning just in time to see Tariq dispatch the other fighter with a well-placed kick.

"Thanks," Tariq panted, offering a tight smile. "Thought I was done for."

Maya clasped his shoulder, a brief moment of solidarity amidst the battle. "We're not losing anyone else. Not today."

As if to challenge her words, a scream rang out nearby. Maya whirled to see one of her own, a girl named Sarah, fall beneath a vicious blow. Time seemed to slow as Maya started forward, knowing she was too far away, too late.

But then Riley was there, pulling Sarah to her feet and shielding her with his own body. He met Maya's gaze across the warehouse floor, his expression grim but determined.

They were all pushed to their limits, battered and bleeding, but still they fought. For survival, for each other, for the hope of a future beyond this brutal present. Maya rallied her group again, her voice rising above the clamor.

"We're almost there! The warehouse is ours! For all we've lost, for all we can still save...keep fighting!"

With a roar of defiance and desperation, her ragtag band surged forward once more into the heart of the battle. Maya led the charge, a flicker of hope kindling within her despite the horror. If they could just hold on, just push a little harder...perhaps there was still a chance for something better on the other side of this long, dark night.

Maya grunted as she parried a blow, her arms aching with the effort. Her opponent, a burly man with a wild look in his eyes, pressed forward relentlessly. She dodged and weaved, trying to find an opening, but he was too fast, too strong.

Despair threatened to overwhelm her as she fought. How could they hope to win against such odds? How could they justify this violence, this brutality?

But then she caught sight of Benji, his face streaked with blood and sweat, standing firm against two attackers. And Tariq, limping but still fighting, still protecting those who couldn't protect themselves.

They were all still here, still fighting for each other. For the chance to build something better.

Maya's resolve hardened. She feinted left, then struck right, her improvised weapon connecting with a sickening crunch. The man fell, and Maya stepped over him, pushing forward.

The tide was turning. Slowly but surely, Maya's group was gaining ground. They fought with the desperate strength of those who had nothing left to lose, and everything to gain.

Yet even as victory seemed within reach, Maya's heart was heavy. The cost had been so high, the toll on her soul so great. She had never wanted this, never wanted to be a warrior, a killer.

But she had no choice. In this brutal new world, it was fight or die. And Maya would fight, would endure the scars on her conscience, if it meant her people could live.

She caught Riley's eye across the battlefield, saw the same grim determination in his gaze. They were in this together, come what may.

With a final, wrenching effort, Maya broke through the enemy line. The warehouse was theirs, but the victory tasted like ashes in her mouth.

As the battle died down and the wounded were tended to, Maya stood apart, her thoughts a tumultuous whirl. They had won, but at what price? How much of their humanity had they sacrificed on the altar of survival?

She didn't have the answers. All she knew was that they had to keep going, keep fighting for a better tomorrow. No matter the cost to her own soul.

Maya squared her shoulders and turned back to her people, ready to lead them into the next challenge. The battle was over, but the war for their future had only just begun.

Maya stood amidst the chaos, her heart heavy with the weight of her choices. The battle raged on around her, the clash of metal and the cries of the wounded filling the air. She parried a blow from one of Jace's followers, her movements automatic, her mind a million miles away.

"Is this the right path?" she wondered, doubt creeping into her thoughts. "Could there have been another way, a path of peace instead of violence?"

But even as the questions plagued her, Maya knew there was no turning back. Her people needed her, needed the supplies and safety the warehouse could provide. If she faltered now, if she let her ideals cloud her judgment, they would all pay the price.

With a shake of her head, Maya refocused on the battle at hand. She couldn't afford to be lost in thought, not when lives hung in the balance. She had to see this through, no matter the cost.

As she fought, Maya caught glimpses of her companions locked in their own struggles. Riley, his face set in grim determination as he took on two of Jace's men at once. Tariq, using his speed and agility to outmaneuver his opponents. And Benji, his strength a bulwark against the enemy onslaught.

They were all counting on her, trusting in her leadership to guide them through this nightmare. Maya couldn't let them down.

But even as her resolve hardened, Maya felt a flicker of doubt. Jace's taunts echoed in her mind, his accusations of weakness and naivety striking a chord. Was she really fit to lead? Could she make the hard choices, the ruthless decisions that survival demanded?

"No," Maya thought fiercely, pushing the doubts aside. "I won't become like Jace, ruling through fear and brutality. There has to be another way, a way to hold onto our humanity even in the darkest of times."

With that thought, Maya's path became clear. She would fight, yes, but she would also show mercy where she could. She would spare those who surrendered, offer a chance at redemption to those who had lost their way.

It wouldn't be easy, walking that line between survival and compassion. But Maya knew it was the only way forward, the only way to build a future worth living in.

As the battle wound down and Jace's followers began to scatter, Maya stood tall amidst the wreckage. Bloodied and bruised, but unbroken.

She had made her choice, and she would bear the consequences, whatever they may be. For the sake of her people, for the sake of the world they hoped to rebuild, Maya would hold fast to her humanity, no matter the cost.

The warehouse was theirs, but the true battle, the battle for the soul of this new world, had only just begun.

The sharp crack of a gunshot pierced the air, shattering the momentary stillness that had settled over the warehouse. Maya whirled around, heart pounding, to see Jace emerging from the shadows, a smoking pistol in his hand and a cold, determined look in his eyes.

"Did you really think it would be that easy?" Jace called out, his voice echoing through the cavernous space. "That I would just let you waltz in here and take what's mine?"

Around him, Jace's followers surged forward, weapons at the ready, their faces twisted with anger and fear. Maya's group tensed, preparing for the counterattack they knew was coming.

"This ends now, Jace!" Maya shouted back, her own voice steady despite the adrenaline coursing through her veins. "We don't have to do this. There's another way, a better way."

Jace laughed, a harsh, mocking sound that sent chills down Maya's spine. "You're still clinging to your naive ideals, even now? Wake up, Maya! The old world is gone, and in this new one, only the strong survive."

With a wave of his hand, Jace signaled his followers to attack. They charged forward, a tidal wave of desperate, furious humanity, ready to crush anything in their path.

Maya's group met them head-on, the clash of bodies and weapons filling the air with a cacophony of violence. Maya found herself in the thick of it, dodging blows and striking out with a fierce determination she hardly recognized in herself.

As she fought, Maya's mind raced. Jace's words echoed in her head, taunting her, challenging her beliefs. Was he right? Was she just a naive fool, clinging to the ghosts of a world long dead?

"No," Maya thought, gritting her teeth as she blocked a vicious swing from one of Jace's followers. "I won't let him break me, won't let him turn me into something I'm not."

She thought of her group, of the trust they had placed in her, the hope they had for a future beyond mere survival. She thought of the promise she had made to herself, to hold onto her humanity no matter what.

With a surge of strength, Maya pushed back against her attacker, sending them sprawling to the ground. Around her, the tide of the battle was turning, Jace's followers falling back under the determined onslaught of Maya's group.

But Jace himself was nowhere to be seen, having vanished into the shadows once again. Maya knew this was far from over, that Jace would not give up his hold on power so easily.

As the last of Jace's followers fled or surrendered, Maya stood amid the wreckage of the battle, breathing hard, her heart still racing. The warehouse was theirs, but at what cost?

She looked around at her group, at the wounds they bore, the haunted looks in their eyes. They had won, but the price had been high, and Maya knew there would be more battles to come.

But for now, they had a moment to catch their breath, to tend to their wounds and regroup. Maya knew that the true test was still ahead and that Jace would be back, more determined than ever to crush her and everything she stood for.

She would be ready for him. Ready to fight, not just for survival, but for the soul of this new world they were building. Ready to prove that humanity, compassion, and hope could still triumph in the face of darkness and despair.

The battle for the warehouse was over. The war for the future had only just begun.

Jace's voice boomed across the warehouse, cutting through the chaos of the battle. "Maya!" he called out, his tone dripping with condescension. "You're too weak to win this fight. Too soft to do what needs to be done to survive in this world."

Maya gritted her teeth, fury rising within her at Jace's taunts. Around her, the battle raged on, her followers clashing with Jace's in a brutal melee of makeshift weapons and desperate hand-to-hand combat. The air was thick with grunts of exertion, cries of pain, and the metallic clang of pipes and crowbars.

I can't let him get to me, Maya thought, dodging a blow from one of Jace's followers. I have to stay focused, stay strong for my people.

But Jace's words continued to echo in her mind, even as she fought on. Was she truly too weak to lead in this harsh new reality? Was her belief in cooperation and compassion nothing more than a liability?

No. She couldn't afford to think like that. Her people needed her, needed the hope and humanity she represented. She would not let Jace break her, no matter how hard he tried.

As if sensing her resolve, Jace plunged into the fray, his powerful frame cutting a swath through the chaos. His eyes locked onto Maya, a predatory gleam in their depths.

"Look around you, Maya!" he shouted, gesturing to the brutal struggle playing out across the warehouse floor. "This is the world we live in now. Only the strong survive. And you? You're nothing but a relic of the past, clinging to outdated ideals."

Maya's heart raced as Jace closed in, his words hitting far too close to home. The battle seemed to fade into the background, narrowing down to just the two of them, locked in a struggle not just for the warehouse, but for the very soul of this new world.

"I can't beat him alone, Maya realized, even as she raised her weapon to meet Jace's charge. But I'm not alone. My people are with me, and together, we're stronger than he could ever be.

With a cry of defiance, Maya met Jace head-on, their weapons clashing in a shower of sparks. Around them, the tide of the battle began to turn, Maya's followers rallying to her side, inspired by her unwavering courage in the face of Jace's onslaught.

But even as they gained ground, Maya knew this was far from over. Jace was too proud, too ruthless to accept defeat easily. He would keep coming at them, keep trying to break them, until one side or the other lay broken on the warehouse floor.

"And it won't be us," Maya vowed silently, even as she traded blows with Jace. We'll keep fighting, keep holding on to our humanity, no matter what he throws at us. We'll show him that compassion isn't weakness, that hope can still light the way in this darkened world.

The battle raged on, the outcome still uncertain. But in that moment, facing down the embodiment of everything she stood against, Maya felt a flicker of something she hadn't felt in a long time: hope. Hope that they could win this fight, hope that a better future was still possible.

And with that hope burning bright within her, she fought on.

The clash of metal on metal rang through the warehouse as Maya and Jace's weapons collided, each blow a testament to the strength of their convictions. Sweat poured down Maya's face, mingling with the grime of battle, but she never wavered, her eyes locked on Jace's in a silent challenge.

"You can't win this, Maya," Jace snarled, his voice rough with exertion. "You're too soft, too weak to do what needs to be done. You'll lead your people to ruin."

Maya shook her head, a grim smile playing at the corners of her mouth. "You're wrong, Jace. Strength isn't about being cruel, about leaving others behind. It's about standing together, about holding on to what makes us human."

She punctuated her words with a flurry of blows, driving Jace back a step. Around them, the battle was turning, Maya's followers gaining the upper hand as they fought with renewed determination.

We can do this, Maya thought fiercely, even as her muscles burned with fatigue. We can beat him, not just here, but in the days to come. We'll build a future based on more than just survival, a future where compassion and unity are our greatest strengths.

Jace's eyes narrowed, and he redoubled his efforts, his attacks becoming more frenzied, more desperate. But Maya met him at every turn, her own resolve unwavering.

This was more than just a physical battle, she knew. It was a battle for the soul of their group, for the kind of world they would create from the ashes of the old. And it was a battle she was determined to win, no matter the cost.

Because if we lose ourselves, she thought as she parried another of Jace's strikes, if we become like him, then what's the point of surviving at all?

The thought gave her new strength, and with a final, mighty effort, she disarmed Jace, sending his weapon skittering across the warehouse floor. He stared at her in shock, his chest heaving, his eyes filled with a mix of fury and fear.

"It's over, Jace," Maya said softly, her own weapon leveled at his chest. "Your way doesn't work, can't you see that? We need each other, now more than ever. We need to remember what it means to be human."

For a long moment, Jace was silent, the only sound the distant echoes of the fading battle. Then, slowly, he raised his hands in surrender, his head bowed in defeat.

As Maya lowered her weapon, she felt a rush of relief, tinged with a bittersweet sense of victory. They had won the battle, but the war for their future was just beginning.

And we'll face it together, she vowed silently, looking out over the faces of her weary, triumphant followers. We'll build a world based on hope, not fear. A world where we never forget the strength that lies in our humanity.

With that thought, she turned to face the challenges ahead, ready to lead her people into the uncertain dawn of a new era.

Maya stood over Jace, her heart pounding in her chest as the weight of her decision settled upon her. The warehouse was eerily quiet now, the sounds of battle replaced by an unsettling stillness. She could feel the eyes of her followers upon her, waiting to see what she would do next.

Jace looked up at her, his face a mask of defeat and resignation. "Well?" he spat. "What are you waiting for? Finish it."

Maya hesitated, her grip tightening on her weapon. It would be so easy to end it here, to ensure that Jace could never threaten them again. But as she looked into his eyes, she saw not just the ruthless leader, but the broken man beneath. A man shaped by the same tragedy that had shaped them all.

"No," she said softly, lowering her weapon. "I won't do it. I won't become like you."

Jace laughed bitterly. "You're a fool, Maya. Do you think mercy will save you in this world? You think your ideals mean anything anymore?"

"They mean everything," Maya replied, her voice growing stronger. "They're what separate us from the animals. They're what give us hope for a better future."

She turned to face her followers, seeing the mix of exhaustion and determination in their faces. "We've won today, but the real work starts now. We have to build something new, something better. And we have to do it together."

Riley stepped forward, placing a hand on Maya's shoulder. "We're with you, Maya. Every step of the way."

Maya nodded, feeling a surge of gratitude and love for her friends. They had been through so much together, and yet here they stood, united in their resolve to create a new world from the ashes of the old.

As they began to gather their wounded and take stock of their supplies, Maya couldn't help but feel a sense of hope rising within her. Yes, the challenges ahead were daunting. Yes, the world had changed in ways they were still struggling to comprehend. But they had each other, and they had their humanity.

And in the end, that was all that mattered.

Maya's fingers tightened around the makeshift blade, the sharp edge hovering mere inches from Jace's throat. His eyes widened, a flicker of fear passing through them before being replaced by a defiant sneer.

"Do it," he spat, his voice dripping with venom. "Prove that you're just like me."

Maya's heart pounded in her ears, the weight of the decision bearing down on her. She could end it all right now—ensure her group's survival, rid the world of Jace's cruelty. But at what cost?

The warehouse seemed to hold its breath, the distant sounds of the ongoing battle fading into the background as Maya wrestled with her conscience. Jace's words echoed in her mind, taunting her, daring her to abandon her principles.

She thought of all the lives lost, all the sacrifices made to get to this point. She thought of the future she wanted to build, a future based on compassion and unity. Could she still claim to fight for those ideals if she let herself be consumed by violence and vengeance?

Maya's hand trembled, the blade quivering against Jace's skin. In that moment, she saw the path before her with startling clarity. She could become like Jace, letting the darkness of this new world twist her into something unrecognizable. Or she could hold fast to her humanity, even in the face of impossible choices.

With a shuddering breath, Maya made her decision. She lowered the blade, stepping back from Jace's prone form. "No," she said, her voice steady despite the turmoil raging inside her. "I won't be like you. I won't let this world turn me into a monster."

Jace's eyes narrowed, a mix of confusion and disgust contorting his features. "You're weak," he snarled, struggling to sit up. "You don't have what it takes to survive."

Maya shook her head, a sad smile tugging at her lips. "You're wrong," she said softly. "It takes more strength to choose mercy than to give in to hate. I'm not weak, Jace. I'm just human."

She turned away from him then, her gaze searching for Riley amidst the chaos of the warehouse floor below. The battle was fizzling out now; Jace's followers were scattering as they realized their leader was down for good. Maya caught Riley's eye across the fray, seeing relief and pride mingled in her expression.

Maya felt drained now that the adrenaline was wearing off—the physical exhaustion of battle compounded by the emotional toll of her choice. But beneath it all was a flicker of something else: hope. Hope that they could rise above the savagery of this new world order. Hope that there was still a place for compassion amid the ruins.

She didn't know what challenges lay ahead beyond these warehouse walls—but with Riley beside her, Benji and Tariq waiting below... Maya felt certain about one thing: they would face those trials hand-in-hand. Not as survivors scrounging in the dirt, but as builders forging something new from dust and dreams alike.

Maya descended the stairs from the catwalk, each step heavy with the weight of her decision. As she reached the warehouse floor, Riley rushed to her side, concern etched across her face. "Are you okay?" Riley asked, her voice barely above a whisper.

Maya nodded, managing a tired smile. "I will be." She glanced back at Jace's crumpled form, a twinge of doubt shadowing her features. "Do you think I made the right choice?"

Riley placed a hand on Maya's shoulder, her touch a steady anchor amidst the turmoil. "You stayed true to yourself," she said firmly. "That's all any of us can do in this world."

Around them, the warehouse was a tableau of the battle's aftermath. Overturned shelves, scattered supplies, and the distant groans of the wounded painted a stark picture of the cost of survival. Benji and Tariq picked their way through the debris, tending to the injured on both sides—a small gesture of the unity Maya hoped to foster.

Maya's gaze drifted to the shattered windows, where the first pale light of dawn was filtering through the cracks. It felt symbolic, somehow—a glimmer of light after the darkness of the night. She drew in a deep breath, squaring her shoulders as she turned to face her people.

"We fought hard for this place," Maya began, her voice growing stronger with each word. "But it's more than just a shelter. It's a chance to build something better." She met the eyes of each person gathered around her, seeing in them the same resilience that had carried them this far.

"We've all lost so much," she continued, her throat tightening with emotion. "But we still have each other. And as long as we hold onto our humanity, as long as we stand together... there's no limit to what we can overcome."

Riley nodded, her eyes shining with unshed tears. Benji and Tariq murmured their agreement, their faces lined with exhaustion but also with determination. And as Maya looked out over the sea of faces, battered but unbroken, she felt a swell of something she hadn't dared to feel in a long time: hope.

The road ahead wouldn't be easy. There would be challenges and setbacks, moments where their resolve would be tested to its limits. But in that moment, standing shoulder-to-shoulder with the people who had become her family, Maya knew they would weather whatever storms came their way.

Together, they would rebuild. Together, they would find a way to thrive in this fractured world. And together, they would never lose sight of what it meant to be human—even when the very foundations of humanity had crumbled around them.

Maya took Riley's hand in hers, feeling the warmth of her touch, the steadiness of her presence. "Let's get to work," she said softly. And with that, they stepped forward into the light of a new dawn—ready to face whatever lay ahead, united by the unbreakable bonds of hope and love.

Maya's grip on Jace loosened as she stepped back, her chest heaving with exertion and emotion. Jace slumped to the ground, his face a mix of disbelief and defeat. Around them, the battle had stilled, all eyes drawn to the scene unfolding in the center of the warehouse.

"It's over, Jace," Maya said, her voice steady despite the tremors running through her body. "Your way... it's not the answer. It never was."

Jace looked up at her, a bitter laugh escaping his lips. "You think this changes anything? You think they'll follow you now, just because you didn't have the guts to finish me off?"

Maya shook her head, a sad smile on her face. "It's not about them following me. It's about all of us working together, building something better than what we had before. Something worth fighting for."

She turned to face the gathered crowds, her voice rising with conviction. "We've all lost so much. We've all had to make impossible choices just to survive. But if we lose sight of what makes us human… if we let go of our compassion, our hope… then what's the point of surviving at all?"

A murmur rippled through the crowd, a mix of uncertainty and dawning realization. Maya pressed on, her eyes shining with unshed tears.

"I know you're scared. I know you're angry. But we can't let those feelings consume us. We can't let them turn us into something we're not." She gestured to Jace's hunched form, her voice softening. "Look at what that path leads to. Is that really the future you want?"

Silence fell over the warehouse, broken only by the distant sound of settling debris. Then, slowly at first, members of Jace's faction began to step forward, their weapons clattering to the ground at their feet. One by one, they moved to stand behind Maya, their faces etched with a fragile new hope.

Jace watched in stunned disbelief as his once-loyal followers abandoned him, his power crumbling before his very eyes. He struggled to his feet, his face contorted with rage and humiliation.

"You'll regret this," he spat, his voice dripping with venom. "You think you can lead them? Do you think you can keep them safe? You're nothing but a naive little girl playing at being a hero."

But even as he spoke, Jace's words rang hollow. The fire in his eyes had dimmed, replaced by a dull, defeated resignation. He knew, as surely as Maya did, that his reign was over.

Maya met his gaze steadily, no trace of fear or doubt in her expression. "Maybe I am naive," she said softly. "Maybe I don't have all the answers. But I know that as long as we hold on to our humanity, as long as we stand together, we have a chance. And that's more than you can say."

With those words, Maya turned her back on Jace, facing her people—both those who had stood with her from the beginning and those who had just now found the courage to join her. The warehouse was theirs, but the victory felt hollow, tainted by the blood and pain it had cost.

Maya's eyes roamed over the battered, weary faces of her followers, taking in the toll the battle had taken. Riley stood at her side, his hand finding hers and gripping it tightly, a silent reminder that she wasn't alone. But even his comforting presence couldn't erase the ache in her heart.

"We won," she said, her voice heavy with exhaustion and grief. "But look around you. Look at the price we paid. Is this really what we wanted? Is this what we were fighting for?"

The survivors shifted uneasily, the weight of Maya's words settling over them like a shroud. They had come here seeking safety, seeking a future, but now that future seemed as uncertain as ever.

Maya's gaze drifted to the shattered windows, to the gray sky beyond. "We have the warehouse," she continued, "but what good is shelter if we lose ourselves in the process? We have to be better than this. We have to find another way."

She took a deep breath, squaring her shoulders as if bracing herself for the burden she knew she had to bear. "We'll stay here tonight, tend to our wounded, bury our dead. But in the morning, we start over. We build something new, something better. And we do it together."

As Maya's words faded into silence, a sense of purpose settled over the group. They had fought hard for this moment, sacrificed so much, and now it was up to them to make it mean something. The road ahead wouldn't be easy, but with Maya to guide them, they knew they could face whatever challenges lay ahead.

The battle was over, but the real work was just beginning.

Maya walked through the warehouse, her footsteps echoing in the eerie silence that had settled over the space. Everywhere she looked, she saw the aftermath of the battle - broken crates, shattered glass, and the still forms of those who had fallen. The metallic scent of blood hung heavy in the air, a bitter reminder of the price they had paid for this victory.

As she moved deeper into the warehouse, Maya caught sight of Riley kneeling beside one of the wounded, his hands steady as he wrapped a makeshift bandage around a gash on the man's arm. He looked up as she approached, his eyes heavy with exhaustion and grief.

"How many?" Maya asked softly, dreading the answer but needing to know.

Riley shook his head. "Too many. At least a dozen of ours, maybe more. And Jace's group..." He trailed off, his gaze drifting to the bodies scattered across the floor.

Maya nodded, her throat tight. She had known the cost would be high, but seeing it laid out before her was almost more than she could bear. Each loss was a wound on her soul, a reminder of the heavy burden of leadership.

She knelt down beside Riley, placing a hand on his shoulder. "You did everything you could," she said gently. "We all did."

Riley looked at her, his eyes searching her face. "But was it enough? Look at this place, Maya. Look at what we've done."

Maya followed his gaze, taking in the destruction that surrounded them. The warehouse had been their goal, the key to their survival, but now that they had it, the victory felt hollow. What good was shelter if they lost their humanity in the process?

She stood up, squaring her shoulders as she faced the survivors of her group. They looked to her now, their eyes filled with a mix of hope and despair, waiting for her to guide them through this new reality.

"We have the warehouse," Maya said, her voice steady despite the emotions churning within her. "But this is not the end. It's only the beginning. We have to build something here, something more than just survival. We have to find a way to live, not just exist."

She looked around at the faces of her people, seeing the flicker of determination in their eyes. They had come this far, fought this hard, and they would not give up now.

"We'll rest tonight," Maya continued. "Tend to our wounded, honor our dead. But in the morning, we start over. We build a new future, one where we don't have to fight each other to survive. We build it together."

As the survivors nodded, a sense of purpose settling over the group, Maya knew that the road ahead would not be easy. The scars of this battle would linger long after the wounds had healed. But with each other to lean on, with the strength of their convictions to guide them, they would find a way forward.

The warehouse was theirs, but the true fight was just beginning - the fight for their humanity, for the future they dared to dream of. And Maya would be there every step of the way, leading them through the darkness and into the light.

Maya stood amidst the ruins of the warehouse, the weight of leadership heavy on her shoulders. The battle was won, but at what cost? Bodies littered the ground, both friend and foe, their blood mingling on the concrete. The air was thick with the metallic scent of death, and the silence that followed the chaos was deafening.

She walked through the carnage, her steps unsteady, her heart heavy. Each lifeless face was a reminder of the price they had paid for survival. These were people she knew, people she had sworn to protect. And now, they were gone, their lives cut short by a war they never asked for.

Tears stung her eyes, but she blinked them back. She couldn't afford to break, not now, not when her people needed her most. They had looked to her for guidance, for strength, and she had led them into this battle. The responsibility for their lives, and their deaths, rested squarely on her shoulders.

"Maya?" Riley's voice cut through the haze of grief, and Maya turned to face her friend. Riley was battered and bruised, her clothes torn and stained with blood, but she was alive. They both were.

"We did it," Riley said, her voice barely above a whisper. "We took the warehouse."

Maya nodded, but the victory felt hollow. "But at what cost, Riley? Look around you. Look at all we've lost."

Riley's gaze swept over the fallen, and her eyes glistened with unshed tears. "I know. But we had no choice. It was either this or…"

"Or we all died," Maya finished, her voice raw with emotion. "I know. But that doesn't make it any easier."

They stood in silence for a moment, the weight of their actions settling over them like a shroud. Maya knew that this was only the beginning, that the road ahead would be long and fraught with challenges. But they had taken the first step, had claimed a foothold in this new world order.

"We have to keep going," Maya said at last, her voice steadier now. "We have to build something here, something more than just survival. We have to find a way to live, not just exist."

Riley placed a hand on Maya's shoulder, a gesture of comfort and solidarity. "We will. Together. You're not alone in this, Maya. We're all behind you, every step of the way."

Maya nodded, drawing strength from her friend's words. She knew that the battles to come would test them in ways they had never been tested before. But with her people by her side, with the hope of a better future guiding them, she knew they could face whatever lay ahead.

The warehouse was theirs, but the true fight was just beginning - the fight for their humanity, for the world they dared to dream of. And Maya would lead them through the darkness, no matter the cost. For in the end, it was not about survival, but about living - truly living - in the face of all that had been lost.

Maya took a deep breath, the weight of her choices and the responsibility of leadership settling heavily on her shoulders. The warehouse stretched out before her, a testament to their hard-fought victory, but also a reminder of the challenges that lay ahead.

She walked slowly through the debris-strewn space, her footsteps echoing in the eerie stillness. The battle had left its mark on every surface, from the shattered windows to the blood-stained floors. But amidst the chaos, there was a glimmer of hope - the hope of a new beginning.

Maya's mind raced with the decisions that needed to be made, the plans that needed to be put in place. They had secured the warehouse, but that was only the first step. They needed to fortify their position, to gather supplies, to establish a system of governance that would ensure their long-term survival.

But more than that, Maya knew that they needed to hold on to their humanity. In a world where the rules had been rewritten, where the strong preyed on the weak and the ruthless thrived, it was all too easy to lose sight of what truly mattered.

She thought of the choices she had made, the impossible decisions she had been forced to confront. Each one had chipped away at her soul, leaving her questioning her own morality, her own sense of right and wrong.

But even in her darkest moments, Maya knew that she could not abandon her principles. She had to stay true to herself, to the ideals that had guided her through the chaos. It was the only way to ensure that they built something more than just a society of survivors - they had to build a community, a place where compassion and empathy could still thrive.

Maya's gaze drifted to the people around her, the faces etched with exhaustion and grief, but also with determination and resilience. They had put their trust in her, had followed her into battle and emerged victorious. She owed it to them to be the leader they needed, to guide them through the dark days ahead with strength and conviction.

"We have a long road ahead of us," Maya said, her voice ringing out in the stillness. "But we have each other. We have the strength of our convictions, the power of our unity. Together, we will build something better, something worthy of the sacrifices we have made."

The words felt heavy on her tongue, but Maya knew that they were true. Leadership was not about power or control - it was about service, about putting the needs of others before your own. And she would bear that burden gladly, would make the impossible choices and stay true to herself, for the sake of the people who depended on her.

With a final glance at the warehouse, Maya squared her shoulders and turned to face her people. The future was uncertain, but one thing was clear - they would face it together, united by their common purpose and their unbreakable bond. And with that knowledge, Maya knew that anything was possible.

Maya took a deep breath, the cool autumn air filling her lungs as she surveyed the devastation before her. The warehouse, once a symbol of their struggle, now lay in ruins, its walls crumbling and its contents scattered across the debris-strewn ground. The battle had been won, but at a terrible cost.

Her mind drifted back to the moment when she had stood over Jace, her makeshift weapon poised to strike the final blow. It would have been so easy to end it then and there, to ensure that he could never threaten them again. But something had stayed her hand.

"I couldn't do it," she whispered, her voice barely audible over the distant sound of shifting rubble. "I couldn't become like him."

It had been the hardest decision of her life, to choose mercy over vengeance. But in that moment, Maya had realized that her humanity was the one thing she could not afford to lose. To kill Jace in cold blood would have been to betray everything she stood for, to become the very thing she had fought against.

"You did the right thing," Riley said, placing a comforting hand on her shoulder. "Killing him wouldn't have solved anything. It would have only added to the cycle of violence."

Maya nodded, grateful for her friend's support. She knew that many in her group might not understand her choice, might see it as a sign of weakness. But she also knew that true strength lay in compassion, in the ability to see the humanity in even the most monstrous of enemies.

She turned to face her people, their faces etched with the weariness and grief of the battle. They had lost so much, had seen horrors that no one should ever have to witness. But they had also shown incredible courage and resilience in the face of overwhelming odds.

"We have won a great victory today," Maya said, her voice growing stronger with each word. "But the fight is far from over. We must rebuild, not just our shelter, but our very way of life. We must create a future that is worth the sacrifices we have made."

She could see the hope kindling in their eyes, the determination to rise from the ashes of their broken world. And in that moment, Maya knew that they would succeed. They had each other, and that was enough.

As the sun began to set over the ruined city, Maya cast one last glance at the warehouse. It had been a crucible, a test of their mettle and their resolve. And they had emerged stronger, more united than ever before.

With a final nod, she turned to lead her people into the gathering darkness, towards an uncertain future that they would face together, come what may.

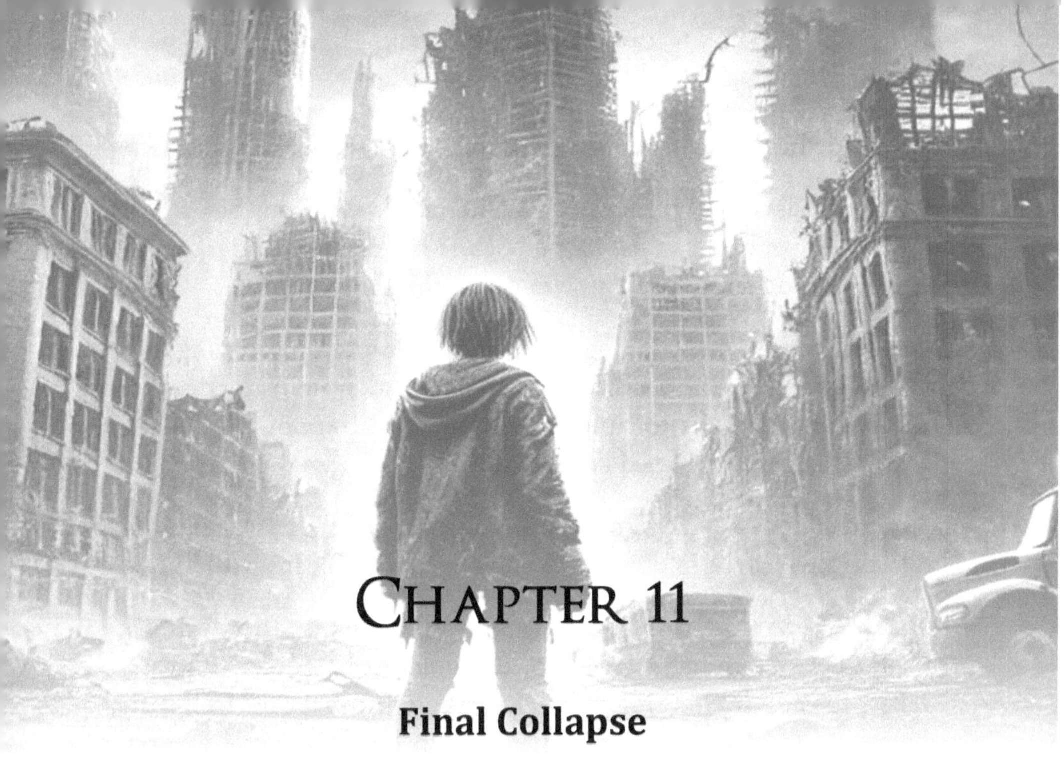

CHAPTER 11

Final Collapse

The stench of blood and gunpowder hung thick in the air as Maya picked her way through the debris-strewn warehouse. Shards of glass crunched beneath her boots, mixing with the soft groans of the wounded. She paused, her eyes fixed on a dark stain spreading across the concrete floor.

"What have I done?" she whispered, her voice barely audible.

Maya's gaze drifted to where Jace lay bound and unconscious, his face a mess of bruises. The sight of him, powerless now, sent a chill through her.

Did I make the right choice? The question echoed in her mind, unanswered.

She turned away, continuing her solitary walk through the carnage. Her group – what was left of it – huddled in small clusters, tending to injuries and murmuring in hushed tones. Maya felt their eyes on her, a mix of gratitude and accusation.

"Maya," a voice called out. It was Tariq, his usually stoic face etched with concern. "We need to decide what to do with the bodies."

She nodded, swallowing hard. "Give me a minute. I'll be right there."

As Tariq walked away, Maya's thoughts raced. We won, but at what cost? The faces of the fallen flashed before her eyes – friends, enemies, all reduced to lifeless forms strewn across the battlefield.

She clenched her fists, feeling the weight of leadership pressing down on her shoulders. The decision to spare Jace had been instinctive, born from a desperate need to cling to her humanity. But now, in the harsh light of day, doubt gnawed at her resolve.

"I couldn't become like him," Maya muttered to herself, glancing back at Jace. "But maybe that's what it takes to survive in this world now."

She shook her head, trying to clear the dark thoughts. There was work to be done, wounded to tend to, decisions to be made. But as she walked towards her waiting group, Maya couldn't shake the feeling that something fundamental had shifted within her. The battle was over, but the war – both outside and within herself – had only just begun.

Riley approached Maya, her bright green eyes dulled by exhaustion and worry. She placed a hand on Maya's shoulder, her touch a mix of comfort and support.

"How are you holding up?" Riley asked softly, her voice barely above a whisper.

Maya shook her head, unable to form words. Riley nodded in understanding, then turned to the group huddled nearby. "Alright, everyone. Let's get the wounded to the east corner. We need to clean those injuries before they get infected."

As Riley directed the survivors, Maya watched her friend's slender frame move with purpose. Despite the visible tremor in her hands, Riley's voice remained steady, a beacon of stability in the chaos.

"You made the right call," Riley murmured to Maya, as she passed by with a bundle of makeshift bandages. "We're alive. That's what matters."

But before Maya could respond, Benji's harsh voice cut through the air. "The right call? Look around you!" He gestured wildly at the destruction surrounding them. "We barely survived, and for what? So Jace can come back and finish the job later?"

Maya flinched at the venom in Benji's words. The stocky boy's usually friendly face was contorted with anger, his curly hair matted with blood and grime.

"Benji, please," Riley started, but he cut her off.

"No, Riley. We need to face facts. Sparing Jace was a mistake. A mistake that could get us all killed."

Maya's mind raced. Was Benji right? Had her decision doomed them all? The doubt that had been gnawing at her threatened to consume her entirely.

Maya's eyes darted to the far corner of the warehouse, where Jace lay slumped against a wall, his hands bound behind his back. Blood seeped through his tattered shirt, and his once-commanding presence had dwindled to that of a broken man. His followers were nowhere to be seen, having fled during the chaos of the battle.

"What are we going to do with him?" someone in the group whispered, their voice trembling.

Maya approached Jace cautiously, her heart pounding. She crouched down, meeting his gaze. His piercing blue eyes, once filled with defiance, now held a mix of pain and defeat.

"You've lost, Jace," Maya said softly, her voice barely audible over the rustling of the group behind her. "Your people are gone. The warehouse is ours now."

Jace let out a bitter laugh, wincing as the movement aggravated his wounds. "And what now, Maya? You going to play judge, jury, and executioner?"

Maya's stomach churned. She hadn't thought this far ahead. The weight of the decision pressed down on her, threatening to crush her resolve. She glanced back at her group, seeing the expectant looks on their faces. They were waiting for her to decide Jace's fate.

"I don't know," she admitted, more to herself than to Jace. Her mind raced with possibilities, each one seeming more impossible than the last. Exile him? Keep him prisoner? The questions swirled in her head, making her dizzy with indecision.

Jace leaned in closer, his voice low and dangerous. "You're weak, Maya. You always have been. That's why you'll never survive in this world."

Maya stood abruptly, taking a step back. She turned to face her group, their expressions a mix of fear, anger, and uncertainty. The warehouse, once a symbol of hope and survival, now felt like a prison, trapping them all with an impossible choice.

"We need to decide what to do with him," Maya announced, her voice shaking slightly. "And we need to decide now."

Benji stepped forward, his usually jovial face hardened into a mask of grim determination. "We should kill him," he said, his voice flat and cold. The words hung in the air, shocking in their bluntness. Maya's eyes widened, unable to reconcile this new Benji with the carefree jokester she'd known.

"He's too dangerous to keep alive," Benji continued, gesturing towards Jace. "If we let him go, he'll just come back with more people. If we keep him here, he'll find a way to turn us against each other. The only way to be safe is to end this now."

Murmurs of agreement rippled through the group. Maya felt her chest tighten, her breath coming in short, sharp gasps. This wasn't the world she wanted to create. This wasn't the leadership she'd envisioned.

"No," she said, her voice barely above a whisper. Then, louder, "No. We're not killers."

Benji's eyes flashed with anger. "Wake up, Maya! Look around you. This isn't the world we used to live in. We have to do whatever it takes to survive."

Maya closed her eyes, trying to block out the carnage surrounding them. The weight of leadership pressed down on her shoulders, threatening to crush her. When she opened her eyes again, she met Benji's gaze steadily.

"If we do this, if we kill him in cold blood, we're no better than he is," she said, her voice growing stronger with each word. "We fought to take back this warehouse, to have a chance at building something better. If we start by executing our enemies, what kind of world are we really creating?"

The tension in the room was palpable. Maya could feel the eyes of her group on her, some supportive, others doubtful. She turned to look at Jace, who watched the exchange with a mixture of contempt and curiosity.

"We're not going to kill you," Maya told him, her voice firm despite the turmoil in her gut. "But you're not staying here either. We'll give you supplies for a few days, and then you're on your own. If you ever come back, if you ever threaten us again, we won't be so merciful."

Benji threw up his hands in frustration. "This is a mistake, Maya. You're going to get us all killed with your misplaced idealism."

Maya felt tears prick at the corners of her eyes, but she blinked them back. "Maybe," she admitted. "But at least we'll still be human."

As the group erupted into heated debate, Maya stood firm, her decision made. She knew the road ahead would be difficult, but in that moment, she clung to the belief that compassion wasn't weakness – it was the only thing that could save them all.

The warehouse echoed with the sound of hushed whispers and muffled sobs. Maya stood in the center of the cavernous space, her eyes scanning the faces of her group. Some looked at her with admiration, others with barely concealed resentment. The victory they'd fought so hard for felt hollow now.

"We need to regroup," Maya said, her voice cracking slightly. "Take stock of our supplies, tend to the wounded."

Benji stepped forward, his jaw clenched. "And what about the price we paid for your 'mercy', Maya? How many of us died because you couldn't make the tough call?"

Maya felt her chest tighten. "Every life lost weighs on me, Benji. But killing Jace wouldn't bring them back."

"No," Benji spat, "but it might have prevented future losses."

Riley moved to Maya's side, her usual cheerfulness replaced by a grim determination. "We can't change what's done. We need to focus on moving forward."

Maya nodded gratefully at Riley, but she could see the doubt in her friend's eyes. The group had fractured, and Maya wasn't sure how to piece it back together.

As she looked around, Maya's thoughts raced. 'How can I keep them united when I'm not even sure of my own choices? Was sparing Jace really the right call, or am I leading us all to ruin?'

"We'll divide into teams," Maya announced, pushing her doubts aside. "Some for inventory, others for medical care. We need to—"

"And who put you in charge?" a voice called out from the back. It was Liam, one of the newer members of the group. "Your leadership nearly got us all killed."

Maya felt her resolve wavering. "I... I'm open to suggestions. We can discuss—"

"Discuss what?" Benji interrupted. "How many more of us need to die before you realize that survival means making hard choices?"

The warehouse erupted into chaos, voices overlapping as accusations and arguments flew. Maya stood in the middle of it all, feeling more alone than ever.

'Is this how it ends?' she thought, her heart racing. 'Not with a victory, but with us tearing ourselves apart?'

Maya raised her hands, trying to calm the escalating tensions. "Everyone, please. We need to work together—"

"Work together?" Liam scoffed. "Look around, Maya. This 'victory' has cost us everything. We should leave this cursed city while we still can."

A chorus of agreement rose from several members, their faces etched with fear and exhaustion. Maya's stomach churned as she realized just how close they were to falling apart.

"Leave?" Riley interjected, her voice hoarse but determined. "And go where? The warehouse is our best chance at survival. We have supplies here, shelter—"

"And a target on our backs," Benji cut in, his eyes dark. "Every desperate soul out there knows what we have now. We'll be under constant threat."

Maya's mind raced, trying to find the right words to bring them back together. She took a deep breath, her voice steadier than she felt. "I know we've all suffered. But leaving isn't the answer. We've fought too hard for this place."

As she spoke, Maya scanned the faces of her group. Some nodded in agreement, while others turned away, unconvinced. The divide was palpable, a chasm threatening to swallow them whole.

'How can I bridge this gap?' Maya thought, her chest tight with anxiety. 'We've come so far, endured so much. But at what cost? And for what future?'

The weight of leadership pressed down on her shoulders, heavier than ever before. Maya wondered if she were truly the right person to guide them through this broken world, or if her idealism would be their downfall.

The warehouse fell into an uneasy silence as the group dispersed, each person retreating to their own corner to process the aftermath of the battle. Maya's eyes found Riley, her closest ally, slumped against a stack of crates. Even from a distance, Maya could see the toll the fight had taken on her friend.

Maya approached cautiously, her footsteps echoing in the cavernous space. "Riley? How are you holding up?"

Riley looked up, her usually bright green eyes now dull with exhaustion. She attempted a smile, but it didn't reach her eyes. "I'm... I'm okay, Maya. Only tired. We all are."

Maya sat down beside her, their shoulders touching. The physical contact was grounding, a reminder that they weren't alone in this chaos.

"I know," Maya said softly. "We've lost so much. But we're still here. That has to count for something, right?"

Riley nodded, but her voice wavered. "It does. I just... I keep seeing their faces. The ones we couldn't save."

Maya's chest tightened at Riley's words. She, too, was haunted by the faces of the fallen. "We did everything we could," she whispered, as much to herself as to Riley.

"Did we?" Riley asked, her tone sharper than usual. "Maybe if we'd been tougher from the start, made different choices..."

Maya flinched internally at the implied criticism, but she knew Riley wasn't wrong. The weight of every decision, every life lost, pressed down on her.

'Am I leading them to survival or to ruin?' Maya thought, her doubts threatening to overwhelm her.

Aloud, she said, "We can't change the past, Riley. All we can do is move forward, try to learn from our mistakes."

Riley sighed, her shoulders sagging. "I know. And I'm with you, Maya. I always will be. It's just... hard sometimes, to keep hoping."

Maya wrapped an arm around Riley's shoulders, drawing strength from her friend's presence even as she offered comfort. "Hope is all we have left," she said quietly. "We have to hold onto it, no matter what."

As they sat there, surrounded by the remnants of their battle, Maya couldn't shake the feeling that their greatest challenges were still to come. The group might have won the warehouse, but keeping it – and themselves – together would be a fight all its own.

The warehouse door creaked open, and Benji stalked in, his face a mask of barely contained fury. Gone was the carefree jokester, replaced by a hardened shell of cynicism. He kicked a piece of debris, sending it skittering across the floor.

"We need to talk, Maya," he growled, his eyes flashing. "This… this 'mercy' of yours? It's going to get us all killed."

Maya straightened, steeling herself for the confrontation. "What would you have me do, Benji? Execute Jace in cold blood?"

Benji laughed, a harsh, bitter sound that echoed through the warehouse. "Maybe! At least then we'd know he wouldn't come back to slit our throats in our sleep."

Maya's stomach churned at the thought, but she held her ground. "That's not who we are. That's not who I am."

"Then maybe you shouldn't be leading us!" Benji shouted, his words cutting through the air like a knife.

Maya flinched, the words hitting her like a physical blow. She opened her mouth to respond, but movement in the corner caught her eye. Tariq, silent as always, was watching the exchange with cold, calculating eyes.

'He's weighing his options,' Maya realized with a sinking feeling. 'Deciding if it's worth staying with us.'

"Benji," she said, trying to keep her voice steady, "I understand you're angry. We all are. But turning on each other isn't the answer."

Benji shook his head, a sneer twisting his features. "Your way isn't working, Maya. Look around you. How many more have to die before you realize that?"

As Maya struggled to find a response, she noticed Tariq silently slipping away, disappearing into the shadows of the warehouse. The gesture spoke volumes, and Maya felt a chill run down her spine.

'We're falling apart,' she thought, panic rising in her chest. 'And I don't know how to hold us together.'

The morning sun filtered weakly through the warehouse's grimy windows, casting long shadows across the concrete floor. Maya stood at the entrance, her eyes scanning the makeshift graves they'd dug in the lot outside. Seven mounds of freshly turned earth, each marked with a crude cross fashioned from scrap wood.

"It's time," she said softly, her voice cracking.

The group gathered silently, their faces etched with grief and exhaustion. Riley stepped forward, clutching a handful of wilted flowers she'd managed to scavenge from the overgrown parking lot.

As they approached the graves, Maya's throat tightened. She'd known each of the fallen - their hopes, their fears, their dreams of a better future. Now, they were nothing but names to be etched into wood.

"We're here to remember," Maya began, her voice barely above a whisper. "To honor those who gave everything for our survival."

She paused, struggling to find the right words. How could she possibly encapsulate the weight of their loss?

Benji's bitter laugh cut through the silence. "Remember? Fat lot of good that'll do them now."

Maya flinched, but Riley stepped in, her green eyes flashing. "They deserve our respect, Benji. They were our friends."

"Friends who'd still be alive if we'd made different choices," Benji muttered, but he fell silent under Riley's glare.

Maya closed her eyes, fighting back tears. 'He's right,' she thought. 'If I'd been stronger, faster, smarter...'

She pushed the thought away, focusing on the task at hand. One by one, they laid the meager flowers on each grave. As Maya placed her last stem, she whispered, "I'm sorry. I'm so sorry."

The group stood in silence, the weight of their loss settling over them like a heavy blanket. Maya looked at their faces - some tear-streaked, others hardened with barely contained anger. She saw their pain, their fear, their doubt.

'How do we move forward from this?' she wondered, her chest tight with grief and uncertainty. 'How do we honor their sacrifice?'

As if sensing her thoughts, Riley reached out and squeezed Maya's hand. It was a small gesture, but in that moment, it meant everything.

"We keep going," Riley said softly. "For them."

Maya nodded, swallowing hard. "For them," she echoed, her voice gaining strength. "We remember, we honor, and we keep fighting for a better world. It's what they would have wanted."

She looked at each member of the group, even meeting Benji's hostile gaze. "We're still here. We're still together. And as long as we have that, we have hope."

The words felt hollow, even to her own ears, but she forced herself to believe them. They had to believe them. It was the only way to survive.

Maya stood alone at the edge of the makeshift graveyard, her eyes fixed on the mounds of freshly turned earth. Each pile represented a life lost, a future stolen. The weight of responsibility pressed down on her shoulders, threatening to crush her.

"I led them here," she whispered, her voice barely audible over the soft autumn breeze. "I made the decisions that brought us to this moment."

She knelt, running her fingers through the cool dirt. The faces of the fallen flashed through her mind - their hopes, their fears, their trust in her leadership. A lump formed in her throat.

"Was it worth it?" Maya asked herself, her internal voice filled with doubt. "Am I truly capable of leading them forward, or am I just prolonging their suffering?"

Riley approached, her footsteps hesitant. "Maya? The others are asking what we should do next."

Maya stood, brushing the dirt from her hands. She turned to face Riley, seeing the exhaustion etched in her friend's face.

"What do you think we should do, Riley?" Maya asked, her voice low.

Riley's eyes widened slightly. "Me? I... I don't know. I thought you would have a plan."

Maya looked back at the graves. "I thought I did. I thought I knew what was right. But now..." She trailed off, her gaze distant.

"We won," Riley said, but her voice lacked conviction. "That has to count for something, right?"

Maya's laugh was bitter. "Did we? Look around, Riley. What have we really won?"

She gestured to the warehouse, to the battered survivors milling about, to the fresh graves. "We've lost our innocence, our hope. Maybe even our unity. Victory shouldn't feel like this."

Riley was silent for a moment. Then, softly, "What are you saying, Maya?"

Maya turned back to her friend, her eyes filled with a mix of determination and uncertainty. "I'm saying that even if we survived this battle, we might have lost something more important. And I don't know if I can get it back for us."

Maya took a deep breath, her shoulders squaring as she faced the remnants of her group. The warehouse, once a symbol of hope and survival, now felt oppressive with its lingering scent of smoke and blood. She cleared her throat, drawing the attention of the weary survivors.

"We've been through hell," Maya began, her voice steady despite the tremor in her hands. "But we're still here. We need to decide our next move."

The group gathered around her, their faces a mosaic of exhaustion, grief, and uncertainty. Maya's gaze swept over them, noting the absence of familiar faces and the haunted look in the eyes of those who remained.

Benji, his arm in a makeshift sling, spoke up. "What's there to decide? We fought for this place. We stay put."

Maya nodded, but hesitated. "That's one option. But we need to consider if it's still safe here, if we have enough supplies—"

"Safe?" Tariq interrupted, his usually quiet voice sharp with bitterness. "Nowhere's safe anymore. This is as good as it gets."

Murmurs of agreement rippled through the group. Maya felt a pang of uncertainty. She had always been the one with the answers, the plans, but now her words felt hollow, even to herself.

"We could try to find other survivors," she suggested, but even as she spoke, she saw the doubt in their eyes.

Riley stepped forward, her loyalty to Maya evident despite her own visible exhaustion. "Maya's right. We should at least consider all our options."

But Maya could see the weariness in Riley's stance, the way her friend's usual optimism seemed forced. She wondered if Riley honestly believed in her leadership anymore, or if she was just going through the motions.

As the group continued to debate, their voices a dull roar in her ears, Maya's thoughts raced. 'Am I still the right person to lead them? Have I brought them this far only to fail them now?'

She looked around at the faces turned towards her, expectant, desperate for guidance. The weight of their trust, their lives, pressed down on her like a physical force. Maya swallowed hard, realizing that the question of her leadership wasn't just brewing in her own mind – it was evident in every uncertain glance, every hesitant word from her group.

"Whatever we decide," Maya said finally, her voice cutting through the chatter, "we decide together. That's how we've survived this far, and that's how we'll keep going."

But even as she spoke, Maya couldn't shake the feeling that her words were falling on deaf ears. The unity they once had seemed to be slipping away, and she wasn't sure if she had the strength to hold them together much longer.

The tension in the warehouse was palpable as Benji stepped forward, his once-jovial face now etched with lines of exhaustion and frustration. He locked eyes with Maya, his voice cutting through the uneasy silence.

"Look, Maya," Benji said, his tone sharp and brittle, "I can't be the only one thinking it. Your leadership... it's costing us too much."

Maya felt a jolt in her chest, but kept her face impassive as Benji continued.

"Sparing Jace? That was a mistake. We need someone who can make the tough calls, someone who understands that in this world, mercy gets you killed."

Murmurs of agreement rippled through the group. Maya's stomach churned as she watched faces she'd come to know turn away from her, unable to meet her gaze.

"We need a leader who can keep us alive," Benji pressed, his words gaining momentum. "Not someone who's going to get us all killed because they can't make the hard choices."

Maya opened her mouth to respond, but Riley beat her to it. "That's not fair, Benji," Riley interjected, stepping between them. "Maya's kept us alive this far. She-"

But even as Riley spoke, Maya could hear the hesitation in her friend's voice. The usual fire was missing, replaced by a quiet uncertainty that cut deeper than Benji's accusations.

'Is this how it ends?' Maya thought, her mind racing. 'Do I fight to keep control, or is it time to step aside?'

She looked around at the faces of her group, seeing the doubt, the fear, the exhaustion mirrored in each of them. The weight of leadership had never felt heavier.

Maya slipped away from the group, their voices fading as she made her way to the far corner of the warehouse. She climbed a stack of crates, settling on the highest one with her back against the cold concrete wall. From here, she could see the entire floor, littered with debris and makeshift sleeping areas.

The morning light filtered through dirty windows, casting long shadows across the space. Maya hugged her knees to her chest, her eyes tracing the cracks spider-webbing across the floor—a stark reminder of the earthquake that had shattered their world.

She closed her eyes, memories of the past weeks flooding her mind. The initial chaos, the desperate scramble for supplies, the hard-fought battles—each decision weighing on her like a physical burden.

"What does it even mean to survive anymore?" she whispered to herself, her voice barely audible.

Opening her eyes, Maya watched as Riley tended to a wounded group member, her movements gentle but her face etched with fatigue. Nearby, Benji paced restlessly, his posture tense and guarded.

Maya's thoughts drifted to the world before—a world of rules, of order, of simple morality. Now, those certainties lay in ruins, much like the city around them.

"We're all just... animals now, aren't we?" she murmured, her words tinged with bitterness. "Fighting over scraps, turning on each other."

She ran a hand through her tangled hair, wincing as her fingers caught on a knot. The gesture reminded her of simpler times—of brushing her hair before school, of worrying about tests and crushes. How quickly it had all fallen away.

"Maya?" Riley's voice called from below. "Are you okay up there?"

Maya peered down at her friend, forcing a smile. "Just... thinking."

Riley's brow furrowed with concern. "Want to talk about it?"

For a moment, Maya considered confiding in Riley, sharing the doubts that plagued her. But the memory of Riley's hesitation earlier held her back.

"I'm fine," Maya replied, her voice steadier than she felt. "Just needed some air."

As Riley nodded and turned away, Maya's gaze drifted back to the warehouse floor. In this broken world, what did it mean to be human anymore? To hold onto compassion when every instinct screamed for self-preservation?

She had no answers, only the weight of responsibility and the gnawing fear that in trying to save everyone, she might end up losing herself.

Maya's fingers traced the rough edge of a broken window frame, the glass long since shattered. The cool autumn air whispered through, carrying the scent of rain and decay. She closed her eyes, letting the chill ground her in the present moment.

"We're not animals," she whispered, her voice barely audible. "We can't be."

Her mind raced, grappling with the weight of leadership in this harsh new reality. Images flashed before her: Jace's defeated form, the anguish in Benji's eyes, the quiet desperation of her fractured group.

"Leadership isn't just about survival," Maya mused aloud, her words meant for no one but herself. "It's about remembering who we are, what makes us... us."

She opened her eyes, gazing out at the ruined cityscape. The overcast sky cast everything in a muted grey, as if the world itself was in mourning.

"Maybe that's what sets us apart," she continued, her voice growing stronger. "The ability to choose compassion, even when it's hard. Especially when it's hard."

A floorboard creaked behind her, and Maya turned to see Benji standing in the doorway, his face a mask of conflicted emotions.

"You really believe that?" he asked, his tone a mixture of skepticism and longing. "After everything we've seen?"

Maya met his gaze, unflinching. "I have to, Benji. The moment we stop believing in our humanity is the moment we truly lose everything."

Benji's shoulders slumped, the anger from earlier seeming to drain out of him. "I want to believe that, Maya. I do. But how can we hold onto those ideals when the world keeps demanding we let them go?"

Maya stepped towards him, her resolve strengthening with each word. "By making the choice, every single day, to be more than just survivors. To be human, in all its messy, complicated glory."

As she spoke, Maya felt something settle within her. The doubts were still there, but alongside them was a renewed sense of purpose. She may not have all the answers, but she knew, with unwavering certainty, that abandoning their humanity was not the solution.

"I don't know what the future holds," Maya admitted, her voice soft but determined. "But I do know that I won't give up on us. On what makes us human. No matter how broken the world becomes."

The warehouse echoed with the shuffling of tired feet and muted whispers as Maya's group gathered in the center, their faces etched with weariness and uncertainty. Maya stood before them, her brown hair pulled back in a messy ponytail, her eyes scanning the faces of those who remained.

"We've fought hard to secure this place," Maya began, her voice steady despite the exhaustion that threatened to overtake her. "The warehouse offers us shelter, supplies, a chance to catch our breath."

She paused, noticing the mix of relief and apprehension on the faces before her. Some nodded in agreement, while others shifted uneasily, their gazes darting towards the exits.

"I propose we stay here, at least for now," Maya continued, her hands gesturing to the vast space around them. "We can use the resources we've gained to rebuild our strength, to heal."

A murmur rippled through the group. Maya could feel the weight of their expectations, their fears, pressing down on her. She took a deep breath, steeling herself for what she needed to say next.

"But I want to be clear," she said, her voice softening. "This isn't an order. It's a suggestion. I know some of you might want to leave, to find your own way. And... that's okay."

The words felt heavy on her tongue, but Maya knew they needed to be said. She'd promised herself she wouldn't become the kind of leader who ruled through fear or force.

Riley stepped forward, her usually bright eyes dimmed with fatigue. "Maya, are you sure about this? Letting people leave could weaken us even further."

Maya nodded, her gaze never wavering. "I'm sure, Riley. We can't force people to stay. That's not who we are. That's not who I want us to be."

As she spoke, Maya's mind raced with doubt. Was she making the right choice? Would this decision lead to the group's collapse? But deep down, she knew that holding onto their humanity, their right to choose, was worth the risk.

"So," Maya concluded, her voice carrying across the warehouse, "the choice is yours. Stay and help us rebuild, or seek your own path. Whatever you decide, know that you have my support."

The silence that followed was deafening, filled with the weight of impending decisions and an uncertain future.

Maya scanned the faces of her group, searching for any sign of hope or unity. Instead, she found a sea of uncertainty and hesitation. The air in the warehouse felt thick with tension, as if the very atmosphere were holding its breath, waiting for someone to make a move.

Tariq, who had been standing near the back, shifted his weight and cleared his throat. "I... appreciate the honesty, Maya," he said, his voice low and measured. "But I'm not sure staying here is the best option for everyone."

Maya's heart sank, but she nodded, forcing herself to maintain a neutral expression. "I understand, Tariq. You've always been one to forge your own path."

As if Tariq's words had broken a dam, others began to murmur among themselves. Maya could see small groups forming, some nodding in agreement with Tariq, others looking conflicted.

"We can't just abandon everything we've fought for," a voice called out. It was Benji, his face still bruised from the battle. "We've bled for this place. Are we really going to let it all fall apart now?"

Maya stepped forward, her hands raised in a placating gesture. "No one's abandoning anything, Benji. We're just... acknowledging that we all have choices to make."

Inside, Maya's thoughts were a whirlwind of doubt and fear. Am I making a terrible mistake? Should I be forcing them to stay together? But she pushed those thoughts aside, clinging to her belief in the importance of free will.

"Look," she said, her voice steady despite her inner turmoil, "I know we're all scared. We're all hurting. But we're stronger together, even if that means our numbers are smaller. Those who want to stay, we'll rebuild. We'll make this place safe again."

She paused, looking each person in the eye. "But I won't hold anyone here against their will. That's not what we fought for."

The silence that followed was heavy with unspoken decisions. Maya could feel the fragile threads of their unity stretching, threatening to snap at any moment. She held her breath, wondering how many would choose to remain, and how many would walk away from everything they'd built together.

Maya turned away from the group, her steps echoing in the cavernous warehouse as she walked towards the large, broken windows overlooking the ruined city. The stark landscape stretched before her, a tapestry of destruction and desolation. Shattered buildings jutted like broken teeth against the pale sky, while smoke still curled from distant fires.

She pressed her palm against the cool glass, her reflection staring back at her - tired eyes, tightened jaw, the weight of responsibility etched into every line of her face. Behind her, she could hear the murmurs of her group, their voices a mix of uncertainty and fear.

"What do you see out there, Maya?" Riley's soft voice broke through her thoughts.

Maya didn't turn around as she answered, "I see... possibility. And danger. Both in equal measure."

She felt Riley's presence beside her, a comforting warmth in the chill of the warehouse. "You really think we can rebuild? After everything?"

Maya's gaze swept over the devastated cityscape. Her voice was low, almost a whisper, "We have to try. What's the alternative?"

She turned to face Riley, noting the doubt clouding her friend's eyes. "This warehouse, it's not just about survival anymore. It's about proving that we can be more than just survivors. That we can rebuild, not just buildings, but... us. Our humanity."

Riley nodded slowly, but Maya could see the hesitation in her stance. "And if we can't? If it's too much?"

Maya's hand clenched at her side, her nails digging into her palm. "Then we'll have tried. That has to count for something, right?"

She looked back out at the ruined city, her thoughts racing. We've won the battle, but at what cost? How many more battles lie ahead? Can I really lead them through this?

The weight of leadership pressed down on her shoulders, threatening to crush her. But as she stood there, looking out over the remnants of their world, a flicker of determination ignited in her chest. They had survived this far. They had fought for this warehouse, for the chance to build something more than just day-to-day survival.

Maya squared her shoulders, her voice gaining strength as she spoke to Riley, but loud enough for the others to hear. "The real fight starts now. We've proven we can survive. Now we need to prove we can live."

Maya's words hung in the air, heavy with promise and uncertainty. She turned away from the window, her eyes scanning the warehouse interior. The flickering light of makeshift lanterns cast long shadows across the faces of her battered group.

"We've all lost something," Maya said, her voice low but firm. "But we're still here. Still standing."

Benji scoffed from his corner, arms crossed tightly over his chest. "Standing on what? The graves of our friends?"

Maya flinched, but held her ground. "On hope, Benji. On the belief that we can be more than just survivors scraping by."

She walked towards the center of the room, feeling the weight of every eye upon her. The choices she'd made - sparing Jace, leading them into battle - they'd cost them dearly. Those decisions would haunt her, she knew, in the quiet moments between breaths, in the darkness before dawn.

But what choice did I have? she thought. To become the very thing, we're fighting against?

"I know I've asked a lot of you," Maya continued, her voice catching. "And I know some of you doubt whether I should be leading at all."

Riley stepped forward, her hand reaching out to touch Maya's arm. "Maya, we-"

"No," Maya cut her off gently. "It's okay. I doubt myself too." She took a deep breath, steeling herself. "But I also know that giving up isn't an option. Not for any of us."

She looked around the room, meeting each pair of eyes in turn. Some were filled with exhaustion, others with a spark of defiance, and still others with a glimmer of hope.

"The path ahead... it's not going to be easy," Maya admitted. "There will be more challenges, more hard choices. But we face them together, or not at all."

As she spoke, Maya could feel the resolve hardening within her. The doubt was still there, a constant companion, but it no longer threatened to overwhelm her.

She walked back to the window, gazing out at the broken skyline of their once-thriving city. The sun was setting, painting the ruins in shades of gold and red. It was beautiful, in its own haunting way.

This is our world now, Maya thought. Broken, but not beyond repair. Changed, but not without hope.

She turned back to her group, her family now, really. "Tomorrow, we start rebuilding. Not just this warehouse, but ourselves. Who's with me?"

The silence that followed seemed to stretch for an eternity. Then, slowly, one by one, hands began to raise. Not everyone, not yet. But enough. Enough to start.

Maya nodded, a small smile tugging at the corners of her mouth. "Then let's get to work."

As the group began to disperse, each to their own tasks, Maya remained by the window. The last rays of sunlight caught her face, illuminating the determination in her eyes and the weight of responsibility etched into the lines of her face.

The future was uncertain, fraught with danger and difficult choices. But they would face it together, one day at a time. And maybe, just maybe, they would find a way not just to survive, but to truly live again.

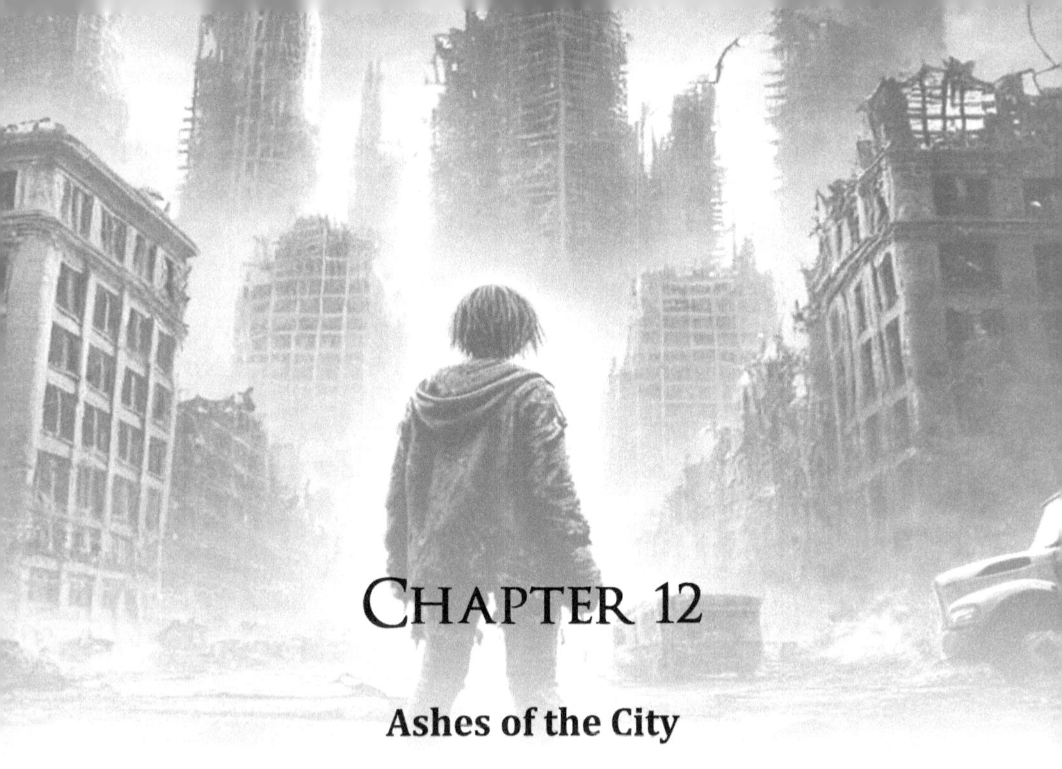

CHAPTER 12

Ashes of the City

The warehouse echoed with the shuffling of feet and whispered conversations as Maya stood before the group, her eyes scanning the faces of those who remained. The flickering light of scavenged lanterns cast long shadows across the concrete floor, a stark reminder of how far they'd fallen from the world they once knew.

Maya took a deep breath, steadying herself. "We can't stay here forever," she began, her voice calm but firm. "This city... it's not our home anymore. It's time we looked for something new, somewhere we can start over."

The words hung in the air, heavy with implication. Maya's gaze fell on Tariq, standing at the edge of the group, his arms crossed and his expression unreadable. She felt a pang of unease as she noticed the distance in his eyes.

"And go where?" a voice called out from the crowd. "There's nothing out there but more ruins."

Maya's jaw tightened. "We don't know that. But what we do know is that staying here means slowly running out of supplies and living in constant fear of the next aftershock or attack."

She paused, looking at each face in turn. Some nodded in agreement, while others looked skeptical or afraid. The weight of their expectations pressed down on her shoulders, threatening to crush her resolve.

"I understand the fear," Maya continued, her voice softening. "But we've survived this far by sticking together, by looking out for each other. We can do this."

A movement caught her eye. Tariq stepped forward, his tall frame casting a long shadow across the floor. "No," he said, his voice low and firm. "We can't."

Maya's heart sank. She had sensed this coming, but hearing it still felt like a blow. "Tariq-"

"I'm leaving," he interrupted, his dark eyes meeting hers with a cold determination. "On my own."

A murmur rippled through the group. Maya fought to keep her expression neutral, even as her mind raced. How many others felt the same way? How many more would she lose?

"We're stronger together," she argued, trying to keep the desperation out of her voice. "The journey will be dangerous-"

Tariq shook his head. "It's more dangerous to rely on others. I've watched, Maya. I've seen how quickly people turn on each other when resources get scarce. My survival depends on me, and me alone."

His words stung, a harsh reminder of the violence and betrayal they'd witnessed in the weeks since the earthquake. Maya wanted to argue, to remind him of all they'd accomplished together, but she knew it would be futile. The distance in Tariq's eyes told her his mind was made up.

"If that's your decision," she said softly, "I won't stop you. But know that you'll always have a place with us, if you change your mind."

Tariq nodded once, then turned and walked away, his footsteps echoing in the sudden silence. Maya watched him go, her chest tight with a mixture of sadness and fear. She wondered how many others would follow his lead, how many more fractures would appear in the fragile community they'd built.

As the group began to disperse, their whispered conversations a buzz of uncertainty, Maya closed her eyes for a moment. The weight of leadership pressed down on her, heavier than ever. She had to be strong, had to believe in the path she was choosing. But as she opened her eyes and looked at the dwindling group before her, she couldn't help but wonder if she was leading them towards salvation or doom.

Benji kicked at a piece of rubble, his once-cheerful face now a mask of conflicted emotions. "You know, Maya," he said, his voice low and gravelly, "Tariq might have a point. Every man for himself and all that jazz."

Maya's heart sank. She'd always counted on Benji's optimism, his ability to lift spirits even in the darkest moments. But now, as she met his eyes, she saw only weariness and doubt.

"Is that what you really believe, Benji?" she asked, trying to keep the desperation out of her voice.

He shrugged, avoiding her gaze. "I don't know what I believe anymore. This world..." he gestured at the ruins around them, "it's not the one we knew. Maybe we need to adapt."

Maya took a step towards him, her mind racing. She couldn't lose another member of their group, not now. "Adapting doesn't mean abandoning each other," she said firmly. "We're stronger together, Benji. You know that."

As Benji wrestled with his decision, Riley stepped forward, her green eyes blazing with determination. "She's right," Riley said, placing a hand on Benji's shoulder. "Look at what we've survived so far. We did that as a team."

Maya felt a surge of gratitude towards Riley. Even as everything else crumbled around them, their bond remained unshakeable. It gave her strength, a reminder of why she fought so hard to keep the group together.

Benji looked between them, his internal struggle visible on his face. Finally, he let out a long sigh. "Alright," he said, a ghost of his old smile flickering across his lips. "I guess I'm not cut out for the lone wolf lifestyle anyway."

Relief washed over Maya, but she knew the battle wasn't over. Trust, once fractured, wasn't easily mended. She'd have to work to rebuild Benji's faith in her leadership, in their shared vision of survival.

"Thank you," she said softly, meeting Benji's eyes. "We need you, Benji. Your humor, your spirit... it's part of what keeps us human."

As the tension eased slightly, Riley turned to Maya, her expression serious but supportive. "So, we're really doing this? Leaving the city?"

Maya nodded, her gaze sweeping over the devastated landscape. "We have to. There's nothing left for us here but ghosts and bad memories."

"It won't be easy," Riley warned, but there was no hesitation in her voice. "We don't know what's out there."

"No," Maya agreed, feeling the weight of the unknown pressing down on her. "But we'll face it together. That's the only way we survive."

As they stood there, the small group united in their decision to venture into the unknown, Maya felt a mix of fear and hope. The city had changed them all, hardened them in ways they never expected. But as she looked at Riley's unwavering support and Benji's tentative trust, she knew that they hadn't lost their humanity. Not yet. And as long as they held onto that, there was hope for a new beginning.

Maya took a deep breath, her eyes scanning the warehouse that had been their temporary sanctuary. "Alright, everyone. We need to gather whatever supplies we can carry. Food, water, medical kits—anything essential."

Riley nodded, her green eyes sharp with focus. "I'll start sorting through our food stores. We should prioritize non-perishables and high-energy snacks."

As Riley moved away, Maya caught Benji's eye. "Benji, can you check our medical supplies? Make sure we have enough first aid materials for the road?"

Benji hesitated for a moment, his jaw clenching. Then he gave a curt nod. "Yeah, I'm on it."

Maya watched him go, her heart heavy. She turned to the rest of the group, raising her voice slightly. "Remember, we can only take what we can carry. Think practical, think survival."

As the others dispersed, Maya began rummaging through a pile of discarded backpacks. Her fingers trembled slightly as she sorted through the items. How did it come to this? Scavenging through the remnants of their old lives, preparing to leave behind everything they'd ever known?

"Hey," Riley's voice broke through her thoughts. "You okay?"

Maya forced a smile. "Just... processing. It's a big step."

Riley's hand found Maya's shoulder, squeezing gently. "We're doing the right thing. This city... it's not home anymore."

Maya nodded, swallowing hard. "I know. I just hope I'm not leading us into something worse."

"You're not," Riley said firmly. "We trust you, Maya. Even Benji, despite everything."

As if on cue, Benji approached, his arms full of medical supplies. "We've got enough bandages and antiseptic to last a while, but we're low on pain meds."

Maya nodded, grateful for his report. "Thanks, Benji. We'll make do. Maybe we can find more along the way."

As they worked, the atmosphere remained somber but determined. Maya could feel the weight of their decision in every carefully packed item, every hushed conversation. They were leaving behind the ruins of their old world, stepping into an unknown future. But as she looked at her small, battered group, Maya felt a flicker of hope. They were survivors. They were together. And maybe, just maybe, that would be enough.

Maya's eyes scanned the desolate cityscape through a broken window, her heart heavy as she witnessed the devastation. Crumbling buildings stood like skeletal remains of a once-thriving metropolis, their jagged edges jutting into the overcast sky. The streets below were littered with debris and abandoned vehicles, a stark reminder of the chaos that had consumed their world.

"It's like a ghost town," she murmured, more to herself than anyone else.

Riley appeared at her side, following Maya's gaze. "Hard to believe this was home just a few weeks ago."

Maya nodded, her throat tight. "We've all changed so much. Sometimes I barely recognize myself, let alone..." She trailed off, gesturing vaguely at their companions.

Benji's gruff voice cut through the somber atmosphere. "We need to get moving. Daylight's wasting."

As they resumed packing, Maya's thoughts drifted to each member of their group. Riley, once carefree and bubbly, now carried a quiet determination in her eyes. Benji, hardened by conflict, moved with a wariness that spoke of battles fought and scars earned. And herself? Maya felt the weight of leadership etched into every decision, every sleepless night.

"Do you think we'll ever find somewhere safe?" Riley asked softly, zipping up a backpack.

Maya paused, choosing her words carefully. "I don't know. But I do know we can't stay here. This city... it's not just broken. It's toxic. We need a fresh start."

As they shouldered their packs and prepared to leave, Maya took one last look at the city that had once been their home. The bittersweet ache of departure mingled with a spark of hope for what lay ahead. Whatever the future held, they would face it together.

Maya took a deep breath, her eyes scanning the remnants of their once-vibrant city. The crumbling buildings and debris-strewn streets felt like a physical manifestation of their shattered lives. She turned to face her small group, her voice steady despite the emotions churning within her.

"Before we go, I think we should take a moment. To say goodbye."

Riley stepped forward, her green eyes bright with unshed tears. "This place... it's where we grew up, where we dreamed. But now, it's also where we learned to survive." She reached out, touching a nearby wall. "Goodbye, old friend. Thanks for sheltering us one last time."

Maya watched as Benji shifted uncomfortably, his usual jokes absent. He cleared his throat, his voice gruff. "Never been good at goodbyes. But... yeah. Thanks for the memories, I guess." His attempt at nonchalance couldn't quite mask the pain in his eyes.

"Benji," Maya said softly, "it's okay to feel."

He shrugged, turning away. "Feeling's what gets you killed these days."

Riley spoke up, her voice filled with quiet determination. "No, it's what keeps us human. We can't forget that, even now." She looked at Maya, a small smile on her freckled face. "Where we're going, we'll build something new. Something better."

Maya felt a surge of gratitude for Riley's unwavering optimism. "You're right. This isn't just an ending. It's a beginning too."

As they stood there, surrounded by the ruins of their past, Maya felt a complex mix of emotions wash over her. Grief for what was lost, fear of the unknown, but also a flickering hope for what they might become.

"We carry this place with us," she said, her voice barely above a whisper. "Not just the rubble and the pain, but the strength we found here too."

Maya's words hung in the air as a figure emerged from the shadows. Tariq, his lean frame silhouetted against the dim light, approached the group. His dark eyes scanned their faces, betraying no emotion.

"So, this is it then," Tariq said, his voice low and measured. "You're all leaving."

Maya stepped forward, her heart heavy. "Yes, we are. And you're not coming with us, are you?"

Tariq shook his head, a ghost of a smile on his lips. "No. My path lies elsewhere."

"Where will you go?" Riley asked, concern evident in her voice.

"Does it matter?" Tariq replied, his tone cool. "In this world, we're all just wanderers now."

Maya watched him, understanding the resolve behind his words. She'd seen it building for days, the distance growing between Tariq and the others. "I wish you'd reconsider," she said softly. "There's strength in numbers."

Tariq's gaze met hers, unwavering. "Perhaps. But there's freedom in solitude." He paused, then added, "I've always walked alone, Maya. This world... it just makes it official."

Maya nodded, respecting his decision even as it pained her. "Then I wish you luck, Tariq. May you find what you're looking for out there."

As Tariq turned to leave, Maya felt a surge of emotions. She closed her eyes, taking a deep breath. In her mind, she saw faces – friends lost, innocence shattered. Her voice barely a whisper, she began to speak.

"For those we've lost," she murmured, "and for the world that was. We remember you. We carry you with us."

Riley's hand found Maya's, squeezing gently. Benji bowed his head, his usual bravado absent.

Maya continued, her voice growing stronger. "We honor your memory by surviving, by holding onto our humanity. In this new world, we'll build something worthy of your sacrifice."

As she finished, Maya opened her eyes, meeting the gazes of her remaining companions. In that moment, surrounded by the ruins of their past, they stood united, ready to face whatever lay ahead.

Maya's footsteps echoed on the cracked pavement as she led her small group away from the warehouse. The weight of leadership pressed down on her shoulders, heavier than the backpack she carried. She glanced back at Riley and Benji, their faces a mix of determination and fear.

"You okay?" Riley asked, catching up to walk beside her.

Maya nodded, her ponytail bobbing with the motion. "Just... thinking."

"Dangerous pastime," Benji quipped, his attempt at humor falling flat in the eerie silence of the abandoned streets.

Maya's mind raced, replaying every decision she'd made since the earthquake. The faces of those they'd lost flashed before her eyes — friends, classmates, strangers who'd become family in the chaos.

"I never asked for this," she murmured, more to herself than the others.

"Asked for what?" Riley prodded gently.

Maya gestured around them. "To lead. To be responsible for lives. Every choice I make... it ripples. People live or die because of me."

Benji scoffed. "People live or die because the world went to shit, Maya. Don't give yourself that much credit."

"Benji!" Riley admonished, but Maya shook her head.

"No, he's right. But that doesn't change the fact that my decisions matter. The warehouse, the supply runs, even this..." She paused, looking at the ruined skyline. "Leaving the city. It all falls on me."

As they walked, Maya's thoughts drifted to the countless nights she'd lain awake, questioning every move. The weight of each life lost, each sacrifice made, bore down on her.

"You know," she said, her voice barely above a whisper, "I used to think leadership was about having all the answers. Being strong, never doubting. But now..."

Riley touched her arm. "Now what?"

Maya stopped, turning to face her friends. "Now I realize it's about making the hard choices, even when you're terrified. It's about carrying the burden, so others don't have to. And sometimes... sometimes it's about admitting you don't have all the answers."

Benji's usually hard expression softened slightly. "For what it's worth, I think you're doing alright. We're still breathing, aren't we?"

Maya managed a small smile. "Yeah, we are. But it's more than just survival now. We have to find a way to live, to build something new. That's the real challenge."

As they resumed walking, the enormity of their situation settled over them. Maya felt the weight of every life she'd touched, every decision that had brought them to this moment. But with that weight came a newfound resolve. Whatever lay ahead, she would face it – not just for herself, but for those who looked to her for guidance in this broken world.

Maya's gaze swept over the desolate cityscape, her heart heavy with the memories of all they'd endured. The crumbling buildings and debris-strewn streets were a stark reminder of the choices she'd been forced to make. Yet, even as she recalled the problematic decisions, a quiet strength began to take root within her.

"You know," she said, her voice soft but steady, "I've made mistakes. We all have. But I've never compromised on what matters most – our humanity."

Riley nodded, her eyes shining with understanding. "That's why we follow you, Maya. You've kept us together, kept us... human."

Maya's hand instinctively reached for the locket around her neck, a gift from her mother before the earthquake. "It would have been easier sometimes to give in to anger, to let aggression rule. But that's not who we are. That's not who I want us to be."

Benji, his face etched with the hardships they'd faced, spoke up. "But has it been enough? Look around us, Maya. The world's gone to hell."

"Maybe," Maya replied, her voice gaining strength. "But we're still here. Still fighting. And not just for survival, but for something more."

As they walked, Maya felt a subtle shift within herself. The burden of leadership remained, but it no longer felt like a crushing weight. Instead, it was a mantle she chose to wear, a responsibility she embraced.

"I've realized something," she said, pausing to face her companions. "Leading isn't about control. It's about showing the way, even when the path isn't clear."

Riley squeezed her hand. "And you've done that, Maya. Even when things were at their worst."

Maya nodded, a quiet determination settling over her. "We're in this together. Whatever comes next, we face it as one. Not because I demand it, but because we choose it."

As they continued their journey, leaving behind the ruins of their old lives, Maya felt a sense of peace amidst the uncertainty. The world might demand brutality, but she would continue to lead with compassion, guiding her people towards a future where humanity could flourish once again.

The crunch of broken glass underfoot echoed through the empty streets as Maya led her group away from the warehouse that had been their temporary sanctuary. The once-bustling city now stood as a silent monument to destruction, its towering skyscrapers reduced to skeletal frames reaching desperately towards a leaden sky.

Maya paused, her eyes scanning the desolate landscape. "This is it," she said, her voice barely above a whisper. "Our last look at what was once home."

Riley stepped up beside her, squinting at the horizon. "It's hard to believe it's the same place."

"Yeah," Benji muttered, kicking at a piece of debris. "Like a nightmare you can't wake up from."

Maya's gaze swept over her companions, noting the weariness etched into their faces. She felt a pang of guilt, wondering if she was leading them towards salvation or further into danger. But there was no turning back now.

"We've survived this long," Maya said, forcing conviction into her voice. "We'll make it through whatever comes next."

As they trudged through the ruins, Maya's mind raced with memories of the life they were leaving behind. The laughter in school hallways, the bustle of weekend markets, the simple joy of a family dinner – all of it seemed like a distant dream now.

"Do you think we'll ever find somewhere... normal again?" Riley asked, breaking the heavy silence.

Maya considered her answer carefully. "Normal might not exist anymore. But we can build something new. Something better, maybe."

Benji scoffed. "Better than this shouldn't be too hard."

Despite the bleakness of their surroundings, Maya felt a flicker of hope. They had endured so much already, and here they were, still standing, still moving forward. She realized that their strength came not just from survival instincts, but from the bonds they had forged.

As they reached the city limits, Maya turned for one last look at the skyline. The devastation was overwhelming, but amidst the rubble and ruin, she could see faint signs of life returning – a determined weed pushing through cracked concrete, a bird's nest perched in a broken window frame.

"This isn't the end," Maya said, more to herself than the others. "It's just the beginning of something different."

With that, she squared her shoulders and led her group towards the unknown, leaving behind the echoes of their past and stepping into the uncertain promise of their future.

Maya's steps were slow but deliberate as she led the group along the crumbling asphalt, Riley matching her pace. The weight of responsibility pressed down on her shoulders, but the presence of her closest friend gave her strength.

"We'll find somewhere," Maya said softly, her eyes scanning the horizon. "It might not be perfect, but it'll be ours."

Riley nodded, her face a mixture of determination and concern. "As long as we're together, we can make it work."

Behind them, Benji's voice carried on the wind. "Hey, maybe we'll stumble upon a secret government bunker. You know, the kind with decades worth of canned goods and those tiny packets of salt."

Maya couldn't help but smile. Even now, Benji was trying to lighten the mood. She glanced back, catching his eye. "I'll settle for a place without collapsing buildings and constant danger."

As they walked, Maya's mind drifted. The path ahead was uncertain, fraught with potential dangers. But staying in the city wasn't an option. They needed a fresh start, a place where the memories of what they'd lost didn't haunt every corner.

"What do you think is out there?" Riley asked, gesturing to the vast unknown before them.

Maya took a deep breath. "I don't know. But whatever it is, we'll face it together."

The group fell into a companionable silence, broken only by the sound of their footsteps and the occasional comment or shared glance. Despite everything they'd been through, their bond remained. Tested, strained, but unbroken.

As they continued their journey, Maya felt a mix of fear and hope swirling in her chest. The future was unknown, but they were moving forward. And for now, that was enough.

Maya paused at the crest of a small hill, her eyes sweeping over the devastated cityscape one last time. Broken skyscrapers jutted into the overcast sky like jagged teeth, their shattered windows reflecting the dull light. The once-bustling streets were now eerily silent, littered with debris and abandoned vehicles.

"It's hard to believe this used to be home," Riley whispered, coming to stand beside Maya.

Maya nodded, her throat tight. "It's not just buildings that fell that day," she said, her voice barely audible. "It's everything we knew, everything we were."

Benji snorted softly behind them. "Well, aren't you just a ray of sunshine, Maya?"

She turned to face him, seeing the pain hidden behind his sarcastic smirk. "I'm serious, Benji. Look at this place. It's... it's..."

"A metaphor?" Riley offered.

Maya nodded. "Exactly. We're like this city now. Broken down, but..." She trailed off, searching for the right words.

"But not beyond repair?" Benji finished, his tone softer now.

"Yeah," Maya said, managing a small smile. "We've been through hell, but we're still standing. Just like some of these buildings."

She gestured to a partially collapsed structure nearby, its framework exposed but still upright. "We might be damaged, but we're not destroyed. And now... now we have the chance to rebuild. To become something new."

As they stood there, taking in the ruins of their former lives, Maya felt a strange mix of grief and hope wash over her. The city's destruction was a stark reminder of all they'd lost, but it also represented the possibility of a fresh start.

"Come on," she said finally, tearing her eyes away from the skeletal remains of their old world. "It's time to move on. Time to find our new beginning."

With one last glance at the ruins behind them, Maya led her group forward, each step taking them further from the past and closer to an uncertain, but hopeful, future.

Maya paused, her eyes drawn to a peculiar sight amidst the urban decay. A vibrant splash of green caught her attention, stark against the gray concrete and rusted metal. Vines had begun to snake their way up the side of a crumbling office building, their tendrils reaching towards the overcast sky.

"Look at that," she murmured, gesturing towards the unexpected burst of life.

Riley followed her gaze, a small smile tugging at her lips. "Nature's already reclaiming the city."

Benji snorted, his cynicism ever-present. "Great. We barely survive the earthquake, and now we've got to worry about getting eaten by plants."

Maya shook her head, her eyes still fixed on the greenery. "No, Benji. It's... it's beautiful, in a way. Don't you see?"

She turned to face her companions, her expression thoughtful. "Everything we knew is gone. Our homes, our schools, our old lives. But life... life finds a way to go on."

"So what?" Benji challenged, crossing his arms. "We're supposed to be inspired by some weeds?"

Maya sighed, her patience wearing thin. "It's not about the plants, Benji. It's about resilience. About hope." She gestured around them.

"This city may have fallen, but something new is already growing from the ashes."

Riley nodded, understanding dawning in her eyes. "Like us, right? We're not who we were before, but we're still here. Still fighting."

"Exactly," Maya agreed, feeling a weight lift from her shoulders. She hadn't realized how much she'd needed this moment of reflection, this glimpse of possibility amidst the ruins.

"So, what now, fearless leader?" Benji asked, his tone softening slightly. "We just... start over?"

Maya took a deep breath, her resolve strengthening. "We move forward. We can't go back to what we were, but we can build something new. Something better."

As she spoke the words, Maya felt a sense of closure wash over her. The city behind them was a graveyard of memories, but the path ahead held the promise of rebirth. They couldn't change the past, but they could shape their future.

"Come on," she said, her voice steady with newfound determination. "Let's see what's waiting for us beyond these ruins."

Maya's gaze swept across the horizon, the unfamiliar landscape stretching endlessly before them. The city's jagged silhouette faded into the distance, a reminder of all they were leaving behind. She felt a knot form in her throat, a mixture of anticipation and fear coursing through her veins.

"What if we don't find anything out there?" Riley's voice was barely above a whisper, her usual optimism wavering.

Maya turned to face her friend, seeing the worry etched on her face. "We'll find something," she said, trying to infuse her words with a confidence she didn't entirely feel. "We have to."

Benji snorted, kicking at a loose stone. "Yeah, maybe we'll stumble upon a magical oasis with unlimited food and no crazy people trying to kill us."

"Enough, Benji," Maya snapped, her patience wearing thin. She took a deep breath, forcing herself to remain calm. "Look, I know this is scary. I'm scared too. But staying in that city... it would've destroyed us."

As they walked, Maya's mind raced with memories of the past weeks - the violence, the desperation, the impossible choices. She shuddered, pushing the thoughts away. "We've learned so much," she continued, her voice softening. "About survival, about each other. Whatever's out there, we face it together."

Riley nodded, squeezing Maya's hand. "You're right. We're stronger now."

"Stronger, maybe," Benji muttered. "But at what cost?"

Maya met his gaze, seeing the haunted look in his eyes. She knew he was thinking of the warehouse, of the lives lost in their struggle to survive. "We carry those costs with us," she said quietly. "But we can't let them define us. We have to keep moving forward."

As they crested a small hill, the group paused, taking in the vast expanse before them. Fields gave way to distant forests, the landscape dotted with abandoned structures. It was beautiful and terrifying in its emptiness.

"So, oh wise one," Benji said, his sarcasm barely masking his fear, "got any idea where we're actually going?"

Maya stared into the distance, her heart pounding. She didn't have all the answers, but she knew they couldn't stay still. "We keep moving," she said firmly. "We look for signs of other survivors, for a place that's defensible. And we don't give up."

As they resumed their journey, Maya felt the weight of leadership pressing down on her. The future was a blank page, full of uncertainty and danger. But as she looked at the determined faces of her companions, she knew that together, they had a chance. Whatever lay ahead, they would face it side by side.

Maya's ponytail swung gently as she led the group down the crumbling asphalt of what was once a bustling highway. The city's jagged skyline receded behind them, a stark reminder of all they'd lost. She paused, allowing the others to catch up, her eyes scanning the horizon.

"We should find shelter before nightfall," Riley suggested, her optimism unwavering despite the exhaustion etched on her face.

Maya nodded, her voice soft but resolute. "Agreed. There's an old gas station about a mile ahead. We'll rest there and plan our next move."

As they walked, Benji fell into step beside Maya. "You know," he said, his voice gruff, "I'm still not sure this was the right call. Leaving everything behind."

Maya's brow furrowed, her internal conflict bubbling to the surface. She understood his doubts; they mirrored her own. "Sometimes," she replied, choosing her words carefully, "the right path isn't the easiest one. We couldn't stay in that city, Benji. It was killing us, inside and out."

The group lapsed into silence, each lost in their own thoughts. Maya's mind raced, replaying every decision that had led them here. The weight of leadership pressed down on her shoulders, a constant reminder of the lives depending on her choices.

As the sun dipped lower, casting long shadows across the desolate landscape, Maya spotted the dilapidated gas station. "There," she pointed, a small spark of hope igniting in her chest. "Let's see what we can salvage."

They approached cautiously, years of survival instincts kicking in. Riley and Benji moved to secure the perimeter while Maya pushed open the creaking door.

Inside, dust motes danced in the fading light. Shelves lay bare, a testament to countless scavengers who had come before. Yet, as Maya's eyes adjusted to the gloom, she spotted a few overlooked cans tucked behind a fallen display.

"Small victories," she murmured to herself, gathering the precious find.

As night fell, the group huddled around a small, carefully concealed fire. The flames cast flickering shadows across their faces, highlighting the weariness and uncertainty that plagued them all.

"What now, Maya?" Riley asked, her voice barely above a whisper.

Maya looked at each of her companions in turn, seeing the same question reflected in their eyes. She took a deep breath, steeling herself for the journey ahead.

"Now," she said, her voice gaining strength, "we keep moving. We keep hoping. And we keep looking out for each other. That's how we survive. That's how we build something new."

The fire crackled, sending sparks into the night sky. As Maya gazed up at the stars, she knew their journey was far from over. Challenges lay ahead, unseen and unknown. But in that moment, surrounded by the people who had become her family, Maya felt a flicker of hope. Whatever the future held, they would face it together.